PENGUIN BOOKS
A Bit of Singing and Dancing

Susan Hill was born in Scarborough in 1942, and educated at grammar schools there and in Coventry. She read English at King's College, London, of which she is now a fellow.

Her novels include *I'm the King of the Castle* (Somerset Maugham Award), *The Albatross* (John Llewellyn Rhys Prize), *Strange Meeting*, *The Bird of Night* (Whitbread Award), *In the Springtime of the Year*, *Air and Angels*, and *The Service of Clouds*. She has also written three collections of short stories, including *A Bit of Singing and Dancing*, and two ghost novels, *The Woman in Black* and *The Mist in the Mirror*, and a number of stories for children. Her autobiographical books are *The Magic Apple Tree*, and *Family* and she has edited three volumes of women's short stories for Penguin.

Susan Hill lives in a Gloucestershire farmhouse, from where she runs her own small publishing company Long Barn Books, and edits and publishes the quarterly journal *Books and Company*.

She is married to the Shakespeare scholar Stanley Wells, and they have two daughters.

A Bit of Singing and Dancing

SUSAN HILL

PENGUIN BOOKS

PENGUIN BOOKS

Published by the Penguin Group
Penguin Books Ltd, 27 Wrights Lane, London w8 5tz, England
Penguin Putnam Inc., 375 Hudson Street, New York, New York 10014, USA
Penguin Books Australia Ltd, Ringwood, Victoria, Australia
Penguin Books Canada Ltd, 10 Alcorn Avenue, Toronto, Ontario, Canada m4v 3b2
Penguin Books (NZ) Ltd, Private Bag 102902, NSMC, Auckland, New Zealand

Penguin Books Ltd, Registered Offices: Harmondsworth, Middlesex, England

First published by Hamish Hamilton 1973
Published in Penguin Books 1975
This edition published with additional stories 2000
10 9 8 7 6 5 4 3 2 1

Some of these stories have appeared in the following: the *Covent Garden Press*, the *Cornhill*, the *London Magazine, Nova, Penguin Modern Stories, The Times* and *Winter's Tales*

The moral right of the author has been asserted

Set in 11/13 pt Monotype Dante
Typeset by Rowland Phototypesetting Ltd, Bury St Edmunds, Suffolk
Printed in England by Clays Ltd, St Ives plc

For John, Valerie, Vivien and David Wilkinson
To thank them

Contents

Halloran's Child

He was eating the rabbit he had shot himself on the previous day, separating the small bones carefully from the flesh before soaking lumps of bread in the dark salt gravy. When they were boys, he and his brother, Nelson Twomey, used to trap rabbits and other animals too, weasels and stoats – it was sport, they thought nothing of it, it was only what Farley the gamekeeper did.

Then, Nate had gone by himself into the wood and found a young fallow deer caught by the leg, and when he had eventually got it free the animal had stumbled away, its foot mangled and dropping a trail of fresh blood through the undergrowth. Nate had gone for his brother, brought him back there and shown him.

'Well, it'll die, that's what,' Nelson had said, and shrugged his thin shoulders. It was the first glimpse Nate had had of his brother's true nature, his meanness.

'Die of gangrene. That's poison.'

He had wept that night, one of the few occasions in his life, and got up at dawn and gone out to search for the wounded animal, remembering the trembling hind quarters and the sweat which had matted its pale coat, the eyes, where sticky rheum had begun to gather in the corners. He found only the blood, dried dark on the bracken. It led him towards where the bank of the stream fell away at his feet, and he could not follow further.

After that he abandoned the traps, though there was nothing he could do to stop his brother from setting them, even if he had been able to talk to him. He was very tall, with long, pale, hairless arms and legs, and beaky features, and he spoke little. He kept his violence well hidden. When he left school he went as apprentice to Layce, the rat-catcher, and took over the job himself three years afterwards when Layce died. Then, for forty-eight years, he had left the village at seven each morning, the rat bag over his shoulder, and the two small dogs at his heels. He always wore the same long, beige raincoat and cap, and when one of the ratting dogs died, it was replaced by another identical dog, so that to everyone in the village the two seemed to have lived forever. He had always given his dogs the same names – Griff and Nip.

Over the years, Nelson Twomey began to stoop at the shoulders until a few years before his death he was bent almost double. His face was sallow and expressionless.

Once, Nate had gone with him to watch the rat-catching in a grain barn over at Salt, and been half-excited, half-sickened at the sight of the dogs, inching forwards, bellies to the ground, snuffling, waiting for the command, and then darting forward like arrows, teeth bared, down onto the hidden rats. He could still remember the look on his brother's face as he stood half in the shadows, thin and pale and grave as a ghost, unmoving; he could still smell the musty smell of the grain. He sensed that Nelson enjoyed it, that his job satisfied some appalling need with him. But he was highly thought of, because of his skills, and well paid too, for rats were a menace and greatly feared. Nate himself went in terror of them until he was a grown man. But he never ceased to be afraid, also, of his brother, so that it was almost a relief when he died and the cottage was empty of him.

But Nate Twomey continued to shoot rabbits, that he did not mind, for he had a keen eye and a sure hand, the animals never lingered, half-alive, and besides, they were pests, there had to be some way of putting them down. Nor did he mind wringing the necks of the hens his sister kept. It was only the traps that he regretted, the traps reminded him that he had been linked by blood to his brother.

*

The flesh of the rabbit fell away moistly from the bones. But in the middle of eating he had to raise his handkerchief to his left eye again and again, where the chip of wood had flown into it that morning, leaving it watery and sore. So that when Bertha spoke to him, he could not see her face and so missed what she was saying. He read her lips more easily than those of anyone else, she had only to mumble and he knew, for it was she who had first taught him, and shown him how to write, too, she had been more patient with his deafness and dumbness than either of their parents, who were uneasy, never knowing what he might be thinking, and frightened of being judged and blamed by the rest of the village. There had been one other child, also a boy, who had died, but he had been quite sound, they felt bitter that it was Nate who grew up in place of him.

Bertha Twomey waited. She always ate her own meal alone, after her brother had gone back to the workshop, and now, she stood beside the wooden kitchen table until he had finished wiping his eyes.

'You damaged yourself then, haven't you?'

He pointed to his eye.

'Splinters. You want to be more careful – putting your head too close to that bench, that's what. I told you before about that.'

He shook his head but his eye was watering freely, he had to wipe it again, and then she insisted on looking at it more closely. It was bloodshot and swimming with tears. In the end, she got the splinter out with the twisted corner of a clean handkerchief. 'You be more careful what you're doing in future, Nate Twomey.' He grinned, nodding at her. They had always been like this together, she treating him like a child, while still knowing that he was not a fool, just because he was deaf and dumb. She was two years older but she had been the first one to push him out, not so long after she had learned to walk herself, they were very close.

Bertha Twomey always wore black – long, full skirts and loose

3

cardigans and heavy black shoes on her wide, painful feet, and so she had looked like an old woman for years. There were lines in her face, they had come there when she was still a young girl, but she had been pretty and her face still had distinction, though she wore her hair scraped back and knotted behind her head, making herself severe.

When she was nineteen, she had been married to Hale, the farrier's son, from Salt, there had been a supper on trestle tables set out in Mid New Common one hot June night, and dancing until sunset, and then Nate had gone to live with them, for his sister had said she would never leave him. Hale had not objected. Nate had an attic room and helped out with the horses, before being apprenticed to Rob Riddy, who was undertaker for all the villages around. Bertha's husband had taught Nate how to shoot. And then, only a year later, he was dead, killed by lightning up on the Top Field, and the very next day, Nate and Bertha had moved back to their own family.

He looked up at her now, at the wide, serious face with the lined forehead, the strong bones. He had never known what she felt about her husband's death, never seen her weeping and she had told him nothing. She had taken a domestic post at the Lodge, and done most of the housework for her mother too, as though she could not bear to be idle for a moment. Otherwise, she kept herself to herself and looked after Nate. But she had changed, age had come to her overnight, and she had never gone out of black.

His eye was easier, it no longer watered. He took up a spoonful of gooseberries, thick with syrup.

Bertha said, 'The doctor was sent for to Halloran's.'

He stopped eating. So she had been waiting to tell him this then.

'I haven't heard more.'

The fruit had turned sickly in his mouth, he could not swallow it. His sister sat down and watched him. She knew. Nate shook his head.

'You'd best finish it.' But she saw that he could not and, after a moment or two, got up slowly and took the dish away.

Nate went to the back door and opened it, and the sun shone full into his face, comforting him, he smelled the fruit bushes and the scarlet bean flowers. At the bottom of the garden the hens were russet coloured, like squirrels, scratching about. He went down to them. When he opened the gate in the wire they took no notice of him at all, only went on pecking at the soil for the last of the meal Bertha had thrown. The sun was very hot here, the air still and dry. Nate's ears rang with silence.

Halloran's child. He tried to believe that it was nothing, that she would certainly be well and coming to talk to him in the workshop, soon enough, that he would see her sitting up on the bench watching his hands move to and fro, planing a piece of oak. But nobody sent for the doctor until it was unavoidable and besides, she had been out of hospital for less than a month.

He stared down at the hens.

In the kitchen, Bertha Twomey cleared the dinner table and took the blue and white checked cloth to shake outside the back door, at the same time looking down the garden at her brother, and then she felt all the old anxiety for him lying heavy as a stone in her chest, though he was sixty-eight years old and she was nearly seventy.

There had always been Twomeys here, but neither Nate nor Nelson the rat-catcher had married, and so they would be the last. She had not wanted to tell him about the Halloran child but he would take it better from her than from some stranger coming into the workshop, and in any case, there was no hope, it was certain that the child would die, though no one knew when.

The thing she was most afraid of was that he would want to go to the Halloran house. He could not do so, because they were

Twomeys, because of the way people thought of him and the work he did, because of all the old suspicion.

He was still standing motionless in the hen run, his head bent under the hot sun. She thought, say something to him, tell him . . . But she would not. He knew for himself. He was deaf and dumb but a grown man. The midday air stirred a little, moving the long lines of tinfoil tops, set across the vegetable patches to scare the birds away. Say something to him.

But she turned and went back inside.

It was common knowledge that a Twomey had been taken for a witch and some said burned, some said drowned to death. So there were superstitions about the family which died hard and when Bertha Twomey's husband was struck by lightning, what people felt was somehow confirmed and they kept their distance. Now, to the children in the village, Bertha looked like a witch, they stared at her from a safe distance, awed by the black clothes, and had nightmares, too, in which she set evil upon them. All of it she knew and was accustomed to it, it only served to make her draw further inside herself. She spoke to no one, not even to her brothers, about how she was feeling. And to them both she had been a rock, taking the place of mother and father and wife, they could not imagine her capable of any weakness.

From Nate Twomey, too, people kept their distance but that was because of the work he did, for he himself was amiable enough, and harmless, nobody blamed him because he could not hear or speak. Nevertheless, the odd noises which he made, the grunts and choking sounds in his throat, which were how he tried to imitate what he saw of laughter, frightened the children. All except Halloran's child.

The Hallorans had come down in the world. Their grandfather had owned land, kept a few dairy cows and called himself a farmer. But when his son inherited, there were more debts than profits, and the land had to be sold. Arthur Halloran had lost heart very quickly, watching his father struggle, and when he was seventeen he left the village altogether and went for a sailor. He returned with a damaged leg, married Amy Criddick and now he was only a casual labourer, working on hedging or hay-making or picking potatoes and paid by the hour. He was a bad-tempered, disappointed man, suffered in the village rather than liked. They had one child, the daughter, Jenny. She had never been strong, never been truly well since the day she was born, and when she was a year old and began to walk her limbs seemed incapable of holding her up, she was unsteady and sickly. At the age of four she had rheumatic fever and almost died, and Halloran had said in public hearing that he wished for it, wished to have it over with, for who wanted an invalid for a child and how could he bear the anxiety? She had been forbidden to run or even walk far, though she went to school when she was five and there was treated like a fragile doll by the others, who had been put in awe of her. She played with no one, though sometimes, as she sat in the classroom or, in fine weather, on a little stool in a corner of the playground, one of them would take pity on her and bring pick-sticks or a jigsaw and do it with her for a little while. But she seemed to be separated from them, almost to be less than human, because of the transparency of her skin and her thin, delicate bones, because of the fine blueness tinging her lips and the flesh below her nervous eyes. She was neither clever nor stupid, she said very little. In the end, they were bored by her.

Then, she began to visit Nate Twomey in the carpenter's shop at the back of Coker's Lane. He could say nothing to her, which seemed to put her at her ease, for she would talk to him more than to anyone else in her life, fascinated by the way he looked straight at her and watched the movements of her lips. She learned what the grunts meant which he uttered occasionally, whether they expressed his approval or not, though most often he would simply nod or shake his head and smile at her, before he went on with his sawing or planing or the hammering in of nails. If there was ever any question that needed a fuller reply, he stopped and wrote it down carefully on a page of his measurement book, with the thick, flat carpenter's pencil.

In the holidays she came almost every day. He gave her a drink of tea from the flask his sister put up for him, and grew used to her presence, it pleased him, made him feel somehow at ease, settled. She sat on the workbench – he had to lift her up there, and she weighed nothing, she was made of air, he was shocked at the frailness of her body between his huge hands.

For much of the time they were both of them silent. She liked the smell of the workshop and the rasping sound of the plane driving evenly over a plank of wood. Only the high-pitched scream of the electric saw terrified her, she would stuff her fingers into her ears and her head rang, though Nate only looked at her and grinned, bending his own head right down over the blade, hearing nothing. He could only try to imagine how the noise pained her by feeling the saw's vibration jar through his body.

Nate was the coffin-maker. Usually, at least once a week, there was a death in one of the villages, and he went there on his bicycle, removing his cap respectfully when he reached the front door, before going inside to measure up and receive the family requirements, written out for him on a slip of paper. The sight of death had never alarmed him, he had been used to it for so long and it quieted him, for he felt that if a man came only to this, this state of calmness and silence, there could be no harm, and nothing in the world could damage him.

And when he leaned over the bodies of the dead, when his hands touched them gently as he worked, he took into himself through them the certainty of resurrection, so that he returned to his workshop to make the coffin confidently, and with a sense of awe. He knew that he was a good craftsman and his work satisfied him when it was finished, it seemed altogether useful, altogether good.

But now, he could not conceive of death in relation to Jenny

Halloran, he disbelieved in the possibility of it, though she was so frail. He had always loved her, they had accepted one another completely, and so he could not accept that she might die, or even worse, might suffer in her body. He was reminded again of the trapped deer.

A year ago, the child had been taken ill with some severe, unidentifiable pain and then, three times in the space of a couple of months, she had fallen over and broken bones which were now as brittle as the bones of birds and would not heal, only crumbled slowly apart within their encasing flesh. She was no longer able to walk or even to sit up in a chair unattended, for fear that she would fall out and, in the end, she was pushed about the village in a wheelchair by her mother – for Halloran himself was ashamed, he would have nothing to do with her. And they refused to let her visit the carpenter's workshop again.

Nate Twomey missed her. But if he thought about it while he was working alone, he knew that it was only what he should have expected, that it was surprising, indeed, that they had ever let her come here at all. For he was a Twomey and Twomeys were not trusted, though none of them had done harm to anyone. But a Twomey had been taken for a witch, and Bertha's husband had been struck down and Nate was born deaf and dumb. It was enough to make anyone wary, and glad that the Twomeys' cottage was a little way out of the village.

But Nate knew that what kept them most in dread of him was his job, for many people believed that if they came face to face with the coffin-maker, it meant death to follow and if you let him into your house, other than on his official business, you were surely tempting fate. Halloran was more suspicious than most men, he expected ill-luck because it was what his family had become accustomed to.

The child came out of hospital, looking even paler and thinner than before, and now people began to keep a little way from her, too, as she was pushed out on fine days in her chair, for she had the look of death about her. Once, Nate met her as he was walking home for dinner and he was shocked at the sight of her, at the small legs poking out like sticks and the neck bent like a stalk, the deadness within the child's eyes. Hers was the only suffering he could not accept. When he went home, he sat pulling at the edges of the tablecloth, rubbing his fingers together, or else standing at the back door, staring down into the garden. He seemed to Bertha to have lost heart for anything.

When she sent him to pick beans or strip the gooseberry and blackcurrant bushes of their fruit, he went heavily down the path and worked mechanically, without any enthusiasm, along the rows. In the old days he would not have to be told, the fruit would be there ready for her, glistening and ripe in great bowls on the kitchen table.

For the first time in his life, too, he began to resent his own condition, to envy those who could hear and chat among themselves, to feel bitter. Why had he been born a Twomey? Why was the child ill and no longer permitted to visit him, what had he done to deserve any of it?

Now, on the day his sister told him the news about the doctor, he was reluctant to go back to his workshop, not wanting to be alone. But old Bart, the stockman from Faze Farm, was dead of a stroke, the funeral was on Wednesday and the coffin was not yet done. Nate envied Bart, who was a year his junior, for it seemed to him suddenly that death was an enviable condition, that Bart was well off and not many had any benefit in this world. He wanted to die himself. He felt exhausted.

While he worked on the coffin, the idea was growing within him, as his sister had feared it would, that he must go round to the Hallorans' cottage, must see the child, see her now, while she was alive and could still speak to him. He would watch her lips moving and be comforted and besides, he wanted reassurance that she was not in pain, that everything was being done for her. He worked on until his head was full to overflowing with pictures of her and he could not concentrate upon his job, was scarcely aware of the smooth wood beneath his fingers, the coldness of the nails. Bart was six and a half feet tall, it was a big coffin, taking shape upon the bench.

He kept the workshop door open so that a beam of sunlight fell onto the pale curled wood chips that strewed the floor, and warmed his back, too – it was a day he would normally have enjoyed, for the sun always smoothed him. But in the end it was too much, in the end he had to go and see Jenny Halloran. At twenty minutes past three, he put his saw away, picked his cap off the hook and blew the dust off it, went out of the door.

The paving stones baked in the heat. There was no one else about as he walked slowly down through the village, a tall, shambling man, his head a little bent, and inside his head, the throbbing of silence.

He went up the front path, put his hand to the door-knocker and then drew it away again. No one saw him. The small front garden was overgrown, with stocks and petunias trying to struggle through thistles and bindweed. Halloran had lost heart.

Because he could not speak, he began to sweat with anxiety that they would not understand why he had come here, would not let him in. He looked up at the bedroom window of the cottage. There were net curtains. Nothing moved. A thin brown cat regarded him from the broken-down fence.

But he could not bear to go away, back to the workshop, without having seen her.

It was some minutes after his knocking ceased before Amy Halloran came to the door, opening it only an inch and peering out. When she saw Nate, her face twitched involuntarily and then closed up in fear, or dislike, he could not tell. She was not an old woman, she was not yet forty, but she looked old, her hair was streaked with grey and her rather square face had long, deep lines, from nose to mouth. Nate took off his cap and moved it nervously round and round in his hands.

'Nate Twomey.'

He smiled. He was very hot and the air was dusty as he breathed it in, and thick with the scent of flowers.

'She's in her bed. She's ill. Doctor came.'

He nodded and pointed into the house and then to himself. She hesitated still, her expression changing as she thought about it, he could see suspicion and tiredness and worry chasing one another like clouds across her face. More than ever before he felt the strain of his own disability. People needed to speak, he needed to reassure her, for he was anxious that she should not be afraid of him.

But in the end she let him in, opening the door slowly and then leading him up the dark stairs. The carpet only reached as far as the bend, and then there were bare boards. The house smelled of old cooking and something else, some medicine or disinfectant. He knew that she was uncertain whether she had done right to let him in.

He was appalled at the sight of the child. She lay in an iron-framed bed, propped up on a single pillow, and she seemed to have shrunk, her flesh was thinner, scarcely covering her bones, and the skin was taut and shiny. Her eyes were very bright, and yet dead, too, there seemed to be no life in her at all. He looked down at her hand, resting on the sheet. It was like a small claw.

'Here's that friend of yours.'

Nate stood uncertainly, cap still in his hand. He wanted to weep. Her lips moved and there was no blood in them, they were thin and dry and oddly transparent, like the skin of a chrysalis.

'I had the doctor come.'

He nodded to encourage her, for while she could speak to him she was alive, there was hope for her. Amy Halloran stood by the door, not moving, only staring vacantly at her child. She seemed too tired, now, even to worry.

'I'm going to the sea. One day. I'm going on a holiday.'

But it seemed to Nate that she did not believe what she told him, that she knew the truth. She turned her head slightly to look out of the window and for a long time she said nothing else, so that he began to be afraid that she was dead. His hands felt weak and sweaty. The room was very hot.

'Will you make me something? Will you make me a toy?'

For he had occasionally taken bits of surplus wood and carved out a rough doll's cradle or a model bird for her, though they were clumsy, he was not good at such delicate work. But she had always been pleased with them. Now he nodded and tried to shape his hands like a boat, looking at her intently, willing her to understand. She frowned. Then, abruptly, began to cough and her face went into a spasm of pain, the bones seemed to tighten, and her mother went to her and lifted her up, touched her hands again and again to the child's cheeks and forehead. He saw that her eyelids looked dusty and faintly mauve, beneath the skin.

'You've seen enough, Nate Twomey. Haven't you stayed here long enough?'

Nate turned at once and went out of the room, his face burning. But as he reached the foot of the stairs, the front door opened and Halloran stood there, with the bright sunlit garden behind him like the background of a picture.

Nate thought that the man was going to hit him. His face went dark and mottled with blood and he clenched his fist. But then, he knew what Halloran was thinking – that the child was dead, for why else would the coffin-maker be here, standing at the bottom of the stairs that led to her bedroom. He put out his hand, thinking to touch Halloran's shoulder, he pointed back up the staircase and smiled, shaking his head, he would have said, 'I saw her, she was speaking to me. I saw her, she is not dead, she is not dead.'

Halloran started forward. Stopped. Looked up, to see his wife there. The three of them stood, unable to move or speak, helpless. The air shimmered with heat in rings like haloes, over the flowerbeds.

Then, Halloran began to shout, though Nate could only see the anger, see his mouth opening and closing, the corners twisted, so that he could scarcely read what the man was saying.

'Get him out of this house. What did you want to let him in for, what right has he got to come here, what have I told you about him? He's not to see her. He can't be trusted. What are you doing letting a Twomey into this house?'

He swung round. Nate was half-way down the front path. The hollyhocks were full of bees, he watched their circling, though he could not imagine their noise. His heart thudded violently, though not because of Halloran's anger. He felt ashamed of himself, ashamed that he should be able to walk out, healthy and strong, while the child lay dying.

The door of the cottage slammed shut.

He could not go back to work, he was trembling and his head swam with the shock of seeing the child, he began to walk aimlessly out of the village in the direction of Salt, between the thick hawthorn hedges, which trailed convolvulus down on to the grass. The cows were all lying down, flies jazzing about their heavy heads under the trees. His own throat was sore and there was a pain in his chest which seemed to choke him. He knew that he had seen the child for the last time.

That evening he could not eat, he only drank two mugs of sweet tea and left the meat and potatoes and pie his sister had put out for him. What he had begun to feel was some sort of rage boiling up within him, he wanted to get up and beat his fists on something, to lash out in protest at his own dumbness, his own misery.

He rolled up his shirt sleeves and went off to the bottom of the garden and into the hen run, captured one of the birds and held it down in a flurry of feathers and clawing feet. From the kitchen doorway Bertha Twomey watched silently, as he wrung the animal's neck. She knew what had happened and could do nothing for him, she only recognized in him the violence that had also been in his brother. Nate was not the same, he was a gentle man, patient, and so he killed the bird swiftly and without pain. But there had been a rage in him, a viciousness she had never seen before. When he came back into the house carrying the dead bird by its feet, she drew back and told him to put it away in the scullery, she would pluck it the next day when the feathers and flesh were no longer warm.

'You'd best eat something.'

He shook his head and his eyes were clouded with unhappiness. He went out again, carrying his gun, and shot crows and jays and pigeons in Faze's fields and over towards the woods, until dark, his aim was as sure as ever, though he had to grip his hands tightly around the gun barrel to quieten their trembling. He was sick with shame at himself, but he went on until he was exhausted, knowing that he had to work out his anger and frustration. When the gun went off, he only saw the puff of smoke and felt his finger jerk sharply back from the trigger. A bird fell somewhere but there was no sound, no sound.

In the west, over High Crop Wood, the sky went dark as damsons, spreading like a stain. The air smelled sweet.

When the gun was empty he went home, his arms and legs aching and his head numb. He was no longer angry. He felt nothing at all. In the kitchen, he tried to eat a slice of pie which his sister had left out for him under a cloth, but his throat contracted, he had to spit the mouthful out. His eyes were still dry and smarting and when he tried to soothe them by weeping, he could not do so, he only lay in his bed, staring up into the darkness remembering the child.

He woke, not abruptly but gradually out of sleep, and when

he opened his eyes he saw that the room was filled with still, pale moonlight. Then he knew. He had been awakened by the death of the child. He lay filled with a sense of relief, as though he had recovered from a long fever.

If he put out his hand, he might touch her. If he could speak to her, she would reply. But he could only think, inside his own head, and so she was there too. Above all, he was thankful that she had suffered no longer. That afternoon she had not seemed to be in pain, only weakened, tired.

Often in his life Nate had known about death. When his brother Nelson Twomey died in the hospital at Garston, he had been selecting a piece of timber for a door panel in the Rectory, and he had known, his head had been filled with the awareness of his brother, whom he had both hated and loved, respected and feared, and when he had gone to the hospital the next day, they had told him the time of the death and it had been the same.

Now, he got up and went to the window. It was open and the scent of stocks drifted up into his face. The moon rode high over the wood. The night was quiet with the presence of this new death.

He had gone out to shoot and kill birds and to wring the neck of the hen and the reason he had done so was the violence boiling up inside him. It had not been necessary shooting. He was to blame. But he knew, sensing the presence of the child, that it was over, that he would do no such shooting again. He knew that some evil had been plucked out of him.

He slept.

They sent for him first thing the next morning and he was afraid to face them, and when he saw their figures standing at the door, he knew how much they hated and blamed him for the child's death. Halloran's face was flushed with anger and weeping, his eyes flickered like tongues over Nate Twomey, as he took off his cap.

'Get up there. Do what you have to. Get it over with.'

For the second time he followed Amy Halloran up the stairs and at the top she turned to him, standing so close that her breath blew onto his face.

'He blamed me. He said I'd never to let you in and I did. He told me.'

Nate stood still. He felt the bitterness and misery which were directed towards him and wanted to find some way of telling her that things were for the best, that it did not matter that the child had died. He could do nothing, say nothing.

He had expected to feel resentment and anger himself, on seeing the child's body, but it was nothing to him except a comfort. He had known more than this. There was nothing to her. The flesh was wasted and the brittle bones showed through, she measured very little. Her face was rather grave but it held no suffering, the brow was smooth and gleaming, like silk. He would not see her in the carpenter's shop again but that no longer mattered, because he had been with her at the time of her dying and he had all that he wanted or had a right to.

But he grieved for the parents, for Amy Halloran, who watched him, twisting her fingers together, standing at the foot of the bed, and for Halloran himself, who would not understand, would not accept. Should he himself not feel as they did? But he did not, for he knew the truth.

He finished his job and put the notebook and pencil away and looked down once more upon the child's body, before going heavily down the stairs.

Halloran was there, waiting for him in the path, his eyes looking swollen and bruised and his mouth working.

He said, 'You came here. You brought it on us. Death. You came here and it killed her. You . . .'

Nate stood looking at him helplessly, unable even to shake his head. It was what he had expected. He was a Twomey, he was the coffin-maker. They could not love or trust him.

'You.'

Amy Halloran was there, plucking at her husband's arm, trying to drag him off.

'It was you.'

Then, suddenly, he lunged forward, his eyes wild with pain and rage, and swung his fist into Nate Twomey's face. The blow hit him like a stroke of lightning, he went down, his head spinning, the blood welling up behind his eyes. As he fell, it seemed to him that this was what he had waited for, because of his own anger of the previous day and the lives of the birds he had so ruthlessly and violently taken, so that it was almost a relief when he felt the impact of the ground and pain went like a blade through his body.

He lay for what seemed like hours and then, getting slowly to his feet again, wiping the blood off his face with the back of his hand, he realized that he was alone, that the Hallorans had gone inside the house, had left him. His skull felt as if it would break open. But he was calm. He knew that it was what had been due to him. Because he had loved the child and known of her dying, because he was a Twomey and maimed. He would not have expected anything else and Halloran was grieving, was beside himself with misery and despair. Halloran was not to blame.

The sun shone down on him and his shadow fell behind him, hard and dark against the brightness. He walked back to the carpenter's shop slowly, to begin work on the small coffin, bearing his own silence.

Mr Proudham and Mr Sleight

That evening, I saw Mr Proudham and Mr Sleight for the first time. I had set out to walk all the way along the sea front but the sleet and a north-easterly wind soon drove me back to the tall, Edwardian house in which I had rented a flat. I had chosen to come here at the bleakest time of year, partly because I gained an obscure satisfaction from physical endurance. But mainly because nobody would trouble me. The flat had no telephone.

The sky was gunmetal grey. Only two or three other people had ventured out, women briskly walking their dogs. They wore long tweed coats padded out with cardigans underneath and sensible, sheepskin-lined boots and scarves wound round their heads for the protection of mouths and ears. Nobody looked at me.

But when I opened the front gate of the house Mr Proudham and Mr Sleight were looking. It was almost dark and they had not put the light on in their ground floor window. They stood side by side, shadowy, improbable figures. I was to see them like that so often during the weeks to come – Mr Proudham, immensely tall and etiolated, with a thin head and unhealthy, yellowish skin: and Mr Sleight, perhaps five feet one or two, with a benevolent, rather stupid moon of a face. He was bald: Mr Proudham had dingy-white hair, worn rather long.

I hesitated, fiddling with the latch. They stood, watching. They made no secret of their curiosity, they had no net curtain behind which they might hide. But their faces were curiously expressionless. The sleet had turned to hail. I went quickly inside. Mr Proudham and Mr Sleight continued to watch me until I had passed out of sight, under the shadow of the porch.

It was a full week before they introduced themselves – or rather, before Mr Proudham introduced them, for little Mr Sleight nodded and beamed and clicked his false teeth but rarely spoke. When he did, it was to murmur with his friend.

Each time I left the house they were watching me. And I began, a little more surreptitiously, to watch them. They had a dog, an overgrown sooty poodle which was clipped in not quite the usual fashion, but in horizontal bands going round its body and up the tail, so that from a distance it appeared to be striped in two-tone grey. Mr Proudham always held the lead and Mr Sleight trotted alongside keeping time with the dog.

They went out three times a day, at ten, at two and at six. In addition, Mr Proudham went out at eleven each morning carrying a shopping bag of drab olive cloth. And it was in a shop, Cox's Mini-Market, that I first came face to face with him. He was buying parsnips and because I was standing at the back of the queue I had a chance to study him. He was considerably older than I had at first thought, with heavy-lidded eyes that drooped at the corners and a mouth very full of teeth. On top of the off-white hair he wore a curious woollen beret, rather like that of a French onion-seller but with a pompom on the top. As he turned to leave the shop he saw me. He stopped. Then, as though he had considered the situation carefully, he bowed, and lifted his hand. For a moment I wondered if he were going to raise the little woollen hat. But he only gave a half-salute.

'Good morning.'

But that time he did not reply.

Later, I was working at my desk in the window when I saw the two of them go off down the path for their two o'clock walk. It was one of those lowering, east coast days which had never come fully light. Both men wore long knitted scarves in bright multi-colours, which hung down their backs like those of children or students. But only Mr Proudham had a hat – the woolly beret. As they reached the gate they turned and looked up at my window. They did not seem in the least disconcerted that I was sitting there, looking back at them. For what can only have been ten seconds but felt considerably longer they stood, so that I almost waved, to prevent embarrassment. But I did not, and eventually they moved off on their walk.

That evening, Mr Proudham spoke. I had been out to post a letter. The temperature had dropped again, so that my breath smoked on the air and the sea was glistening with reflected frost. It was quite dark. As I came up the alleyway between two houses, which led from the High Street on to the sea front, I saw them a few yards away. The dog was sniffing busily around the concrete bollard. Some decision must have been reached by them earlier for, as though they had been waiting for this moment, Mr Proudham stepped forward to meet me.

'I am Mr Proudham, this is Mr Sleight. How do you do?'

It was a formal little speech. He had a rather high-pitched voice, and I saw that there were even more teeth than I had first noticed, long and crowded together. We shook hands and the dog turned its attention from the bollard and began to sniff me.

'We do hope you are comfortable at number forty-three? We do hope you have everything you require?'

Yes, I said, I was very comfortable. And I looked at Mr Sleight, who at once blushed and glanced at Mr Proudham, and then away, and then down at the dog. He did not speak, though I thought that the movement of his mouth indicated that he might wish to.

'We do hope you were not expecting better weather. Alas, it is never better than this in late November.'

I told him it was what I had been prepared for.

'Yes. I see, I see, I see.'

Then abruptly he pulled at the dog's lead and touched the arm of Mr Sleight. Mr Sleight jumped and his eyes began to swivel about again. He was smiling into space.

'I'm afraid there is not much entertainment here,' Mr

Proudham said. They were already moving off, so that when he repeated the sentence, his words were carried away down the sea front on the wind.

'No entertainment . . .'

'Goodbye.' But they were already out of earshot. I looked back at them, the tall, thin figure and the short round one with the brightly coloured scarves hanging like pigtails down behind. The striped dog was pulling at the end of the lead, so that Mr Proudham had to bend forward. I smiled. But there was something about them that was not altogether funny.

At the front door I looked for their names above the bell. 'Proudham and Sleight' were written, like a firm of solicitors. No initials. Proudham and Sleight.

I drew my curtains and switched on the electric fire. I would work for another couple of hours before supper. A little later, I heard them come in, heard doors open and close gently. They were very quiet, Mr Proudham and Mr Sleight, they did not seem to have a television or wireless set, or to shout to one another from room to room, as is sometimes the habit of those who live together. Most of the time, there might have been no one at all in the flat below.

I had gone there to work undisturbed, but I also spent a good time walking, either along the beach itself for several miles or on the promenade which followed the shore from the south side, where I was living, right up to the breakwater at the most northerly point of the town. It was here that a few amusements were situated. Most of them were closed at this time of year but I liked to wander past the canvas-shrouded dodgem cars and the shuttered gift stalls, I enjoyed the tawdriness of it all, the blank lights and peeling paint. There was an open air swimming pool, drained for the winter, and sand and silt had been washed over the rim by the storm tides. Near to this was a café and one amusement centre, called Gala Land, both of which remained open.

I could not keep away from Gala Land. It had a particular smell which drew me down the steep flight of concrete steps to the pay desk below. It was built underground in a sort of valley between two outcrops of rock, over which was a ribbed glass roof, like those of Victorian railway stations and conservatories. The walls were covered in greenish moss and the whole place had a close, damp, musty smell and although it was lit from end to end with neon and fluorescent lights, everything looked somehow dark, furtive and gone to seed. Some of the booths were closed down here, too, and those which kept open must have lost money, except perhaps on the few days when parties of trippers came from inland, in the teeth of the weather, and dived down for shelter to the underground fun palace. Then, for a few hours, the fruit and try-your-strength and fortune card machines whirred, loud cracks echoed from the riffle ranges, hurdy-gurdy music sounded out, there was a show of gaiety. For the rest of the time the place was mainly patronized by a few unemployed men and teenage boys, who chewed gum and fired endless rounds of blank ammunition at the bobbing rows of duck targets, and by older schoolchildren after four o'clock. At the far end was a roller skating rink which drew a good crowd on Saturday afternoons.

I liked that sad, shabby place, I liked its atmosphere. Occasionally I put a coin into a fruit machine or watched What the Butler Saw. There was a more gruesome peepshow, too, in which one could watch a condemned man being led on to a platform, hooded and noosed and then dropped snap, down through a trapdoor to death. I watched this so often that, long after I had left the town, this scene featured in my nightmares, I smelled the brackish, underground smell.

It was in Gala Land, early one Thursday afternoon, that I saw Mr Proudham. He was alone, and operating one of the football machines. A dropped coin set a small ball rolling among a set of figures which could be swivelled from side to side by means of a lever. The aim was to make one of them bang the ball into the goal before it rolled out of sight down a slot in the side. Mr Proudham was concentrating hard, bending over the machine and manipulating the handles with great energy. He wore, as usual, the woolly pompom hat and a grey mackintosh. I watched him as he had three tries and then succeeded in knocking the ball into a goal with the fourth. He stood upright and retrieved his coin from the metal dish.

'Well done!' I said.

He turned, and for a moment I thought he was going to scuttle away, pretending that he had not recognized me. Instead he smiled, showing all those teeth. I would have asked if he came here often. But at once, he said, 'Today is Mr Sleight's day at the clinic. I always come down here to pass the time you know, until he is due to return. I have somehow to pass the time.'

I hoped that Mr Sleight was not seriously ill. Mr Proudham leaned forward a little, lowering his voice. 'It's the massage, you see. He goes for the massage.'

I did not like to inquire further and I would have made some excuse to leave quickly then, in case Mr Proudham felt embarrassed at being caught in Gala Land. But he asked, with a rather strange, cat-like expression on his face, if I would care for some tea.

'There is quite a *clean* café, just beside the pool, they do make a very reasonable cup of tea. I generally go there on Mr Sleight's day at the clinic. It passes the time. I like to give myself something to do. Yes.'

And so he escorted me out of the damp-smelling, half-empty funfair and up to ground level, where Timpson's Seagull Café was also half-empty, and smelled of china tiles and urn-tea.

I did not know what I might talk to Mr Proudham about, over our pot of tea, but I need not have worried because, as though he wanted to deflect any attention from himself, he began to ask me questions, about my work, my life in London, London itself.

They were not personal, probing questions – I could answer them in detail and yet not give much away. Mr Proudham listened, smiling every now and again with all those teeth. He was the one who poured out the tea. I noticed that his eyes were bloodshot and that the yellowish cheeks were shot through here and there with broken veins. How old was he? Seventy? Perhaps not quite, or perhaps a year or two more, it was hard to tell.

Suddenly he said, 'Behind you is a photograph of my mother.' I looked round.

The picture was an old one, in an oak frame, of the grandstand which had been demolished during the last war. There were flowers, mostly hydrangeas, banked around the base and awnings draped above, hung with tassels. Sitting in the bandstand was a Ladies Orchestra. They were all dressed in white, Grecian style garments, hanging in folds to the floor, with floral headbands. They looked wide-eyed, vacant and curiously depressed.

'My mother,' said Mr Proudham, 'is the Lady Conductor.'

And there she was, a large-bosomed woman with wildly curling hair, who clutched her baton like a fairy's wand.

I said, how interesting.

'She died in 1937,' Mr Proudham said. 'I myself was never musical. It was her great sadness.'

'So you have always lived here.'

Mr Proudham inclined his head. Then, as if he were afraid of having given too much away, he looked up brightly, clapping his hands together.

'Now – I hope you are not a believer in blood sports.'

We stayed in Timpson's Seagull Café until just before five o'clock, when he jumped up and began to pull on gloves and wind his scarf anxiously, for Mr Sleight would be home from the clinic.

'And I make a point of being in,' Mr Proudham said, 'I think that is so important, don't you? To be in. I am always waiting.'

He shook hands with me, across the green formica table,

as though one of us were departing on a journey, and rushed away.

After that I saw them together most days, and Mr Proudham always spoke and Mr Sleight smiled and looked nervous, and once or twice I bumped into Mr Proudham alone. But Mr Sleight was never alone. I wondered if he might be a little simple, unable to cope with the outside world by himself. On Thursday afternoons a taxi drew up and he went off in it to 'the clinic'. Mr Proudham left the house shortly after, to walk in the direction of the funfair and the Seagull Café.

The week before Christmas they issued an invitation. I had been for a walk along the beach, in the snow, and when I returned there was an envelope pushed underneath my door.

> *Would you care to take tea with us on Saturday next? Unless we hear to the contrary, we greatly look forward to seeing you at 4.30 p.m.*

The note was written in a neat, rather childish hand on cream paper. I replied to it, putting my own card underneath the door while they were out on their six o'clock walk. For I wanted to satisfy my curiosity about them, I wanted to see inside their flat. And I felt rather sorry for them, a pair of elderly men who never had a visitor.

On that Saturday morning, Mr Proudham went out alone not once but twice and returned each time with a full shopping bag. I put on a red dress, and wished that I had some gift I could take with me.

Mr Proudham opened the door. He was wearing a canary yellow waistcoat, over a boldly checked shirt and matching cravat. In the sitting room I found Mr Sleight with his bald head almost invisible over the polo neck of a bright orange jumper. We made a highly coloured trio standing uncertainly together in the centre of the room, which was stiflingly hot, with a log fire and three radiators turned on to full. 'Now please sit down, please sit down.' I picked a chair well away from the hearth and, for a moment, Mr Proudham and Mr Sleight both stood over me, their faces beaming proudly. Perhaps no one had been here to tea before.

When Mr Proudham did speak, it was a little 'Ah!' like a sigh of satisfaction, as though he were a photographer who had arranged a perfect tableau. 'Ah!' and he glanced at Mr Sleight and nodded and smiled and held out a hand in my direction. Mr Sleight smiled. I smiled. The hot room was full of *bonhomie*.

They might have been expecting a party of schoolboys for tea. There was white and brown bread and butter, muffins, toast, gentleman's relish, honey, crab apple jelly, fruit loaf, fruit cake, chocolate gâteau, éclairs, meringues, shortbread fingers. I ate as much as I could, but Mr Proudham and Mr Sleight ate a good deal more, cake after cake, and drank cups of sugary tea. Conversation lapsed. The poodle dog watched from the other side of the room. I wondered how we would get through the time after tea, and whether Mr Sleight were dumb.

They had bought or inherited some beautiful furniture – a set of Chippendale chairs, a Jacobean oak table, a dresser hung with Crown Derby china. The carpet was Persian, there were Cotman and Birkett Foster watercolours on the walls. And in an alcove near the window stood an enormous tropical fish tank. In another corner, a parrot in a cage sat so perfectly still and silent I thought it might be a dummy.

Eventually, Mr Proudham wiped crumbs of meringue from around his mouth with a purple handkerchief. He said, 'I think that Mr Sleight has something to *show* you.' It was the tone a mother would use about her child which has some drawing or piece of handiwork to proffer. Mr Sleight gave a little, nervous cough.

I could not have been in the least prepared for what I was to see. Mr Sleight led me, with a slightly flustered air, out of the

27

room and down a short passage, and through a heavily beaded curtain which he held aside for me, and which rattled softly as he let it go. Mr Proudham stood well back.

'Now this is Mr Sleight's territory. I never interfere. This is *all* his own.'

It was rather dark, apart from two spotlights attached to the wall above a long workbench. Shelves had been fitted all round the room, and displayed on the shelves, as well as on the window-ledge and several small tables, were rows of wax-work models. They were a little larger than children's puppets, and similarly grotesque, but a good deal more carefully made.

Mr Sleight stood back, his eyes flicking here and there about the room, occasionally resting on me for a second, as he tried to judge what I was thinking. I stepped closer to the bench and looked down at the two models which were in progress, at enamel bowls of wax, rubber moulds and papier mâché bases, and small chisels and blades and neat little piles of hair. And, looking round, I saw the faces of Mr Proudham and Mr Sleight, smiling and motionless like two, larger waxworks, dressed in those startling colours.

'Well? Well?' Mr Proudham said, and lifted a hand to finger his cravat.

'Does he . . .' I corrected myself. 'Do you make all these yourself, by hand?' Mr Sleight blushed and nodded, and at once glanced for confirmation at Mr Proudham.

'Oh yes, yes, nothing to do with *me*. I was never at all a handyman, I wouldn't be the slightest help, oh no! Everything is done by Mr Sleight, all by himself.'

The waxworks were very bizarre characters from Japanese Nō plays and from Grimm, African warriors in war paint, animal masks attached to human bodies, hideous Punch and Judy figures: and then, familiar, ordinary-looking men in ordinary clothes who were, I realized with a shock, tiny replicas of the figures in the Chamber of Horrors – Crippen and Haigh and Christie. The clothes, down to the last button and shoelace and cufflink, were perfect.

'They're superb.'

'We don't *sell* them, you know,' Mr Proudham said. 'We don't do this for money, it's a craft, what you might call a pastime. Mr Sleight works away in here day after day. But we are not a *commercial* enterprise.'

The room smelled of old, spent matches and cooling wax, like a church after candles have been snuffed out. I wondered whether Mr Sleight would gradually fill the whole, already crowded flat with his shelves of models. They were disturbing, curiously lifelike, utterly dead. I wanted to leave.

Later, as I was thanking them for the tea, Mr Sleight disappeared, and came scurrying back with one of the puppets in his hand, his face very pink.

'Well!' Mr Proudham clasped his hands together. 'Well, you *are* honoured!'

Mr Sleight was pressing the model into my hands. It was a Chinese Court Lady, with exquisitely small hands, and feet covered in beaded slippers. She wore a gold brocade kimono and a sash embroidered with flights of tiny butterflies and bumble bees.

'All for you!'

I was touched by Mr Sleight's gesture, and by the silent, beaming face. But oddly repelled by the small figure which felt so stiff and cold in my hands. I knew it was generous of him to give it. I wished very much that he had not.

I had reached the door of my own flat when Mr Proudham caught up with me. He was out of breath and his face was suddenly very old and anxious. 'I had to say – you see Mr Sleight takes to people so very rarely, he knows no one here, he . . . You will keep it, won't you? You do appreciate . . . He never gives them away, he has never done it before. You will *treasure* it, won't you?'

I reassured him. Inside my flat I examined the doll more closely. The workmanship was astonishing. I imagined Mr Sleight's pale, plump hands moulding, embroidering. I did not think I had heard him speak at all, there were only the nods and smiles, the shifting glances. I put the wax doll on the mantelpiece.

On Christmas Eve it snowed. The tide was running high and there was the hardest frost of the year. In the middle of the night I was awakened by the sound of raised voices. I had worked late and not been very long in bed. It was perhaps one o'clock. Mr Proudham and Mr Sleight were quarrelling. Ever since I was a young child in the home of unhappy, incompatible parents I had been used to hearing the sound of bitter argument in another room, so that now I felt the old misery and apprehension, wanting it to stop, wanting a reconciliation. The voices went on. A door banged, then another.

It was after two before I went to sleep. When I woke again it was past five. The shouting had ceased. My room was bitterly cold. I got up and went to the window. There was a full moon and the pebbles of the beach gleamed pale, the sea was very still. A light shone out of the flat below onto the small front garden. I stood looking down for a long time, until I began to shiver and had to go in search of another blanket. There might have been no one else awake in the whole world. It was a quiet house in any case, the top floor flat was closed up for the winter. I thought of Mr Sleight's workroom behind the beaded curtain, of the rows of wax figures. It was a long time before I went back uneasily to sleep.

On Christmas morning, I went out early to spend the day with friends inland, and it was gone midnight when I returned. The ground floor flat was in darkness, all the curtains were drawn. I was not woken up that night.

The next day, a thaw set in. I spent most of it working, and beyond the window I could see sky and sea merged together in the rain, everything was leaden grey. At eleven o'clock and at two Mr Proudham went out alone with the dog, at six it was Mr Sleight, draped in a mackintosh that reached to his ankles. Neither of them glanced up at my window. I was puzzled by the small changes in routine.

The rain continued all night, rolling down the gutters and lashing against the glass. For the first time, I felt lonely here, I missed London where there was always someone to call on, something to do, the streets were always lighted and full of people. I began to be sick of the endlessly rolling grey sea and the cawing of gulls. So I was glad of any company when, the following evening, Mr Proudham came to my door. I asked him to go back and fetch his friend, we would all have a festive drink.

Mr Proudham stood half in and half out of the hallway, his hands moving about nervously inside the pockets of his long, beige cardigan. He looked ill, the skin was markedly more yellow than usual and there were dark smears like thumb-prints beneath his eyes. His hair was uncombed, his shirt, open at the neck, was not particularly clean. He had always struck me as a fastidious man.

'Is everything all right, Mr Proudham?'

'No. Oh no, I'm afraid it is not – I'm afraid . . . I'm sorry, but it is not possible for me to fetch Mr Sleight – you are very kind but Mr Sleight has gone.' He was biting the side of his mouth anxiously.

'Really, I should not have come up, it has nothing to do with you – why should you have any idea what has happened?'

'Where has Mr Sleight gone to?'

'If I knew that . . .' He jumped suddenly, as though there were somebody behind him. I persuaded him to come inside, and in the light of the sitting room he looked even more ill and distressed.

'It isn't the first time you see, it has happened before.'

Outside the sea roared up and hit the shingle and hissed back again into the darkness.

'He is not well, that is the point, he cannot manage alone, wherever he may have gone. He is not at all well.'

I wondered whether it were physically or mentally, but did not like to ask.

'We had – there were *words*, you see, I was impatient. Oh, it is a long story, it was nothing . . . But then everything seemed to blow over again, we had settled down. But he is not an easy man, I can never tell, you see, never be quite sure . . . he says so little. Well, you will have noticed. But now, today, he has disappeared again, and how can he manage, in this weather? I did wonder if perhaps you had heard something, seen something? I have been searching all over the town, asked everyone. I wondered if you . . .'

I had not, of course, and had to tell him so.

'No. No, you would not know. You could not be expected.'

'Does he have friends to go to? Have you tried telephoning relatives?'

'He has none. There is no one.'

'Has he taken anything with him? Clothes? A suitcase?'

'Nothing. But he is not *well* – he has, fits, he cannot manage alone.' His face crumpled, the mouth sagged suddenly, until I thought that he would cry.

'I shall go out again. There is nothing else for it. I shall go out looking for him. I shall find him in the end.'

At the door he turned and gave a little, formal bow, like that with which he had first greeted me.

'Perhaps I can help? Would you like me to come with you?'

'It is better for me to go alone.'

I watched him go down the stairs.

The next five days were extremely distressing for Mr Proudham, who paced the beaches and the streets of that bleak little town, and telephoned ceaselessly to hospitals and police stations, and for me, too, who watched him and could not help, could not even inquire too closely. The rain did not cease, twice the tide spilled over the sea wall and flooded part of the front garden. Mr Proudham went out in Wellington boots, carrying the poodle dog. I tried to work and could not. Every so often my eye fell on the tiny wax doll.

And then, just before six o'clock one evening, when I had drawn my curtains against the cold, wet night, I heard footsteps coming quickly up the stairs, the doorbell rang urgently.

'He is found!' Mr Proudham's eyes were full of excited tears, he clasped and unclasped his hands. 'He is found! Oh, he has been very ill, *is* very ill, he wandered away for miles, got onto a bus . . . he is in hospital. But he is not drowned, not dead, I made sure that he would be dead. But he is alive!'

I was delighted, and said so, and he stood on the doorstep for several minutes, chattering with relief.

'But I must go to see him, I thought I would just tell you, but now I must get everything ready, I am sure they will let him come home soon.'

As it happened they did not, not for another three weeks. He was perhaps more seriously ill than was at first thought. Every afternoon, Mr Proudham went off to visit him, every evening he came upstairs to report on his friend's progress – though I thought that there was something he was keeping back. Once or twice I gave him a meal or a drink for he was not accustomed to managing on his own.

'It is Mr Sleight who cooks and keeps us tidy, you know. It has always been Mr Sleight who has managed things.' I was surprised, the partnership seemed to have been based upon the quickness and efficiency of the talkative Mr Proudham.

I did not really come to know him, though we talked a good deal, he told me stories about the past, about his childhood, in theatrical boarding-houses with his mother, of the ladies' orchestra. But although I knew selected facts I felt that he was holding anything of himself, of his own emotions or beliefs, back from me. He framed his formal, old-fashioned sentences, but that was all. Of his life with Mr Sleight he told me nothing, except that they had been together for more than twenty years.

The day before Mr Sleight was to come home, I offered to go downstairs and help with any cleaning there might be to do. Mr Proudham seemed offended and rather shocked, he would not hear of such a thing, and I was embarrassed. I had not intended to seem curious or interfering.

'I shall take a pleasure in it,' he said stiffly. 'It is the least I can do, after all, the proper way for me to welcome him home.'

I understood, and listened all that day to the sounds of cleaning, saw Mr Proudham shake rugs and mops out of the window, wearing a mauve plastic apron. The poodle dog had been freshly clipped, so that brownish pink skin showed through the shaven, horizontal bands and a red bow was tied around the top knot between its ears.

An ambulance brought Mr Sleight home. And as soon as I saw him, wrapped in a blanket and wheeled up the path in a chair, I knew that something was very wrong. He was much smaller, he seemed to have shrunk into himself, the skin was creased and folded, and his eyes darted wildly in the bony face. His hands, resting on the padded arms of the wheelchair, were white as claws. Mr Proudham, wearing the canary yellow waistcoat, fluttered around in attendance, smiling, smiling.

I had intended to wait a day or so until Mr Sleight had settled in, and then to take down some magazines and fruit, for he seemed unlikely to have any other visitors. But the morning after his return, Mr Proudham met me by the front door. He looked tired.

'In case you were wondering . . . in case you thought of paying Mr Sleight a visit.'

I told him what I had planned.

'Oh no. No, really you had far better not. You are very kind, but you see . . . things are not quite as they were, Mr Sleight has . . . is a little changed, not up to seeing visitors, he may not know you, or rather . . . Well, he is disturbed just at the moment. He has had a shock. They found him wandering, you know, he had had nothing to eat, his clothes . . . I really do think . . .'

I interrupted to save his obvious embarrassment, told him that of course I understood and would not dream of causing either of them any distress. Mr Proudham's face relaxed, but there was still something, an anxiety, a fear in the bloodshot eyes, he fidgeted more than ever. 'Thank you, thank you, thank you,' he said and went into the flat, closing the door behind him very quickly.

Every day after that he went out with the dog, and to do the shopping, always alone. He grew paler and more worn looking, he took on a dishevelled, even a grubby appearance. I worried about him from time to time, about both of them, so isolated and dependent. The winter weather was the worst for several years, snow and frost set in and showed no signs of thawing by early March.

My work was coming to an end, and I began to think I had had enough of the place. Once or twice, during those last weeks, I felt strongly that all was not as it should be with Mr Proudham and Mr Sleight. Several times I heard raised voices and now and then a loud banging on the floor, as though with a stick.

I came home as it was getting dark one evening, and as I turned from the gate, I caught sight of a pale, still face in the ground floor window. Mr Sleight was propped up on a sofa and he was staring intently at me. The beam, and the rather amusing self-consciousness had quite gone. His face was thin. He did not take his eyes off me and I saw that they had the intense yet oddly blank look of the very mad. He held in his hands one of the wax models: it was unfinished, without clothes and without any features moulded in its smooth, oval face. He held it up a little and, as I stared, began to twist one of the legs. If I had stayed there I should have seen it come away in his hands. I did not, I ran up the path and Mr Sleight watched me, unblinking, unsmiling. That night, the quarrelling began again, one of the voices rose to a scream. In the morning, I saw Mr Proudham go out with the dog, and his face was grey.

A week later, I left. When I met Mr Proudham in the path, he seemed alarmed, we shook hands, and he ducked back at once into the flat. I heard the key turn in the lock. When I shut the gate behind me for the last time, I saw the two figures, so changed, watching me as they had watched when I arrived, Mr Proudham standing a little bent at the shoulders behind the chair of Mr Sleight. I hesitated, half-raised a hand to them. There was no response. I moved quickly away.

It was on Good Friday that the name of the town happened to catch my eye, in the daily paper. There was a small paragraph. Police were investigating the deaths of Mr Albert Proudham and Mr Victor Sleight, whose bodies were found in a gas-filled room. A poodle dog and a parrot were also dead. I would have thought it an accident on the part of poor, harassed Mr Proudham, if it had not also been reported that the flat was in considerable disorder, a large number of 'dolls and puppets' having been found, broken and mutilated, and strewn about the floor.

In the Conservatory

From the beginning, theirs was a very public love affair. That is, they conducted it mainly in public places, and that out of choice, rather than of necessity. They both had a certain amount of time and money to spend on the relationship, so that it might have been nurtured in the quietness and privacy of town and country hotels, perhaps even of a flat. But they met in public, wanting somehow to prove the reality of it to themselves, by seeing and being seen.

It began at the party to celebrate the opening of Nancy's bookshop, in one of the Dickensian alleyways off Chancery Lane. *He* knew Nancy quite well, because he had been prevailed upon to help her select the stock, though he had had misgivings, it was not his field. He sold only – and sold very successfully – anti-quarian books.

She scarcely knew Nancy at all, she had gone to the party in place of her husband, Boris, to whom the invitation was addressed. Boris never went to parties of any kind, but that did not stop the invitations coming. And she had gone with this purpose in mind – to meet someone. For she had decided some weeks beforehand that it ought to be her next experience. I am thirty-two years old, she told herself, eight years married and childless, what else is there for me? I am not unattractive, not unintelligent, yet I have never had any sort of an affair, before marriage or since, there is a whole world about which my friends talk and people write, and about which *I* know nothing. There are emotions, passions, jealousies and anxieties, which I do not understand. It is time, surely it is time . . .

Perhaps, after all, it was not as clear-cut, as fully conscious as that, perhaps there were many doubts and moments of disillusionment. But the decision was in some sort made, and afterwards, she felt herself to be suddenly more vulnerable, more aware, she was receptive to glances and questions and implications. And then, it was only a question of time. Time, and the right choice.

She had arrived at Nancy's party, flushed and pretty with anticipation. Of course, Boris would never mind. Indeed, her dull certainty that Boris would not mind took a little of the edge off it all. Boris, preoccupied with his books on military history, Boris with his little leaden soldiers, drawn up in battalions all over the dining-table, Boris who was more of a stranger to her, now, than any of the people at Nancy's party – this was the Boris who would not mind.

And so, that was where they had met, one evening in Nancy's new shop, and then the following day, too, because *he* had half said, and *she* had half said, that they might be somewhere in the British Museum at some point tomorrow. She had rushed all about that great mausoleum, up and down marble staircases, until her legs ached, among all the Malay students and school parties from Lancashire, in and out of manuscript rooms and sculpture rooms and print rooms, galleries full of Egyptian mummies and Anglo-Saxon drinking vessels and oriental porcelain, and still she had not found him anywhere. Only later, after she had drunk a cup of grey coffee and slipped off her shoes under the table, and then gone wearily back, there he had been, looking at her behind one of the racks of postcards in the publications hall. His eyes were the colour of pebbles on a winter beach.

After that, for several weeks, they always met in the British Museum, a different room each day, she had never seen so much of it, never learned so much, by accident, in her life before. They moved on to the National Portrait Gallery, then, and the Tate, and the musical instruments rooms of the V and A, they sat on innumerable, leather-covered benches, and stood before important paintings and drank tea in the dreary tea-rooms, talked to one another, touched one another rather formally, explored the initial avenues of their affair.

Soon, they took to going farther afield, as though they now felt able to extend the boundaries of their relationship, to view it against a new background. He had to travel, in any case, buying his books, and she herself was a free agent, neither children nor work claimed her, and Boris did not care. They took their time over finding country hotels, first of all for lunch or tea, but later, when the spring came, they began to sleep together. Sparingly, at first. In the mornings, she awoke and got out of bed to stare in the mirror at herself, expecting to see a change. Here I am, she said, and there he is and it must be that I am now truly living, that this is experience . . .

It was at about this time, in their search for public places out of London, for castles and abbeys and country homes, that they came across Fewings. And Fewings seemed to them to be some kind of architectural terminus, a statement, in bricks and mortar, of all that they were experiencing in their affair. Once they had found Fewings, and the convenient Inn called the Four in Hand, in a village close by, they went nowhere else.

Fewings was the ugliest house either of them had ever seen, a Victorian Gothic fantasy, like one of mad Ludwig's Bavarian castles, all turrets and towers and crenellations of rose-pink brick. It *had* in fact been built, in the heart of the Kent countryside, by an Anglophile German count, who had seen it as his gift to England.

When he died, at the turn of the century, he had left Fewings, together with a wealthy trust for its upkeep, to the British nation. The nation, being obliged to accept it, had made a virtue out of necessity and erected signposts along all the main roads and posters in selected railway stations. Paragraphs about Fewings appeared in local guide books, a caretaker was installed, gardeners and a curator were employed, and from March until October, the visitors came.

The grotesqueness of the house was more than matched by its bizarre contents, for the Count had been a collector. A whole wing, for instance, was given over to Chinoiserie, with life-size waxworks dressed as Mandarins and Cantonese executioners, lurking on the bends of stairs. In the cellars were instruments of torture, and, at the top of the building, galleries full of dolls, and miniature dolls' houses. There were the usual libraries full of morocco-bound books in glass cases, the usual guns and pistols and suits of armour, the usual oils and watercolours and prints – and other things besides, less usual and more alarming. There was something sinister about Fewings, the rooms had a certain smell. Very few people who came once ever wanted to return.

The gardens were rather a different matter, for the German Count had handed over the construction of them to an Englishman called Captain Smithers, who combined the enthusiasm of the amateur with the application and authority of a professional. He took twenty years to make, at Fewings, one of the great landscape gardens of England.

There was much topiary work, casting dark shadows of birds and lions couchant on to the sunlit grass, there were colonnades and formal terraces and large fountains, a Gothic arch of beeches and raised, circular lawns. It was a dramatic garden, devoid of prettiness except for one or two arbours hidden in the topiary here and there, overlooking the sunken flower beds. It was all rather severe, to complement the extravagances of the house, satisfying in its proportions yet wholly dramatic, a public garden, larger than any of the life that surrounding Kent might have to offer.

The drama of Fewings and its gardens was what appealed to them. That and its unexpectedness. For her part, too, she found it sinister, she had nightmares centred upon the place, and all of this contributed to her sense of heightened awareness, of real, true living. Each time they visited, they felt excitement, they discovered more and more rooms, new spiral staircases leading up into the towers and new corridors, ending in sudden window seats that gave startling views of the gardens below, and the rich countryside beyond. They experienced themselves through their experience of the house.

She liked to be frightened there, to have him leave her alone in the cellars, with all the black and grey steel instruments of torture and the cold whitewashed walls, the smell of dampness that came from being below the level of the earth. The long passages echoed to the ring of his footsteps, as he walked quickly away from her, and she was forced to run in terrified search of him, frantically going from room to room, getting lost and coming upon one of the costumed waxworks, before she did, at last, find him, and sobbed with relief. Fewings excited them, indeed, as nowhere else could have done. And afterwards, there was the small back bedroom at the Four in Hand.

But above all, she found herself drawn, in fear and fascination, to the conservatory that was built into the centre of the house like a great, covered courtyard, the glass roof ribbed and vaulted in the style of the Victorian railway stations. It had a wrought-iron gallery running all the way around it, close to the sky. The German Count had spent most of his time here, in his last years, pacing around and around, wearing a long red dressing-gown. He had talked to himself all day and terrified the maids if they sought him out with news of a guest or a letter or a meal. As he walked, he had looked down upon the jungle he had made below.

He had imported every kind of tropical plant and creeper and now, years later, they crept up over the glass walls and then knitted together, to overhang the narrow pathways, trailing down their dark green leaves like great flat hands. The stems were thick as legs and arms, and all the time, one or other of the plants was throwing up gigantic flowers in vivid unlikely colours, flame and scarlet, yellow and fuchsia pink, all striped and spotted and fantastically shaped. The conservatory was heated to a steaming temperature, by long, old-fashioned radiators hidden in the undergrowth, so that, however hard they cut everything back, it grew again twice as fast, the foliage and the flowers rampaged up and over the conservatory roof and the light that filtered through was a pale and curious green.

Down below, in the centre of it all, was the pond, thick with reeds and water-plants, below which slid the fish, slow, fat-bodied fish taken from the rivers of Central Africa and South America, dramatically coloured and marked. You could sit on the flat stone ledge that surrounded the pool, under the green umbrella of leaves, and smell the hot, sweet smell of the jungle. They came in here more and more, stayed for hours, shoulders and thighs touching, mesmerized by the stillness and the soft green light, saying nothing at all. Though once, at the very beginning, she had told him, 'This is the heart of the house, this is where we should always come,' and at once, she had felt foolish, for saying that had brought into the open some truth she did not wish to acknowledge, about the unreality, the *risibility* of their affair, and she had shrunk back at once. It does not do, she said, to analyse things, we should never make definitive statements about a relationship. She had read precisely that, somewhere recently.

To cover the moment's embarrassment, she had leaned forward and slid her hand into the warm, slightly glutinous water. It had come up against the body of a fish, and she cried out in horror, got up at once, pulling him after her, had made him take her away from the conservatory and from Fewings altogether. But before very long, she had to go back, she now seemed only able to savour their relationship to the full in the strange atmosphere of Fewings. She forced herself to sweat gently under the dark green canopy of leaves, watching the slow opening of an orange Hulura flower pointed and starred and with purple stamens like long, furred tongues.

He, for his part, was not at all alarmed by the atmosphere at

Fewings, it merely amused him, but he was excited by the effect it had upon her, it shocked him to see her violent delight and fear. He had always thought himself a dull man, leading a dull life, he had been too lethargic to seek out the experiences he thought he needed, if life were not entirely to pass him by, but he had so far had only the usual, the predictable relationships. She startled him profoundly, therefore, because she had sought him out, yet he had still not altogether shrugged off the lethargy, for he himself had done nothing, and he did nothing still. It was she who worked up their affair as she chose, and gave it its pattern and character; he watched and was manipulated by her and that seemed to be enough.

It was in the conservatory that she first caught sight of the boy, and was at once aware that she had, in fact, seen him several times before, about the house – disappearing ahead of them up some staircase, or standing in the corners of rooms, half hidden by the furniture. Until now, he had not registered himself upon her consciousness, and so she had paid no attention to him. Now, here he was, in the conservatory, looking at them between the thick, fleshy leaves, and yet not looking, his eyes focused elsewhere, or focused upon nothing at all. She moved suddenly, but he did not start. He stayed where he was, for several moments, and then turned and went slowly away with a curious, shuffling walk. A door scraped shut behind him, the sound muffled by the undergrowth.

One of the violently coloured tropical birds, that lived up near the roof of the conservatory, flapped down, in a rush of wings and darting, turquoise-blue tail.

'I want to go,' she said, pulling him to his feet. 'Now, quickly.'

The next time they came to Fewings, they saw the boy again.

The Musrys had come as caretakers to Fewings as soon as everything got under way again, after the war. Arthur wasn't well, his leg would never get properly better, they said, and it had seemed too good an opportunity to miss, with living in the country and a self-contained flat, and so forth. You thought twice about turning down jobs with self-contained flats, in those days. So they had come, though she had not been at all sure, not really, and the moment they had started to open up all the rooms, and get the stuff out of store, she knew why.

'It's a very funny place,' she had said, 'a very funny place indeed.' But that was all, because Arthur seemed keen, it had taken his fancy, and he didn't think so much about his leg and feel sorry for himself. So she kept her real feelings to herself, and made the most of the self-contained flat, tucked away in the east wing, not venturing farther than she must, into the rest of the house. In time, she had an army of morning cleaners, who came in a coach from the town, nine miles away, and she was in her element then, organizing them. They could always be sent into those parts of the house she didn't much care for.

So they had been here for twenty-four years, and the boy Leonard for thirteen of them.

It was her younger sister's boy, and she had known about him right from the beginning, from the very first day that Amy was sick. It was what they had all expected of Amy sooner or later, but they hadn't expected her to die, nor that their mother would die, six days after. Amy had been going to live on at home, with her mother and the child, it was all arranged. Nobody knew anything at all about the child's father.

They were the only ones left, and so they had taken him themselves, and, although neither of them knew anything about children, they fitted their lives around him without any difficulty, because he was a good boy, he had not been a moment's trouble.

They didn't exactly know what was wrong with him, just that, as it were, something was not quite right. He was very slow. He picked up his fork and spoon slowly and it was hard for him to grip things, or to separate his toys into piles, or judge how many stairs he had to clamber down, so that at first he was forever falling. He was nine before he was sure which shoe to put on which foot, and even now, they had trouble over laces.

But he was a gentle child, he touched people and objects with the same soft, delicate touch, and he smiled a good deal, at almost anything. He loved Fewings. He went everywhere about the place with his father from being a tiny baby – because they called themselves mother and father to him and never told him the truth: where was the point? He would only be upset and never properly understand. They carried him about, and he was left on the window seats, or the carved oak settle, and he would wait, looking about him, quite content. He was very late in walking, almost three before he could climb the stairs, but after that, he was always going off into the house, they never knew exactly where. And because he was such an obedient child and would never touch anything after they had told him once that he was not to, they let him go, by himself, wherever he pleased. She was worried for a long time about the cellars, there were so many terrible things on which he could have accidents but his father told him that he could only walk about down there and never touch anything. He never touched.

Some things, of course, he *was* allowed to touch, mostly in winter, when there were no visitors and the curator only came once a month. They let him take the dolls and hold them, and when the guns were being cleaned, his father would balance one upon his outstretched hands. But not the books, for he had once let a book slip off his knees, and grabbed it back, in panic, by a single page, which tore. It was a big book of maps. He had sobbed for two hours, and on and off through the night, and for weeks afterwards, if he went by the doors of the library.

If they had been willing to send him away from them, he could have boarded in London at a special school, but they knew that Amy would not have let him go, and besides, what good would it do? To their own surprise, they found that they loved him, and so he went to the village school, where he learned what little he

45

could, and was happy. At eleven, he had been taken by a school in the next town, and so, Arthur Musry had bought a motor bicycle and side-car and learned to drive it very cautiously, so that he could take the boy, and bring him back, each day. It was worst in winter, when his leg and the weather were bad.

They knew that he would always stay with them at Fewings, that he was never going to make his own way in the world, and they were only worried about how he might be if anything should happen to them. But he was happy enough, meanwhile, in the house and gardens after school and all through the holidays, doing little jobs, fetching and carrying. He knew every corner, every room and staircase and corridor, and he only wanted to be left to wander about, looking at everything, making sure that it was safe. He did not get in the way of the summer visitors, only watched them, fascinated, and sometimes, he would be able to direct them to this or that room, to the tea bar or the lavatories, and this delighted him, it made him feel necessary, though his speech was thick and slow, they could not always understand him. He never seemed to hold their subsequent impatience against them.

But it was the conservatory that he loved most of all. There were lizards hidden among the stones in the undergrowth, and small toads about the pond. He let them run over his hands, unafraid. Feeding the fish was the one job he had done quite by himself for some years, the keeper, who lived down in the village, had come to trust him over that. It was to the conservatory that the couple went first, if they wanted to find him.

He was there, just sitting, when they came upon him the next time they visited Fewings. She had been saying something about Boris, and his floor-to-ceiling maps of German battlefields, laughing at the childishness of it, when they came around the path, towards the pond, and saw him. She stopped dead.

'He's there,' she said, 'he's there again.' The boy took no

notice of them, though she felt that he was aware, was listening.

'I keep on seeing him, now,' she said, 'why does he follow us?'

'Oh, surely he does not!' They always spoke half in whispers in the conservatory, there was something about the place that encouraged secrecy. 'I think he's just the caretaker's boy.'

'I don't like him, he watches us. I wish he would go away.'

They sat, some distance from him, under the leaves beside the pond. She laid each one of her fingers upon his. One of the birds began to chatter, Kuu-uup, Kuu-uup, Kuu-uup, in the branches above.

Later, they went up into the tower room at the remote, north end of the house, climbing up a dark staircase. They had found the bench seat, let into a narrow gap in the wall, quite by chance, and the tower housed only a few dull maps and suits of armour, nobody else bothered to come up here. The window looked directly down hundreds of giddy feet on to the top of the fountain. But this time, they arrived breathless, to find the boy already in the window seat staring down. She jumped back, giving a little cry of alarm, and then she was angry, for she felt spied upon, and the boy frightened her because there was something not right. This particular place was now quite spoiled for her. The boy got up and went at once, moving forward with his odd, slow walk, knees a little bent. He had still taken no notice of them. But she said in a hysterical voice, 'I don't like him, I wish we didn't have to keep seeing him here. He isn't quite right, he shouldn't be wandering about alone, I shall find somebody and complain.'

He calmed her eventually, and they forgot about the boy, they talked of themselves and their continuing amazement at the complexities of their affair. She was still absorbed in it, in the emotions she experienced and in the sense of acute awareness, of unreality. She had begun to keep a diary, for everything seemed too significant to lose. Now, when she read novels and saw plays, and talked to friends about such affairs, she understood everything exactly, it was all personally confirmed, and she felt herself to be part of the great, adult world of experience. For she said to him that she had never felt herself to be truly adult, until now.

Her one disappointment was that Boris did not care. She could not quite tell whether he knew about them or not, but whichever it was, she smarted under his indifference, and began to think of ways in which she might bring matters to a head with him, for surely the time had come for there to be some jealousy, some quarrels ending in tears and forgiveness. But Boris only marched his leaden soldiers up and down the dining-table, and smiled vaguely at a point beyond her shoulder, when she was going out. And did not care.

'You must see it,' she said, one afternoon in July, 'he *spies* upon us. If we manage to get away from the other visitors, we cannot get away from him. He is everywhere.'

'No, no, surely not. You've started to notice him, be irritated by him, that's all. I think perhaps he was always there.'

'No. He looks, he lies about in wait for us.'

That day, they had been walking through the Chinese rooms, and suddenly, he was there, sitting in a sedan chair, his eyes glistening, very still.

'He ought not to be *allowed* to,' she said, 'he will damage something.' And she had made a vague movement of her hands towards the boy, frowned very sternly, in order to shoo him away.

He laughed at her, the anger and discontent excited him. 'Poor child,' he said mildly, 'I'm sure he cannot help it,' and touched his hand to her bare arm, moving her away. They could have three nights, this time, in the bedroom at the Four in Hand, though he must spend some part of the days buying books at house sales.

But she could not stop thinking about the boy, even when they were away from Fewings. And while they were there, if she saw the back of him, disappearing along some corridor, or in the distance, pushing a barrow-load of grass cuttings across the lawn, the rest of their day was spoiled for her, she could not concentrate upon themselves.

While he went to one of his sales, therefore, she came alone, and looked about purposefully, for someone in charge.

'Surely it is not safe,' she said firmly. 'We have seen him poking about in this and that, sitting on the furniture, going up and down steep stairs. Surely he ought to be watched more carefully.'

Arthur Musry stared, reaching down to rub at the back of his bad leg. He didn't like her, had never liked her, and he had often wondered about them, always coming here, spending so much money on entrance tickets, wondered what they did all those afternoons, in the deserted rooms.

'Mightn't he hurt himself? How can he be safe, when he walks the way he does? He isn't the sort of boy who should have the run of a place like this on his own.'

'He's all right,' Arthur Musry said, 'there's nothing wrong with him, he's a good boy. He'll not touch anything, not do anything. This is his home, isn't it? He's all right.'

'He *follows us*.' Her voice rose in desperation.

'Why should he do that?'

'*I* don't know why, I only know he does.'

He shook his head, and looked away from her, down the gravelled drive. If he could have been rid of her, turned her away the next time, he would have done so.

'He's all right,' he said again, sullen.

'I just don't like it when he watches us, and listens. When he follows.' She was almost in tears of rage, knowing there was nothing she could do, that she was in the wrong and the man could never be made to take her word, could never begin to understand.

'He was stupid,' she said later, in the bedroom, 'a stupid little man.'

The next time they went to Fewings, she caught hold of the boy in one of the dark passages and held his arm tightly, pushed her face into his and told him not to come near them, to go now, right away, to stop following and spying. He backed from her, eyes huge with alarm, and disappeared into the shadows, she heard his uncertain tread, fast as it could go on the staircase. He had made straight for the conservatory, and that was where they too came, some time later, and found him hiding under the branches, with a small brown lizard resting on his hand.

He got up at once and backed away.

'That's all right,' she said, walking round and round the pond, trying to see down into the water, looking for the fish. 'He's gone, he won't do it again, that's all right.' And later, she said also, 'Poor child, he ought to be away somewhere, he ought to be looked after. How can you blame him?' She sat down and began to talk to him about how she wanted to quarrel violently with Boris.

For three weeks, the boy would not go out of the flat, and at night he wet his bed and called out. They couldn't make sense of it, and got the doctor, who could find nothing wrong. He sat all day with a picture book or looking at the television, and he wanted to be near to them both, wherever they went, he went, and his shoes were suddenly on the wrong feet, he wore his jersey back to front until she noticed and helped to dress him.

It was a long time before he would go back into the house alone. They had to coax him like a mouse out of a hole, his father had to keep calling to him, for reassurance. Gradually he grew better, but his hands still trembled when he lifted anything, and he began to sleep-walk every night, they grew accustomed to lying tensely listening for him.

During this time, Boris developed pleurisy, and she was pre-occupied with her sense of guilt, and with her alarm at the idea that she would no longer want to continue with the affair, if Boris were to die.

But Boris did not die, he got better and went to convalesce in Ischia, and then they could visit Fewings again. She sat up in bed very early each morning to write a blue air-mail letter to her absent husband.

At Fewings, it was almost the end of the season. The lines of poplars were half-bare, half-brown, and Arthur Musry was out on the circular lawn with a besom, sweeping up leaves.

'We must go everywhere,' she said, her eyes very bright, '*every*where. This is the last time, there is such a lot to see and remember.' 'But it is only till March.' He laughed at her. 'There will be next year.' But she would not have him spoil her sense of occasion.

They left the conservatory until the very last.

The boy was better, much better, except that he still would not go up on to the landing where she had frightened him. He no longer wet the bed, or clutched at them suddenly, he ate his meals without making any mess. But something had happened, something was different, his mother knew that, and they had noticed it at school and wondered what had happened, and if he would improve. Arthur Musry remembered the woman, and said nothing.

For some time, he would not go into the conservatory either, but they talked to him about the fish, and asked didn't he want to feed them again? 'It's to build up his confidence,' his father said, 'we've got to do it, it's for the best. Let him get back to the fish and the animals, they'll help him, bring him round.'

In some way, they did, so that before very long he would venture in alone, as long as the door was left slightly open.

Shortly after this, he had a kind of fit, one of the cleaners found him just outside the library, his eyes rolled back into his head, legs twitching. He came round before the doctor arrived and seemed quite all right, was only a little pale, and confused over which hand ought to hold his fork. They gave him tablets and he went for a day to the hospital for tests, but nothing was told them, nothing was said.

She had been talking about the winter, and how different everything would be, for they would be meeting in London again, and she wanted to start visiting his flat, because it happened to be quite close to the college at which Boris gave his military lectures. She foresaw new dangers in the continuation of their affair, she wanted to take risks and be in suspense, to be speculated over and talked about.

'Whatever you want,' he told her, laughing again, 'whatever you say.' For he saw how much even the anticipation of the winter was affecting her and knew that she would continue to act violently upon his emotions.

'Now,' she said, jumping up, '*now* the conservatory!'

She began to run down the staircases and along the corridors, he panted and could scarcely keep up with her, the blood began to make a rushing sound in his ears.

The conservatory was very still, very quiet, the glass door slipped shut and she smelled the thick jungle smell and shivered a little, her skin shadowed green by the overhanging branches.

They found the boy upside down in the pond, his head and shoulders underneath the flat water-plants, among the slow-moving fish, and only his legs sticking out over the side. She saw that the shoes were carefully fitted on to the wrong feet. The little canister of meal for the fish lay, overturned, on the floor.

He was making for the door to get help, he would have left her there, not thinking, if she had not stumbled out after him, making an odd, low noise in her throat and putting her hands up to her face. The glass door clicked gently shut behind her.

*

They never came to Fewings again. She had known that they would not, even before it happened, known that events do not repeat themselves, and that by the end of the winter, she would have grown bored and started to look for something, someone else, the next experience.

In the event, it could not go on even for as long as that, everything was changed, she surfaced like a diver into a grey and chilling world. For weeks, she could think of nothing but the boy, dead, among the fish, in the conservatory. They had to go to the nearby town, for the inquest, but she made him drive her straight back to London when it was over.

On his side, he sensed the change, saw that there was a deadness about her, and, knowing that it was at an end, was unexpectedly relieved. There was no final scene, no quarrel, no dramatic parting, as she had always anticipated. He gave her dinner that evening, and then drove her all the way home, got out of the car, and shook hands, strangely, on the doorstep. Once, a couple of months later, they did see one another in the Food Hall at Harrods, and he half-waved, she half-waved, hesitated, and moved on. She bought veal and a whole Cheddar cheese, and when she got home with them, Boris had arranged his battalions of soldiers on the kitchen table, because there were workmen decorating the dining-room.

In the bathroom, she looked at her own face in the mirror and for the first time she saw a change.

Arthur Musry sold the motor bicycle and side-car but that was all, they stayed on at Fewings because there was nowhere else for them to go, not after twenty-four years, even if she did not really like it. Whenever he could, he avoided the conservatory. She resigned herself, said nothing, knowing that it would not be easy, these days, to find another job with a self-contained flat.

How Soon Can I Leave?

The two ladies who lived together were called Miss Bartlett and Miss Roscommon.

Miss Roscommon, the older and stouter of the two, concealed her fear of life behind frank reference to babies and lavatories and the sexing of day-old chicks. It was well known that she had travelled widely as a girl, she told of her walking tours in Greece, and how she had driven an ambulance during the Spanish Civil War.

Miss Bartlett, who was only forty, cultivated shyness and self-effacement, out of which arose her way of leaving muttered sentences to trail off into the air, unfinished. Oh, do not take any notice of anything *I* may say, she meant, it is of no consequence, I am sorry to have spoken . . . But the sentences drew attention to her, nevertheless.

'What was that?' people said, 'I beg your pardon, I didn't quite catch . . . Do speak up . . .' And so, she was forced to repeat herself and they, having brought it upon themselves, were forced to listen. She also protested helplessness in the face of everyday tools. It was Miss Roscommon who peeled all the potatoes and defrosted the refrigerator and opened the tins.

Their house, one of two white bungalows overlooking the bay, was called Tuscany.

When Miss Bartlett had finally come to live with Miss Roscommon, seven years before, each one believed that the step was taken for the good of the other. Miss Bartlett had been living in one of the little stone cottages, opposite the harbour, working through the winter on the stock that she sold, from her front room and on a trestle outside, in summer. From November until

March, there were no visitors to Mountsea. Winds and rain scoured the surface of the cliffs and only the lifeboat put out to sea. Miss Roscommon had taken to inviting Miss Bartlett up to the bungalow for meals.

'You should have a shop,' she had begun by saying, loading Miss Bartlett's plate with scones and home-made ginger jam, 'properly equipped and converted. It cannot be satisfactory having to display goods in your living-room. Why have you not thought of taking a shop?'

Miss Bartlett made marquetry pictures of the church, the lighthouse and the harbour, table-lamps out of lobster pots and rocks worked over with shells. She also imported Italian straw baskets and did a little pewter work.

The idea of a shop had come to her, and been at once dismissed, in the first weeks after her coming to Mountsea. She was too timid to take any so definite a step, for, by establishing herself in a shop, with her name written up on a board outside, was she not establishing herself in the minds of others, as a shop*keeper*? As a girl, she had been impressed by her mother's constant references to her as dreamy and artistic, so that she could not possibly now see herself in the role of shopkeeper. Also, by having her name written up on that board, she felt that she would somehow be committing herself to Mountsea, and by doing that, finally abandoning all her hopes of a future in some other place. As a girl, she had looked out at the world, and seen a signpost, with arms pointing in numerous different directions, roads leading here, or here, or there. She had been quite unable to choose which road to take for, having once set out upon any of them, she would thereby be denying herself all the others. And what might I lose, she had thought, what opportunities shall I miss if I make the wrong choice?

So that, in the end, she had never chosen, only drifted through her life from this to that, waking every morning to the expectation of some momentous good fortune dropped in her lap.

'That cottage is damp,' said Miss Roscommon, allowing her persuasions to take on a more personal note, as they got to know one another better. 'I do not think you look after yourself properly. And a place of business should not have to double as a home.'

At first, Miss Bartlett shrank from the hints and persuasions, knowing herself to be easily swayed, fearful of being swept along on the tide of Miss Roscommon's decision. I am only forty years old, she said, there is plenty of opportunity left for me, I do not have to abandon hope by retreating into middle age, and life with another woman. Though certainly she enjoyed the meals the other cooked; the taste of home-baked pasties and stews and herb-flavoured vegetables.

'I'm afraid that I cannot cook,' she said. 'I live on milk and cheese and oven-baked potatoes. I would not know where to begin in the kitchen.' It did not occur to her that this was any cause for shame, and Miss Roscommon tut-tutted and floured the pastry-board, relieved to have, once again, a sense of purpose brought into her life.

'There were nine of us in the family,' she said, 'and I was the only girl. At the age of seven, I knew how to bake a perfect loaf of bread. I am quite content to be one of the Marthas of this world.'

But I will not go and *live* there, Miss Bartlett told herself, towards the end of that summer. I am determined to remain independent, my plans are fluid, I have my work, and besides, it would never do, we might not get on well together and then it would be embarrassing for me to have to leave. And people might talk.

Though she knew that they would not, and that it was of her own judgement that she was most afraid, for Mountsea was full of ladies of indeterminate age, sharing houses together.

The winter came, and the cottage was indeed damp. The stone walls struck cold all day and all night, in spite of expensive electric heaters, and Miss Bartlett spent longer and longer afternoons at Tuscany, even taking some of her work up there, from time to time.

At the beginning of December, the first of the bad storms sent waves crashing up over the quayside into the front room.

Of course, Miss Roscommon is lonely, she said now, she has need of me, I should have realized. That type of woman, who appears to be so competent and strong, feels the onset of old age and infirmity more than most, but she cannot say so, cannot give way and confess to human weakness. She bakes me cakes and worries about the dampness in my house because she needs my company and concern for herself.

And so, on Christmas Eve, when the second storm filled Miss Bartlett's living-room with water up to the level of the window seat, she allowed herself to be evacuated by the capable Miss Roscommon up to the white bungalow.

'It will not be for good,' she said anxiously, 'when the weather improves, I shall have to go back, there is the business to be thought of.' 'We shall make plans for a proper shop,' said Miss Roscommon firmly, 'I have a little money . . .'

She filled up a pottery bowl with leek soup, having acquired her faith in its restorative powers when she had set up a canteen at the scene of a mining disaster in the nineteen-twenties.

Miss Bartlett accepted the soup and a chair close to the fire and an electric blanket for her bed, thereby setting the seal on the future pattern of their relationship. By the beginning of February, plans for the shop were made, by mid-March, the work was in hand. There was no longer any talk of her moving, she would sell her goods from the new shop during the summer days, but she would live at Tuscany. The garage was fitted with light, heat and two extra windows, and made into a studio.

'This is quite the best arrangement,' said Miss Roscommon, 'here you will be properly fed and looked after, I shall see to that.'

Over the seven years that followed, Miss Bartlett came to rely upon her for many more things than the comforts of a well-kept home. It was Miss Roscommon who made all the business arrangements for the new shop, who saw the bank manager, the estate agent and the builder, Miss Roscommon who advised with the orders and the accounts. During the summer seasons, the shop did well, and after three years, at her friend's suggestion, Miss Bartlett started to make pink raffia angels and pot-pourri jars, for the Christmas postal market.

She relaxed, ceased to feel uneasy, and if, from time to time, she did experience a sudden shot of alarm, at seeing herself so well and truly settled, she said, not, 'Where else would I go?' but, 'I am needed here. However would she manage without me? It would be cruel to go.' All the decisions were left to Miss Roscommon. 'You are so much better at these things . . .' Miss Bartlett said, and drifted away to her studio, a small woman with pastel-coloured flesh.

Perhaps it was her forty-seventh birthday that jolted her into a renewed awareness of the situation. She looked into the mirror on that morning, and saw middle-age settled irrevocably over her features. She was reminded of her dependence upon Miss Roscommon.

I said I would not stay here, she thought, would never have my name written up above a permanent shop, for my plans were to remain fluid. And now it is seven years, and how many opportunities have I missed? How many roads are closed to me?

Or perhaps it was the visit of Miss Roscommon's niece Angela, and her husband of only seven days, one weekend in early September.

'I shall do a great deal of baking,' Miss Roscommon said, 'for they will certainly stay to tea. We shall have cheese scones and preserves and a layer cake.'

'I did not realize that you had a niece.'

Miss Roscommon rose from the table heavily, for she had put on weight, over the seven years. There had also been some suspicion about a cataract in her left eye, another reason why Miss Bartlett told herself she could not leave her.

'She is my youngest brother's child. I haven't seen her since she was a baby.'

Miss Bartlett nodded and wandered away from the break-fast table, not liking to ask why there had been no wedding invitation. Even after seven years, Miss Roscommon kept some of her secrets, there were subjects upon which she simply did not speak, though Miss Bartlett had long ago bared her own soul.

The niece Angela, and her new husband, brought a slab of wedding cake, which was put to grace the centre of the table, on a porcelain stand.

'And this,' said Miss Roscommon triumphantly, '*this* is my friend, Miss Mary Bartlett.' For Miss Bartlett had hung behind in the studio for ten minutes after their arrival, out of courtesy and because it was always something of a strain for her to meet new people.

'Mary is very shy, very retiring,' her own mother had always said, 'she is artistic you see, she lives in her own world.' Her tone had always been proud and Miss Bartlett had therefore come to see her own failure as a mark of distinction. Her shyness had been cultivated, readily admitted to.

The niece and her husband sat together on the sofa, a little flushed and self-conscious in new clothes. Seeing them there, Miss Bartlett realized for the first time that no young people had ever been inside the bungalow, since her arrival. But it was more than their youthfulness which struck her, there was an air of suppressed excitement about them, a glitter, they emanated pride in the satisfactions of the flesh.

Miss Roscommon presided over a laden tea-table, her face still flushed from the oven.

'And Miss Bartlett is very clever,' she told them, 'she makes beautiful things. You must go down to the shop and see them, buy something for your new home.'

'You make things?' said Angela, through a mouthful of short-bread, 'what sort of things?'

Miss Bartlett made a little gesture of dismissal with her hand. 'Oh, not very much really, nothing at all exciting. Just a few little . . . I'm sure you wouldn't . . .' She let her voice trail off, but it was Miss Roscommon and not the niece Angela who took her up on it.

'Now that is just nonsense,' she said firmly. 'There is no virtue in this false modesty, I have told you before. Of course Angela will like your things, why should she not? Plenty of visitors do, and there is nothing to be ashamed of in having a talent.'

'I wore a hand-embroidered dress,' said the niece Angela, 'for my wedding.'

Miss Bartlett watched her, and watched the new husband, whose eyes followed Angela's slim hand as it moved over to the cake plate and back, and up into her mouth. Their eyes met and shone with secrets, across the table. Miss Bartlett's stomach moved a little, with fear and excitement. She felt herself to be within touching distance of some very important piece of knowledge.

'Do you help with this shop, then –?' asked the husband though without interest.

'Oh, no! Well, here and there with the accounts and so forth, because Mary doesn't understand any of that, she is such a dreamer! No, no, that is not my job, that is not what keeps me so busy. My job is to look after Mary, of course. I took that upon myself quite some time ago, when I saw that I was needed. She is such a silly girl, she lives in a world of her own and if I were not here to worry about her meals and her comforts, she would starve, I assure you, simply starve.'

'Oh, I don't think I really . . .'

'Of course you would,' said Miss Roscommon. 'Now let me have your cup to be filled.'

The young couple exchanged another glance, of comprehension and amusement. How dare you, thought Miss Bartlett, almost in tears with anger and frustration, at being so looked upon and judged and misunderstood. What do you know of it, how can you sit there so smugly? It is because you are young and know nothing. It is all very well for you.

'All the same,' said the niece Angela, sitting back in her chair, 'it's nice to be looked after, I must say.'

She smiled like a cat.

'Yes, that has always been my role in life, that is *my* talent,' said Miss Roscommon, 'to do all the looking after.' She leaned over and patted Miss Bartlett on the hand. 'She is my responsibility now, you see,' she told them confidently. 'My little pussy-cat.'

Miss Bartlett pushed the hand away and got to her feet, her face flushed with shame and annoyance. 'What a foolish thing to say! Of course I am not, how very silly you make me look. I am a grown woman, I am quite capable of looking after myself.'

Miss Roscommon, not in the least discomfited, only began to pour the tea dregs into a slop basin, smiling.

When they were about to leave, Miss Bartlett said, 'I will walk down the hill with you, and we shall drop in for a minute at the shop. Yes, I insist . . . But not for you to buy anything. You must choose a wedding present from my stock, it is the very least I can do.' For she wanted to keep them with her longer, to be seen walking in their company down the hill away from the bungalow, wanted to be on their side.

'You will need a warm coat, it is autumn now, the evenings are drawing in. Take your mohair.'

'Oh, leave me, leave me, do not *fuss*.' And Miss Bartlett walked to the end of the gravelled drive, while the niece and her new husband made their goodbyes.

'I am afraid it is all she has to worry over nowadays,' she said hastily, the moment they had joined her. 'It gives her pleasure, I suppose, to do all that clucking round and I have not the heart to do anything but play along, keep up appearances. If it were not for me, she would be so lonely. Of course, I have had to give up a good deal of my own life, on that account.'

The niece Angela took her husband's arm. 'It must be very nice and comfortable for you there,' she said, 'all the same.'

Miss Bartlett turned her face away and looked out to sea. Another winter, she thought, and I am now forty-seven years old. You do not understand.

She detained them in the shop for as long as possible, fetching out special items from the stock room and taking time over the wrapping paper. Let me be with you, she wanted to say, let me be on your side, for do you not see that I still have many opportunities left, I am not an old woman, I know about the world and the ways of modern life? Take me with you.

But when they had gone she stood in the darkening shop and saw that they had already placed and dismissed her, that she did not belong with them and there was no hope left. She sat on the stool beside the till and wept, for the injustice of the world and the weakness of her own nature. I have become what I always dreaded becoming, she said, everything has slipped through my fingers.

And for all of it, after a short time, she began to blame Miss Roscommon. She has stifled me, she thought, she preys upon me, I am treated as her child, her toy, her *pussy-cat*, she has humiliated me and fed off my dependence and the fact that I have always been so sensitive. She is a wicked woman. And then she said, *but I do not have to stay with her*. Fortified by the truth of this new realization, Miss Bartlett blew her nose, and walked back up the hill to Tuscany.

'You cannot leave,' said Miss Roscommon, 'what nonsense, of course you cannot. You have nowhere else to go and besides in ten days' time we set off for our holiday in Florence.'

'You will set off. I am afraid my plans have now changed.' Miss Bartlett could not now bear the thought of being seen with her friend in all the museums and art galleries of Florence, discussing the paintings in loud, knowledgeable voices and eating wholemeal sandwiches out of neat little greaseproof bags, speaking very slowly to the Italians. This year Miss Roscommon must go alone. She did not allow herself to think of how, or whether she would enjoy herself. We are always hearing of how intrepid she was as a girl, she thought. Then let her be intrepid again.

Aloud, she said, 'I am going back to live at the cottage.' For she had kept it on, and rented it to summer visitors.

Miss Roscommon turned herself, and her darning, a little more towards the light. 'You are being very foolish,' she said mildly. 'But I understand why, it is your age, of course.'

Appalled, Miss Bartlett went through to her room, and began to throw things furiously, haphazardly, into a suitcase. I am my own mistress, she said, a grown-up woman with years ahead of me, it is time for me to be firm. I have pandered to her long enough.

The following day, watched by Miss Roscommon, she moved back down the hill to the cottage. She would, she decided, stay there for a while, give herself time to get accustomed, and to gather all of her things around her again, and then she would look out and make plans, take steps towards her new life.

That evening, hearing the wind around her own four walls, she said, I have escaped. Though she woke in the night and was aware of being entirely alone in the cottage, of not being able to hear the loud breathing of Miss Roscommon in the room next door.

She expected the Italian holiday to be cancelled, on some pretext, and was astonished when Miss Roscommon left, on the appointed day and alone. Miss Bartlett took the opportunity of going up to Tuscany and fetching some more of her things down, work from the studio to keep her busy in the evening, and during the days, too, for now it was October and few people came into the shop.

Here I am, she said, twisting the raffia angels and winding ribbon around the pot-pourris, etching her gift cards, here I am, living my own life and making my own decisions. She wanted to invite someone down to stay, someone young, so that she could be seen and approved of, but there was no one. A search through all the drawers and cupboards at the bungalow did not yield her the address of the niece Angela. She would have sent a little note, with a Christmas gift, to tell of her removal, prove her independence.

Miss Roscommon returned from Italy, looked rather tired and not very suntanned. She came in with a miniature plaster copy of a Donatello statue, and some fine art postcards. Miss Bartlett made tea, and the conversation was very stilted.

'You are not warm enough here,' said Miss Roscommon, 'I will send down some extra blankets.'

'Oh no, thank you. Please don't do that.'

But the following day the blankets, and a Dutch apple pie, arrived with the butcher's boy.

Miss Bartlett bought huge slabs of cheese and eggs, which she could boil quite well, and many potatoes, and ate them off her knee while she read detective stories through the long evenings. She thought that she might buy a television set for company, though she was busy too, with the postal orders for Christmas. When all this is over, she told herself, that is when I shall start looking about me and making my plans. She thought of all the things she might have done as a girl, the studio in London and the woodblock engravings for the poetry press, the ballet company for whom she might have been asked to do some ethereal costume designs. She read in a newspaper of a woman who had started her own firm, specializing in computer management, at the age of fifty and was now rather wealthy, wholly respected in a man's world. Miss Bartlett looked at herself in the mirror. I am only forty-seven, she said.

In her white bungalow, lonely and lacking a sense of purpose, Miss Roscommon waited.

On November the seventh, the first of the storms came, and Miss Bartlett sat in her back room and heard the wind and the crashing of the sea, terrified. The next morning, she saw that part of the pierhead had broken away. Miss Roscommon sent down a note, with a meat pasty, via the butcher's boy.

'I am worried about you,' she wrote, 'you cannot be looking after yourself, and I know that it is damp in that cottage. Your room here is ready for you at any time.'

Miss Bartlett tore the note up and threw the pasty away, but she thought of the warm bed, the fires and soft sofas at Tuscany.

Two days later, when the gales began again, Miss Roscommon came herself, and hammered at the door of the cottage, but Miss Bartlett hid upstairs, behind a cheval mirror, until she went away. This time, there was no note, only a thermos flask of lentil soup on the doorstep.

She is suffocating me, thought Miss Bartlett, I cannot bear all these unwanted attentions, I only wish to be left alone. It is a poor thing if a woman of her age and resources can find nothing else to occupy her, nothing else to live for. But in spite of herself, she drank the soup, and the taste of it, the smell of the steam rising up into her face reminded her of all the meals at Tuscany, the winter evenings spent happily sitting beside the fire.

When the storms came again, another section of the pier broke away, the lifeboat put out to sea and sank with all hands, and the front room of Miss Bartlett's cottage was flooded, rain broke in through a rent in the roof. She lay all night, too terrified by the roaring of the wind and seas to get out of bed and do anything about it, only whimpering a little with cold and fright, remembering how close the cottage came to the water, how vulnerable she was.

As a child, she had been afraid of all storms, gales and thunder and cloudbursts drumming on the roof, and her mother had understood, wrapped her in a blanket and taken her into her own bed.

'It is because you have such a vivid imagination,' she had said, 'you feel things that the other, ordinary little children, cannot ever feel.' And so, nothing had been done to conquer this praise-worthy fear of storms.

Now, I am alone, thought Miss Bartlett, there is no one, my mother is dead, and who is there to shelter and understand me? A flare rocket, sent up from the sinking lifeboat, lit up the room faintly for a second, and then she knew who there was, and that everything would be all right. On the stormy nights, Miss Roscommon always got up and made sandwiches and milky hot drinks, brought them to her as she lay awake in bed, and they would sit reading nice magazines, in the gentle circle of the bedside lamp.

I have been very foolish, Miss Bartlett thought, and heard herself saying it aloud, humbly, to Miss Roscommon. A very foolish, selfish woman, I do not deserve to have you as a friend.

She did not take very much with her up the hill on the following morning, only a little handcase and some raffia work. The rest could follow later, and it would be better to arrive like that, it would be a real indication of her helplessness.

The landscape was washed very clean and bare and pale, but the sea churned and moved within itself, angry and battleship grey. In the summer, Miss Bartlett thought, refreshed again by the short walk, it will be time to think again, for I am not committing myself to any permanent arrangements and things will have to be rather different now, I will not allow myself to be treated as a pet plaything, that must be understood. For she had forgotten, in the cold, clear morning, the terrors of the previous night.

She wondered what to do, ring the bell or knock or simply

open the back door into the kitchen, where Miss Roscommon would be working, and stand there, case in hand, waiting to be forgiven. Her heart beat a little faster. Tuscany was very settled and reassuring in its low, four-square whiteness on top of the hill. Miss Bartlett knocked timidly at the blue kitchen door.

It was some time before she gave up knocking and ringing, and simply went in. Tuscany was very quiet.

She found her in the living-room, lying crumpled awkwardly on the floor, one of her legs twisted underneath her. Her face was a curious, flat colour, like the inside of a raw potato. Miss Bartlett drew back the curtains. The clock had stopped just before midnight, almost twelve hours ago.

For a moment, she stood there, still holding her little case, in the comfortable, chintzy room, and then she dropped down on to her knees, and took the head of Miss Roscommon into her lap and, rocking and rocking, cradling it like a child, Miss Bartlett wept.

The Custodian

At five minutes to three he climbed up the ladder into the loft. He went cautiously, he was always cautious now, moving his limbs warily, and never going out in bad weather without enough warm clothes. For the truth was that he had not expected to survive this winter, he was old, he had been ill for one week, and then the fear had come over him again, that he was going to die. He did not care for his own part, but what would become of the boy? It was only the boy he worried about now, only he who mattered. Therefore, he was careful with himself, for he had lived out this bad winter, it was March, he could look forward to the spring and summer, could cease to worry for a little longer. All the same he had to be careful not to have accidents, though he was steady enough on his feet. He was seventy-one. He knew how easy it would be, for example, to miss his footing on the narrow ladder, to break a limb and lie there, while all the time the child waited, panic welling up inside him, left last at the school. And when the fear of his own dying did not grip him, he was haunted by ideas of some long illness, or incapacitation, and if he had to be taken into hospital, what would happen to the child, then? *What would happen?*

But now it was almost three o'clock, almost time for him to leave the house, his favourite part of the day, now he climbed on hands and knees into the dim, cool loft and felt about among the apples, holding this one and that one up to the beam of light coming through the slats in the roof, wanting the fruit he finally chose to be perfect, ripe and smooth.

The loft smelled sweetly of the apples and pears laid up there since the previous autumn. Above his head, he heard the scrabbling noises of the birds, house martins nesting in the eaves, his heart lurched with joy at the fresh realization that it was almost April, almost spring.

He went carefully down the ladder, holding the chosen apple. It took him twenty minutes to walk to the school but he liked to arrive early, to have the pleasure of watching and waiting, outside the gates.

The sky was brittle blue and the sun shone, but it was very cold, the air still smelled of winter. Until a fortnight ago there had been snow, he and the boy had trudged back and forwards every morning and afternoon over the frost-hard paths which led across the marshes, and the stream running alongside of them had been iced over, the reeds were stiff and white as blades.

It had thawed very gradually. Today, the air smelled thin and sharp in his nostrils. Nothing moved. As he climbed the grass bank onto the higher path, he looked across the great stretch of river, and it gleamed like a flat metal plate under the winter sun, still as the sky. Everything was pale, white and silver, a gull came over slowly and its belly and the undersides of its wings were pebbly grey. There were no sounds here except the sudden chatter of dunlin swooping and dropping quickly down, and the tread of his own feet on the path, the brush of his legs against grass clumps.

He had not expected to live this winter.

In his hand, he felt the apple, hard and soothing to the touch, for the boy must have fruit, fruit every day, he saw to that, as well as milk and eggs which they fetched from Maldrun at the farm, a mile away. His limbs should grow, he should be perfect.

Maldrun's cattle were out on their green island in the middle of the marshes, surrounded by the moat of steely water, he led them across a narrow path like a causeway, from the farm. They were like toy animals, or those in a picture seen from this distance away, they stood motionless, cut-out shapes of black and white.

Every so often, the boy was still afraid of going past the island of cows, he gripped the old man's hand and a tight expression came over his face.

'They can't get at you, don't you see? They don't cross water, not cows. They're not bothered about you.'

'I know.'

And he did know – and was still afraid. Though there had been days, recently, when he would go right up to the edge of the strip of water, and stare across at the animals, he would even accompany Maldrun to the half-door of the milking parlour, and climb up and look over, would smell the thick, sour, cow-smell, and hear the splash of dung on to the stone floor. Then, he was not afraid. The cows had great, bony haunches and vacant eyes.

'Touch one,' Maldrun had said. The boy had gone inside and put out a hand, though standing well back, stretched and touched the rough pelt, and the cow had twitched, feeling the lightness of his hand as if it were an irritation, the prick of a fly. He was afraid, but getting less so, of the cows. So many things were changing, he was growing, he was seven years old.

Occasionally, the old man woke in the night and sweated with fear that he might die before the boy was grown, and he prayed, then, to live ten more years, just ten, until the boy could look after himself. And some days it seemed possible, seemed, indeed, most likely, some days he felt very young, felt no age at all, his arms were strong and he could chop wood and lift buckets, he was light-headed with the sense of his own youth. He was no age. He was seventy-one. A tall bony man with thick white hair, and without any spread of spare flesh. When he bathed, he looked down and saw every rib, every joint of his own thin body, he bent an arm and watched the flicker of muscle beneath the skin.

As the path curved round, the sun caught the surface of the water on his right, so that it shimmered and dazzled his eyes for a moment, and then he heard the familiar, faint, high moan of the wind, as it blew off the estuary a mile or more away. The reeds rustled dryly together like sticks. He put up the collar of his coat. But he was happy, his own happiness sang inside his head, that he was here, walking along this path with the apple inside his hand inside his pocket, that he would wait and watch and then, that he would walk back this same way with the boy, that none of those things he dreaded would come about.

Looking back, he could still make out the shapes of the cows, and looking down, to where the water lay between the reed-banks, he saw a swan, its neck arched and its head below the surface of the dark, glistening stream, and it too was entirely still. He stopped for a moment, watching it, and hearing the thin sound of the wind and then, turning, saw the whole, pale stretch of marsh and water and sky, saw for miles, back to where the trees began, behind which was the cottage and then far ahead, to where the sand stretched out like a tongue into the mouth of the estuary.

He was amazed, that he could be alive and moving, small as an insect across this great, bright, cold space, amazed that he should count for as much as Maldrun's cows and the unmoving swan.

The wind was suddenly cold on his face. It was a quarter past three. He left the path, went towards the gate, and began to cross the rough, ploughed field which led to the lane, and then, on another mile to the village, the school.

Occasionally, he came here not only in the morning, and back again in the afternoon, but at other times when he was overcome with sudden anxiety and a desire to see the boy, to reassure himself that he was still there, was alive. Then, he put down whatever he might be doing and came, almost running, stumbled and caught his breath, until he reached the railings and the closed, black gate. If he waited there long enough, if it was dinner or break time, he saw them all come streaming and tumbling out of the green painted doors, and he watched desperately until he saw him, and he could loosen the grip of his hands on the railings, the thumping of his heart eased, inside his chest. Always, then, the boy would come straight down to him, running over the asphalt, and laughed and called and pressed himself up against the railings on the other side.

'Hello.'

'All right are you?'

'What have you brought me? Have you got something?'

Though he knew there would be nothing, did not expect it, knew that there was only ever the fruit at home-time, apple, pear or sometimes, in the summer, cherries or a peach.

'I was just passing through the village.'

'Were you doing the shopping?'

'Yes. I only came up to see . . .'

'We've done reading. We had tapioca for pudding.'

'That's good for you. You should eat that. Always eat your dinner.'

'Is it home-time yet?'

'Not yet.'

'You will be here won't you? You won't forget to come back?'

'Have I ever?'

Then, he made himself straighten his coat, or shift the string shopping bag over from one hand to the other, he said, 'You go back now then, go on to the others, you play with them,' for he knew that this was right, he should not keep the child standing here, should not show him up in front of the rest. It was only for himself that he had come, he was eaten up with his own concern, and fear.

'You go back to your friends now.'

'You will be here? You will be here?'

'I'll be here.'

He turned away, they both turned, for they were separate, they should have their own ways, their own lives. He turned and walked off down the lane out of sight of the playground, not allowing himself to look back, perhaps he went and bought something from the shop, and he was calm again, no longer anxious, he walked back home slowly.

He did not mind all the walking, not even in the worst weather. He did not mind anything at all in this life he had chosen, and which was all-absorbing, the details of which were so important. He no longer thought anything of the past. Somewhere, he had read that an old man has only his memories, and he had wondered at that, for he had none, or rather, they did not concern him, they were like old letters which he had not troubled to keep. He had, simply, the present, the cottage, and the land around it, and the boy to look after. And he had to stay well, stay alive, he must not die yet. That was all.

But he did not often allow himself to go up to the school like that, at unnecessary times, he would force himself to stay and sweat out his anxiety and the need to reassure himself about the child, in some physical job, he would beat mats and plant vegetables in the garden, prune or pick from the fruit trees or walk over to see Maldrun at the farm, buy a chicken, and wait until the time came so slowly around to three o'clock, and he could go, with every reason, could allow himself the pleasure of arriving there a little early, and waiting beside the gates, which were now open, for the boy to come out.

'What have I got today?'

'You guess.'

'That's easy. Pear.'

'Wrong!' He opened his hand, revealing the apple.

'Well, I like apples best.'

'I know. I had a good look at those trees down the bottom this morning. There won't be so many this year. Mind, we've to wait for the blossom to be sure.'

'Last year there were hundreds of apples. *Thousands*.' He took the old man's hand as they reached the bottom of the lane. For some reason he always waited until just here, by the white-beam tree, before doing so.

'There were *millions* of apples!'

'Get on!'

'Well, a lot anyway.'

'That's why there won't be so many this year. You don't get two crops like that in a row.'

'Why?'

'Trees wear themselves out, fruiting like that. They've to rest.'

'Will we have a lot of pears instead then?'

'I daresay. What have you done at school?'

'Lots of things.'

'Have you done your reading? That's what's the important thing. To keep up with your reading.'

He had started the boy off himself, bought alphabet and word picture books from the village, and, when they got beyond these, had made up his own, cut out pictures from magazines and written beside them in large clear letters on ruled sheets of paper. By the time the boy went to school, he had known more than any of the others, he was 'very forward', they had said, though looking him up and down at the same time for he was small for his age.

It worried him that the boy was still small, he watched the others closely as they came out of the gates and they were all taller, thicker in body and stronger of limb. His face was pale and curiously old looking beside theirs. He had always looked old.

The old man concerned himself even more, then, with the fresh eggs and cheese, milk and fruit, watched over the boy while he ate. But he did eat.

'We had meat and cabbage for dinner.'

'Did you finish it?'

'I had a second helping. Then we had cake for pudding. Cake and custard. I don't like that.'

'You didn't leave it?'

'Oh no. I just don't like it, that's all.'

Now, as they came on to the marshes, the water and sky were even paler and the reeds beside the stream were bleached, like old wood left out for years in the sun. The wind was stronger, whipping at their legs from behind.

'There's the swan.'

'They've a nest somewhere about.'

'Have you seen it?'

'They don't let you see it. They go away from it if anybody walks by.'

'I drew a picture of a swan.'

'Today?'

'No. Once. It wasn't very good.'

'If a thing's not good you should do it again.'

'Why should I?'

'You'll get better then.'

'I won't get better at drawing.' He spoke very deliberately, as he so often did, knowing himself, and firm about the truth of things, so that the old man was silent, respecting it.

'He's sharp,' Maldrun's wife said. 'He's a clever one.'

But the old man would not have him spoiled, or too lightly praised.

'He's plenty to learn. He's only a child yet.'

'All the same, he'll do, won't he? He's sharp.'

But perhaps it was only the words he used, only the serious expression on his face, which came of so much reading and all that time spent alone with the old man. And if he was, as they said, so sharp, so forward, perhaps it would do him no good?

He worried about that, wanting the boy to find his place easily in the world, he tried hard not to shield him from things, made him go to the farm to see Maldrun, and over Harper's fen by himself, to play with the gamekeeper's boys, told him always to mix with the others in the school playground, to do what they did.

Because he was most afraid, at times, of their very contentment together, of the self-contained life they led, for in truth they needed no one, each of them would be entirely happy never to go far beyond this house: they spoke of all things, or of nothing, the boy read and made careful lists of the names of birds and moths, and built elaborate structures, houses and castles and palaces out of old matchboxes, he helped with the garden, had his own corner down beside the shed in which he grew what he chose. It had been like this from the beginning, from the day the old man had brought him here at nine months' old and set him down on the floor and taught him to crawl, they had fallen naturally into their life together. Nobody else had wanted him. Nobody else would have taken such care.

Once, people had been suspicious, they had spoken to each other in the village, had disapproved.

'He needs a woman there. It's not right. He needs someone who knows,' Maldrun's wife had said. But now, even she had accepted that it was not true, so that, before strangers, she would have defended them more fiercely than anyone.

'He's a fine boy, that. He's all right. You look at him, look. Well, you can't tell what works out for the best. You can never tell.'

By the time they came across the track which led between the gorse bushes and down through the fir trees, it was as cold as it had been on any night in January, they brought in more wood for the fire and had toast and the last of the damson jam and mugs of hot milk.

'It's like winter. Only not so dark. I like it in winter.'

But it was the middle of March now, in the marshes the herons and redshanks were nesting, and the larks spiralled up, singing through the silence. It was almost spring.

So, they went on as they had always done, until the second of April. Then, the day after their walk out to Derenow, the day after they saw the kingfisher, it happened.

From the early morning, he had felt uneasy, though there was no reason he could give for his fear, it simply lay, hard and cold as a stone in his belly, and he was restless about the house from the time he got up.

The weather had changed. It was warm and clammy, with low, dun-coloured clouds and, over the marshes, a thin mist. He felt the need to get out, to walk and walk, the cottage was dark and oddly quiet. When he went down between the fruit trees to the bottom of the garden the first of the buds were breaking into green but the grass was soaked with dew like a sweat, the heavy air smelled faintly rotten and sweet.

They set off in the early morning. The boy did not question, he was always happy to go anywhere at all but when he was asked to choose their route, he set off at once, a few paces ahead, on the path which forked away east, in the opposite direction from the village and leading, over almost three miles of empty marsh, towards the sea. They followed the bank of the river, and the water was sluggish, with fronds of dark green weed lying below the surface. The boy bent, and put his hand cautiously down, breaking the skin of the water, but when his fingers came up against the soft, fringed edges of the plants he pulled back.

'Slimey.'

'Yes. It's out of the current here. There's no freshness.'

'Will there be fish?'

'Maybe there will. Not so many.'

'I don't like it.' Though for some minutes he continued to peer between the reeds at the pebbles which were just visible on the bed of the stream. 'He asks questions,' they said. 'He takes an interest. It's his mind, isn't it – bright – you can see, alert, that's what. He's forever wanting to know.' Though there were times when he said nothing at all, his small, old-young face was crumpled in thought, there were times when he looked and listened with care and asked nothing.

'You could die here. You could drown in the water and never, never be found.'

'That's not a thing to think about. What do you worry over that for?'

'But you could, you could.'

They were walking in single file, the boy in front. From all the secret nests down in the reed beds, the birds made their own noises, chirring and whispering, or sending out sudden cries of warning and alarm. The high, sad call of a curlew came again and again, and then ceased abruptly. The boy whistled in imitation.

'Will it know it's me? Will it answer?'

He whistled again. They waited. Nothing. His face was shadowed with disappointment.

'You can't fool them, not birds.'

'You can make a blackbird answer you. You can easily.'

'Not the same.'

'Why isn't it?'

'Blackbirds are tame, blackbirds are garden birds.'

'Wouldn't a curlew come to the garden?'

'No.'

'Why wouldn't it'

'It likes to be away from things. They keep to their own places.'

As they went on, the air around them seemed to close in further, it seemed harder to breathe, and they could not see clearly ahead to where the marshes and mist merged into the sky. Here and there, the stream led off into small, muddy pools and hollows, and the water in them was reddened by the rust seeping from some old can or metal crate thrown there and left for years, the stains which spread out looked like old blood. Gnats hovered in clusters over the water.

'Will we go onto the beach?'

'We could.'

'We might find something on the beach.'

Often, they searched among the pebbles for pieces of amber

or jet, for old buckles and buttons and sea-smooth coins washed up by the tides, the boy had a collection of them in a cardboard box in his room.

They walked on, and then, out of the thick silence which was all around them came the creaking of wings, nearer and nearer and sounding like two thin boards of wood beaten slowly together. A swan, huge as an eagle, came over their heads, flying low, so that the boy looked up for a second in terror at the size and closeness of it, caught his breath. He said urgently, 'Swans go for people, swans can break your arm if they hit you, if they beat you with their wings. Can't they?'

'But they don't take any notice, so come on, you leave them be.'

'But they *can*, can't they?'

'Oh, they might.' He watched the great, grey-white shape go awkwardly away from them, in the direction of the sea.

A hundred yards further on, at the junction of two paths across the marsh, there was the ruin of a water mill, blackened after a fire years before, and half broken down, a sail torn off. Inside, under an arched doorway, it was dark and damp, the walls were coated with yellowish moss and water lay, brackish, in the mud hollows of the floor.

At high summer, on hot, shimmering blue days they had come across here on the way to the beach with a string bag full of food for their lunch, and then the water mill had seemed like a sanctuary, cool and silent, the boy had gone inside and stood there, had called softly and listened to the echo of his own voice as it rang lightly round and round the walls.

Now, he stopped dead in the path, some distance away.

'I don't want to go.'

'We're walking to the beach.'

'I don't want to go past that.'

'The mill?'

'There are rats.'

'No.'

'And flying things. Things that are black and hang upside down.'

'Bats? What's to be afraid of in bats? You've seen them, you've been in Maldrun's barn. They don't hurt.'

'I want to go back.'

'You don't have to go into the mill, who said you did? We're going on to where the sea is.'

'I want to go back now.'

He was not often frightened. But, standing there in the middle of the hushed stretch of fenland, the old man felt again disturbed himself, the fear that something would happen, here, where nothing moved and the birds lay hidden, only crying out their weird cries, where things lay under the unmoving water and the press of the air made him sweat down his back. Something would happen to them, something . . .

What could happen?

Then, not far ahead, they both saw him at the same moment, a man with a gun under his arm, tall and black and menacing as a crow against the dull horizon, and as they saw him, they also saw two mallard ducks rise in sudden panic from their nest in the reeds, and they heard the shots, three shots that cracked out and echoed for miles around, the air went on reverberating with the waves of terrible sound.

The ducks fell at once, hit in mid-flight so that they swerved, turned over, and plummeted down. The man with the shotgun started quickly forward and the grasses and reeds bent and stirred as a dog ran, burrowing, to retrieve. 'I want to go back, *I want to go back.'*

Without a word, the old man took his hand, and they turned, walked quickly back the way they had come, as though afraid that they, too, would be followed and struck down, not caring that they were out of breath and sticky with sweat, but only wanting to get away, to reach the shelter of the lane and the trees, to make for home.

Nothing was ever said about it, or about the feeling they had both had walking across the marshes, the boy did not mention the man with the gun or the ducks which had been alive and in flight, then so suddenly dead. All that evening, the old man watched him, as he stuck pictures in a book, and tore up dock leaves to feed the rabbit, watched for signs of left-over fear. But he was only, perhaps, quieter than usual, his face more closed up, he was concerned with his own thoughts.

In the night, he woke, and got up, went to the boy and looked down through the darkness, for fear that he might have had bad dreams and woken, but there was only the sound of his breathing, he lay quite still, very long and straight in the bed.

He imagined the future, and his mind was filled with images of all the possible horrors to come, the things which could cause the boy shock and pain and misery, and from which he would not be able to save him, as he had been powerless today to protect him from the sight of the killing of two ducks. He was in despair. Only the next morning, he was eased, as it came back to him again, the knowledge that he had, after all, lived out the winter and ahead of them lay only light and warmth and greenness.

Nevertheless, he half-expected that something would still happen to them, to break into their peace. For more than a week, nothing did, his fears were quieted, and then the spring broke, the apple and pear blossom weighed down the branches in great, creamy clots, the grass in the orchard grew up as high as the boy's knees, and across the marshes the sun shone and shone, the water of the river was turquoise, and in the streams, as clear as glass, the wind blew warm and smelled faintly of salt and earth. Walking to and from the school every day, they saw more woodlarks than they had ever seen, quivering on the air high above their heads, and near the gorse bushes, the boy found a nest of leverets. In the apple loft, the house martins hatched out and along the lanes, dandelions and buttercups shone golden out of the grass.

It was on the Friday that Maldrun gave the boy one of the farm kittens, and he carried it home close to his body beneath his coat. It was black and white like Maldrun's cows. And it was the day after that, the end of the first week of spring, that Blaydon came, Gilbert Blaydon, the boy's father.

He was sitting outside the door watching a buzzard hover above the fir copse when he heard the footsteps. He thought it was Maldrun bringing over the eggs, or a chicken – Maldrun generally came one evening in the week, after the boy had gone to bed, they drank a glass of beer and talked for half an hour. He was an easy man, undemonstrative. They still called one another, formally, 'Mr Bowry', 'Mr Maldrun'.

The buzzard roved backwards and forwards over its chosen patch of air, searching.

When the old man looked down again, he was there, standing in the path. He was carrying a canvas kitbag.

He knew, then, why he had been feeling uneasy, he had expected this, or something like it, to happen, though he had put the fears to the back of his mind with the coming of sunshine and the leaf-breaking. He felt no hostility as he looked at Blaydon, only extreme weariness, almost as though he were ill.

There was no question of who it was, yet above all he ought to have expected a feeling of complete disbelief, for if anyone had asked, he would have said that he would certainly never see the boy's father again. But now he was here, it did not seem surprising, it seemed, indeed, somehow inevitable. Things had to alter, things could never go on. Happiness did not go on.

'Will you be stopping?'

Blaydon walked slowly forward, hesitated, and then set the kitbag down at his feet. He looked much older.

'I don't know if it'd be convenient.'

'There's a room. There's always a room.'

The old man's head buzzed suddenly in confusion, he thought

The Custodian

he should offer a drink or a chair, should see to a bed, should ask
questions to which he did not want to know the answers, should
say something about the boy. *The boy.*

'You've come to take him . . .'

Blaydon sat down on the other chair, beside the outdoors
table. The boy looked like him, there was the same narrowness
of forehead and chin, the same high-bridged nose. Only the
mouth was different, though that might simply be because the
boy's was still small and unformed.

'You've come to take him.'

'Where to?' He looked up. 'Where would I have to take him
to?'

But we don't want you here, the old man thought, we don't
want anyone: and he felt the intrusion of this younger man, with
the broad hands and long legs sprawled under the table, like a
violent disturbance of the careful pattern of their lives, he was
alien. *We don't want you.*

But what right had he to say that? He did not say it. He was
standing up helplessly, not knowing what should come next, he
felt the bewilderment as some kind of irritation inside his own
head.

He felt old.

In the end, he managed to say, 'You'll not have eaten?'

Blaydon stared at him. 'Don't you want to know where I've
come from?'

'No.'

'No.'

'I've made a stew. You'll be better for a plate of food.'

'Where is he?'

'Asleep in bed, where else would he be? I look after him, I
know what I'm about. It's half-past eight, gone, isn't it? What
would he be doing but asleep in his bed, at half-past eight?'

He heard his own voice rising and quickening, as he defended
himself, defended both of them, he could prove it to this father

or to anyone at all, how he'd looked after the boy. He would have said, what about you? Where have you been? What did you do for him? But he was too afraid, for he knew nothing about what rights Blaydon might have – even though he had never been near, never bothered.

'You could have been dead.'

'Did you think?'

'What was I to think? I knew nothing. Heard nothing.'

'No.'

Out of the corner of his eye, the old man saw the buzzard drop down suddenly, straight as a stone, on to some creature in the undergrowth of the copse. The sky was mulberry coloured and the honeysuckle smelled ingratiatingly sweet.

'I wasn't dead.'

The old man realized that Blaydon looked both tired and rather dirty, his nails were broken, he needed a shave and the wool at the neck of his blue sweater was unravelling. What was he to say to the boy then, when he had brought him up to be so clean and tidy and careful, had taken his clothes to be mended by a woman in the village, had always cut and washed his hair himself? What was he to tell him about this man?

'There's hot water. I'll get you linen, make you a bed. You'd best go up first, before I put out the stew. Have a wash.'

He went into the kitchen, took a mug and a bottle of beer and poured it out, and was calmed a little by the need to organize himself, by the simple physical activity.

When he took the beer out, Blaydon was still leaning back on the old chair. There were dark stains below his eyes.

'You'd best take it up with you.' The old man held out the beer.

It was almost dark now. After a long time, Blaydon reached out, took the mug and drank, emptying it in four or five long swallows, and then, as though all his muscles were stiff, rose slowly, took up the kitbag, went towards the house.

When the old man had set the table and dished out the food, he was trembling. He tried to turn his mind away from the one thought. That Blaydon had come to take the boy away.

He called and when there was no reply, went up the stairs. Blaydon was stretched out on his belly on top of the unmade bed, heavy and motionless in sleep.

While he slept, the old man worried about the morning. It was Saturday, there would not be the diversion of going to school, the boy must wake and come downstairs and confront Blaydon.

What he had originally said, was, your mother died, your father went away. And that was the truth. But he doubted if the boy so much as remembered; he had asked a question only once, and that more than two years ago.

They were content together, needing no one.

He sat on the straight-back chair in the darkness, surrounded by hidden greenery and the fumes of honeysuckle, and tried to imagine what he might say.

'This is your father. Other boys have fathers. This is your father who came back, who will stay with us here. For some time, or perhaps not for more than a few days. His name is Gilbert Blaydon.'

Will you call him 'father'?, will you . . .

'This is . . .'

His mind broke down before the sheer cliff confronting it and he simply sat on, hands uselessly in front of him on the outdoors table, he thought of nothing, and on white plates in the kitchen the stew cooled and congealed and the new kitten from Maldrun's farm slept, coiled on an old green jumper. The cat, the boy, the boy's father, all slept. From the copse, the throaty call of the night-jars.

'You'll be ready for breakfast. You didn't eat the meal last night.'

'I slept.'

'You'll be hungry.' He had his back to Blaydon. He was busy with the frying pan and plates over the stove. What had made him tired enough to sleep like that, from early evening until now, fully clothed on top of the bed! But he didn't want to know, would not ask questions.

The back door was open on to the path that led down between vegetable beds and the bean canes and currant bushes, towards the thicket. Blaydon went to the doorway.

'Two eggs, will you have?'

'If . . .'

'There's plenty.' He wanted to divert him, talk to him, he had to pave the way. The boy was there, somewhere at the bottom of the garden.

'We'd a hard winter.'

'Oh, yes?'

'Knee deep, all January, all February, we'd to dig ourselves out of the door. And then it froze – the fens froze right over, ice as thick as your fist. I've never known like it.'

But now it was spring, now outside there was the bright, glorious green of new grass, new leaves, now the sun shone.

He began to set out knives and forks on the kitchen table. It would have to come, he would have to call the boy in, to bring them together. What would he say? His heart squeezed and then pumped hard, suddenly, in the thin bone-cage of his chest.

Blaydon's clothes were creased and crumpled. And they were not clean. Had he washed himself? The old man tried to get a glimpse of his hands.

'I thought I'd get a job,' Blaydon said.

The old man watched him.

'I thought I'd look for work.'

'Here?'

'Around here. Is there work?'

'Maybe. I've not had reason to find out. Maybe.'

'If I'm staying on, I'll need to work.'

'Yes.'

'It'd be a help, I daresay?'

'You've a right to do as you think fit. You make up your own mind.'

'I'll pay my way.'

'You've no need to worry about the boy, if it's that. He's all right, he's provided for. You've no need to find money for him.'

'All the same . . .'

After a minute, Blaydon walked over and sat down at the table.

The old man thought, he is young, young and strong and fit, he has come here to stay, he has every right, he's the father. He is . . .

But he did not want Blaydon in their lives, did not want the hands resting on the kitchen table, and the big feet beneath it.

He said, 'You could try at the farm. At Maldrun's. They've maybe got work there. You could try.'

'Maldrun's farm?'

'It'd be ordinary work. Labouring work.'

'I'm not choosy.'

The old man put out eggs and fried bread and bacon onto the plates, poured tea, filled the sugar basin. And then he had no more left to do, he had to call the boy.

But nothing happened as he had feared it, after all.

He came in. 'Wash your hands.' But he was already half-way to the sink, he had been brought up so carefully, the order was not an order but a formula between them, regular, and of comfort.

'Wash your hands.'

'I've come to stay,' Blaydon said at once, 'for a bit. I got here last night.'

The boy hesitated in the middle of the kitchen, looked from one to the other of them, trying to assess this sudden change in the order of things.

'For a week or two,' the old man said. 'Eat your food.'

The boy got on to his chair. 'What's your name?'

'Gilbert Blaydon.'

'What have I to call you?'

'Either.'

'Gilbert, then.'

'What you like.'

After that, they got on with eating; the old man chewed his bread very slowly, filled, for the moment, with relief.

Maldrun took him on at the farm as a general labourer and then their lives formed a new pattern, with the full upsurge of spring. Blaydon got up, and ate his breakfast with them and then left, there was a quarter of an hour which the old man had alone with the boy before setting off across the marsh path to school, and in the afternoon, an even longer time. Blaydon did not return, sometimes, until after six.

At the weekend, he went off somewhere alone, but occasionally, he took the boy for walks; they saw the heron's nest, and then the cygnets, and once, a peregrine, flying over the estuary. The two of them were at ease together.

Alone, the old man tried to imagine what they might be saying to each other, he walked distractedly about the house, and almost wept, with anxiety and dread. They came down the path, and the boy was sitting up on Blaydon's shoulders, laughing and laughing.

'You've told him.'

Blaydon turned, surprised, and then sent the boy away. 'I've said nothing.'

The old man believed him. But there was still a fear for the future, the end of things.

The days lengthened. Easter went by, and the school holidays, during which the old man was happiest, because he had so much time with the boy to himself, and then it was May, in the early mornings there was a fine mist above the blossom trees.

'He's a good worker,' Maldrun said, coming over one evening with the eggs and finding the old man alone. 'I'm glad to have him.'

'Yes.'

'He takes a bit off your shoulders, I daresay.'

'He pays his way.'

'No. Work, I meant. Work and worries. All that.'

What did Maldrun know? But he only looked back at the old man, his face open and friendly, drank his bottled beer.

He thought about it, and realized that it was true. He had grown used to having Blaydon about, to carry the heavy things and lock up at night, to clear out the fruit loft and lop off the overhanging branches and brambles at the entrance to the thicket. He had slipped into their life, and established himself. When he thought of the future without Blaydon, it was to worry. For the summer was always short and then came the run down through autumn into winter again. Into snow and ice and cold, and the north-east wind scything across the marshes. He dreaded all that, now that he was old. Last winter, he had been ill once, and for only a short time. This winter he was a year older, anything might happen. He thought of the mornings when he would have to take the boy to school before it was even light, thought of the frailty of his own flesh, the brittleness of his bones, he looked in the mirror at his own weak and rheumy eyes.

He had begun to count on Blaydon's being here to ease things, to help with the coal and wood and the breaking of ice on pails, to be in some way an insurance against his own possible illness, possible death.

Though now, it was still only the beginning of summer, now, he watched Blaydon build a rabbit hutch for the boy, hammering nails and sawing wood, uncoiling wire skilfully. He heard them laugh suddenly together. This was what he needed, after all, not a woman about the place, but a man, the strength and ease of a man who was not old, did not fear, did not say 'Wash your hands', 'Drink up all your milk', 'Take care'.

The kitten grew, and spun about in quick, mad circles in the sun.

'He's a good worker,' Maldrun said.

After a while, the old man took to dozing in his chair outside, after supper, while Blaydon washed up, emptied the bins and then took out the shears, to clip the hedge or the grass borders, when the boy had gone to bed.

But everything that had to do with the boy, the business of rising and eating, going to school and returning, the routine of clothes and food and drink and bed, all that was still supervised by the old man. Blaydon did not interfere, scarcely seemed to notice what was done. His own part in the boy's life was quite different.

In June and early July, it was hotter than the old man could ever remember. The gnats droned in soft, grey clouds under the trees, and over the water of the marshes. The sun shone hard and bright and still the light played tricks so that the estuary seemed now very near, now very far away. Maldrun's cows tossed their heads, against the flies which gathered stickily in the runnels below their great eyes.

He began to rely more and more upon Blaydon as the summer reached its height, left more jobs for him to do, because he was willing and strong, and because the old man succumbed easily to the temptation to rest himself in the sun. He still did most of the cooking but he would let Blaydon go down to the shops and the boy often went with him. He was growing, his limbs were filling out and his skin was berry-brown. He lost the last of the pink-and-whiteness of babyhood. He had accepted Blaydon's presence without question and was entirely used to him, though he did not show any less affection for the old man, who continued to take care of him day by day. But he became less nervous and hesitant, more self-assured, he spoke of things in a casual, confident voice, learned much from his talks with Blaydon. He still did not know that this was his father. The old man thought there was no reason to tell him – not yet, not yet, they could go on as they were for the time being, just as they were.

He was comforted by the warmth of the sun on his face, by the scent of the roses and the tobacco plants in the evening, the sight of the scarlet bean-flowers clambering higher and higher up their frame.

He had decided right at the beginning that he himself would ask no questions of Blaydon, would wait until he should be told. But he was not told. Blaydon's life might have begun only on the day he had arrived here. The old man wondered if he had been in prison, or else abroad, working on a ship, though he had no evidence for either. In the evenings they drank beer together and occasionally played a game of cards, though more often, Blaydon worked at something in the garden and the old man simply sat, watching him, hearing the last cries of the birds from the marshes.

With the money Blaydon brought in, they bought new clothes for the boy, and better cuts of meat, and then, one afternoon, a television set arrived with two men in a green van to erect the aerial.

'For the winter,' Blaydon said. 'Maybe you won't bother with it now. But it's company in the winter.'

'I've never felt the lack.'

'All the same.'

'I don't need entertainment. We make our own. Always have made our own.'

'You'll be glad of it once you've got the taste. I told you – it's for the winter.'

But the old man watched it sometimes very late in the evenings of August and discovered things of interest to him, new horizons were opened, new worlds.

'I'd not have known that,' he said. 'I've never travelled. Look at what I'd never have known.'

Blaydon nodded. He himself seemed little interested in the television set. He was mending the front fence, staking it all along with old wood given him by Maldrun at the farm. Now, the gate would fit closely and not swing and bang in the gales of winter.

It was on a Thursday night towards the end of August that Blaydon mentioned the visit to the seaside.

'He's never been,' he said, wiping the foam of beer from his top lip. 'He told me. I asked him. He's never been to the sea.'

'I've done all I can. There's never been the money. We've managed as best we could.'

'You're not being blamed.'

'I'd have taken him, I'd have seen to it in time. Sooner or later.'

'Yes.'

'Yes.'

'Well – I could take him.'

'To the sea?'

'To the coast, yes.'

'For a day? It's far enough.'

'A couple of days, I thought. For a weekend.'

The old man was silent. But it was true. The boy had never been anywhere and perhaps he suffered because of it, perhaps at school the others talked of where they had gone, what they had seen, shaming him; if that was so, he should be taken, should go everywhere, he must not miss anything, must not be left out.

'Just a couple of days. We'd leave first thing Saturday morning and come back Monday. I'd take a day off.'

He had been here three months now, and not missed a day off work.

'You do as you think best.'

'I'd not go without asking you.'

'It's only right. He's at the age for taking things in. He needs enjoyment.'

'Yes.'

'You go. It's only right.'

'I haven't told him, not yet.'

'You tell him.'

When he did, the boy's face opened out with pleasure, he licked his lips nervously over and over again in his excitement, already counting until it should be time to go. The old man went upstairs and sorted out clothes for him, washed them carefully and hung them on the line, he began himself to anticipate it all. This was right. The boy should go.

But he dreaded it. They had not been separated before. He could not imagine how it would be, to sleep alone in the cottage, and then he began to imagine all the possible accidents. Blaydon had not asked him if he wanted to go with them. But he did not. He felt suddenly too tired to leave the house, too tired for any journeys or strangers, he wanted to sit on his chair in the sun and count the time until they should be back.

He had got used to the idea of Blaydon's continuing presence here, he no longer lived in dread of the coming winter. It seemed a long time since the days when he had been alone with the boy.

They set off very early on the Saturday morning, before the sun had broken through the thick mist that hung low over the marshes. Every sound was clear and separate as it came through the air, he heard their footsteps, the brush of their legs against the grasses long after they were out of sight. The boy had his own bag, bought new in the village, a canvas bag strapped across his shoulders. He had stood up very straight, eyes glistening, already his mind was filled with imaginary pictures of what he would see, what they would do.

The old man went back into the kitchen and put the kettle on again, refilled the teapot for himself and planned what he was going to do. He would work, he would clean out all the bedrooms of the house and sort the boy's clothes for any that needed mending; he would polish the knives and forks and wash the curtains and walk down to the village for groceries, he would bake a cake and pies, prepare a stew, ready for their return.

So that, on the first day, the Saturday, he scarcely had time to think of them, to notice their absence and in the evening, his legs and back ached, he sat for only a short time outside, after his meal, drunk with tiredness, and slept later than usual on the Sunday morning.

It was then that he felt the silence and emptiness of the house. He walked about it uselessly, he woke up the kitten and teased it with a feather so that it would play with him, distract his attention from his own solitude. When it slept again, he went out, and walked for miles across the still, hot marshes. The water between the reed beds was very low and even dried up altogether in places, revealing the dark, greenish-brown slime below. The faint, dry whistling sound that usually came through the rushes was absent. He felt parched as the countryside after this long, long summer, the sweat ran down his bent back.

He had walked in order to tire himself out again but this night he slept badly and woke out of clinging nightmares with a thudding heart, tossed from side to side, uncomfortable among the bedclothes. But tomorrow he could begin to count the strokes of the clock until their return.

He got up feeling as if he had never slept, his eyes were pouched and blurred. But he began the baking, the careful preparations to welcome them home. He scarcely stopped for food himself all day, though his head and his back ached, he moved stiffly about the kitchen.

When they had not returned by midnight on the Monday, he did not go down to the village, or across to Maldrun's farm to telephone the police and the hospitals. He did nothing. He knew.

But he sat up in the chair outside the back door all night with the silence pressing in on his ears. Once or twice his head nodded down on to his chest, he almost slept, but then jerked awake again, shifted a little, and sat on in the darkness.

He thought, they have not taken everything, some clothes are left, clothes and toys and books, they must mean to come back. But he knew that they did not. Other toys, other clothes, could be bought anywhere.

A week passed and the summer slid imperceptibly into autumn, like smooth cards shuffled together in a pack, the trees faded to yellow and crinkled at the edges.

He did not leave the house, and he ate almost nothing, only filled and refilled the teapot, and drank.

He did not blame Gilbert Blaydon, he blamed himself for having thought to keep the boy, having planned out their whole future. When the father had turned up, he should have known what he wanted at once, should have said, 'Take him away, take him now,' to save them this furtiveness, this deception. At night, though, he worried most about the effect it would have on the boy, who had been brought up so scrupulously, to be tidy and clean, to eat up his food, to learn. He wished there was an address to which he could write a list of details about the boy's everyday life, the routine he was used to following.

He waited for a letter. None came. The pear trees sagged under their weight of ripe, dark fruit and after a time it fell with soft thuds into the long grass. He did not gather it up and take it to store in the loft, he left it there for the sweet pulp to be burrowed by hornets and grubs. But sometimes he took a pear and ate it himself, for he had always disapproved of waste.

He kept the boy's room exactly as it should be. His clothes were laid out neatly in the drawers, his books lined on the single shelf, in case he should return. But he could not bother with the rest of the house, dirt began to linger in corners. Fluff accumulated greyly beneath beds. The damp patch on the bathroom wall was grown over with moss like a fungus when the first rain came in October.

Maldrun had twice been across from the farm and received no answer to his questions. In the village, the women talked. October went out in fog and drizzle, and the next time Maldrun came the old man did not open the door. Maldrun waited, peering through the windows between cupped hands, and in the end left the eggs on the back step.

The old man got up later and later each day, and went to bed earlier, to sleep between the frowsty, unwashed sheets. For a short while he turned on the television set in the evenings and sat staring at whatever was offered to him, but in the end he did not bother, only stayed in the kitchen while it grew dark around him. Outside, the last of the fruit fell onto the sodden garden and lay there untouched. Winter came.

In the small town flat, Blaydon set out plates, cut bread and opened tins, filled the saucepan with milk.

'Wash your hands,' he said. But the boy was already there, moving his hands over and over the pink soap, obediently, wondering what was for tea.

A Bit of Singing and Dancing

There was no one else on the beach so late in the afternoon. She walked very close to the water, where there was a rim of hard, flat sand, easier on her feet than the loose shelves of shingle, which folded one on top of the other, up to the storm wall. She thought, I can stay out here just as long as I like, I can do anything I choose, anything at all, for now I am answerable only to myself.

But it was an unpromising afternoon, already half dark, an afternoon for early tea and banked-up fires and entertainment on television. And a small thrill went through her as she realized that that, too, was entirely up to her, she could watch whichever programme she chose, or not watch any at all. There had not been an evening for the past eleven years when the television had stayed off and there was silence to hear the ticking of the clock and the central heating pipes.

'It is her only pleasure,' she used to say, 'She sees things she would otherwise be quite unable to see, the television has given her a new lease of life. You're never too old to learn.' But in truth her mother had watched variety shows, Morecambe and Wise and the Black and White Minstrels, whereas she herself would have chosen BBC 2 and something cultural or educational.

'I like a bit of singing and dancing, it cheers you up, Esme, it takes you out of yourself. I like a bit of spectacular.'

But tonight there might be a play or a film about Arabia or the Archipelagoes, or a master class for cellists, tonight she would please herself, for the first time. Because it was two weeks now, since her mother's death, a decent interval.

*

It was February. It was a cold evening. As far as she could see, the beach and the sea and the sky were all grey, merging into one another in the distance. On the day of her mother's funeral it had been blowing a gale, with sleet, she had looked round at all their lifeless, pinched faces under the black hats and thought, this is right, this is fitting, that we should all of us seem bowed and old and disconsolate. Her mother had a right to a proper grief, a proper mourning.

She had wanted to leave the beach and walk back, her hands were stiff with cold inside the pockets of her navy-blue coat – navy, she thought, was the correct first step away from black. She wanted to go back and toast scones and eat them with too much butter, of which her mother would have strongly disapproved. 'We never had it, we were never allowed to indulge ourselves in rich foods, and besides, they've been discovering more about heart disease in relation to butter, haven't you read that in the newspapers, Esme? I'm surprised you don't pay attention to these things. I pay attention. I don't believe in butter at every meal – butter on this, butter with that.'

Every morning, her mother had read two newspapers from cover to cover – the *Daily Telegraph* and the *Daily Mirror*, and marked out with a green ball-point pen news items in which she thought that her daughter ought to take an interest. She said, 'I like to see both sides of every question.' And so, whichever side her daughter or some visitor took, on some issue of the day, she was informed enough by both her newspapers to take the opposing view. An argument, she had said, sharpened the mind.

'I do not intend to become a cabbage, Esme, just because I am forced to be bedridden.'

She had reached the breakwater. A few gulls circled, bleating, in the gunmetal sky, and the waterline was strewn with fishheads, the flesh all picked away. She thought, I am free, I may go on or go back, or else stand here for an hour, I am mistress of myself. It was a long time since she had been out for so long, she could not quite get used to it, this absence of the need to look at her watch, to scurry home. But after a while, because it was really very damp and there was so little to see, she did turn, and then the thought of tomorrow, and the outing she had promised herself to buy new clothes. It would take some months for her mother's will to be proven, the solicitor had explained to her, things were generally delayed, but there was no doubt that they would be settled to her advantage and really, Mrs Fanshaw had been very careful, very prudent, and so she would not be in want. Meanwhile, perhaps an advance for immediate expenses? Perhaps a hundred pounds?

When the will was read, her first reaction had been one of admiration, she had said, 'The cunning old woman' under her breath, and then put her hand up to her mouth, afraid of being overheard. 'The cunning old woman.' For Mildred Fanshaw had saved up £6,000, scattered about in bank and savings accounts. Yet they had always apparently depended upon Esme's salary and the old age pension, they had had to be careful, she said, about electricity and extra cream and joints of beef. 'Extravagance,' Mrs Fanshaw said, 'it is a cardinal sin. That is where all other evils stem from, Esme. Extravagance. We should all live within our means.'

And now here was £6,000. For a moment or two it had gone to her head, she had been quite giddy with plans, she would buy a car and learn to drive, buy a washing machine and a television set, she would have a holiday abroad and get properly fitting underwear and eat out in a restaurant now and again, she would . . .

But she was over fifty, she should be putting money on one side herself now, saving for her own old age, and besides, even the idea of spending made her feel guilty, as though her mother could hear, now, what was going on inside her head, just as, in life, she had known her thoughts from the expression on her face.

She had reached the steps leading up from the beach. It was almost dark.

She shivered, then, in a moment of fear and bewilderment at her new freedom, for there was nothing she had to do, she could please herself about everything, anything, and this she could not get used to. Perhaps she ought not to stay here, perhaps she could try and sell the house, which was really far too big for her, perhaps she ought to get a job and a small flat in London. London was the city of opportunity . . .

She felt flushed and a little drunk then, she felt that all things were possible, the future was in her power, and she wanted to shout and sing and dance, standing alone in the February twilight, looking at the deserted beach. All the houses along the seafront promenade had blank, black windows, for this was a summer place, in February it was only half alive.

She said, 'And that is what I have been. But I am fifty-one years old and look at the chances before me.'

Far out on the shingle bank the green warning light flashed on-on-off, on-on-off. It had been flashing the night of her mother's stroke, she had gone to the window and watched it and felt comforted at three a.m. in the aftermath of death. Now, the shock of that death came to her again like a hand slapped across her face, she thought, my mother is not here, my mother is in a box in the earth, and she began to shiver violently, her mind crawling with images of corruption, she started to walk very quickly along the promenade and up the hill towards home.

When she opened the front door she listened, and everything was quite silent, quite still. There had always been the voice from upstairs, 'Esme?' and each time she had wanted to say, 'Who else would it be?' and bitten back the words, only said, 'Hello, it's me.' Now, again, she called, 'It's me. Hello,' and her voice echoed softly up the dark stair well, when she heard it, it was a shock, for what kind of woman was it who talked to herself and was afraid of an empty house? What kind of woman?

She went quickly into the sitting-room and drew the curtains and then poured herself a small glass of sherry, the kind her mother had preferred. It was shock, of course, they had told her, all of them, her brother-in-law and her Uncle Cecil and cousin George Golightly, when they had come back for tea and ham sandwiches after the funeral.

'You will feel the real shock later. Shock is always delayed.' Because she had been so calm and self-possessed, she had made all the arrangements so neatly, they were very surprised.

'If you ever feel the need of company, Esme – and you will – of course you must come to us. Just a telephone call, that's all we need, just a little warning in advance. You are sure to feel strange.'

Strange. Yes. She sat by the electric fire. Well, the truth was she had got herself thoroughly chilled, walking on the beach like that, so late in the afternoon. It had been her own fault.

After a while, the silence of the house oppressed her, so that when she had taken a second glass of sherry and made herself a poached egg on toast, she turned on the television and watched a variety show, because it was something cheerful, and she needed taking out of herself. There would be time enough for the educational programmes when she was used to this new life. But a thought went through her head, backwards and forwards, backwards and forwards, it was as though she were reading from a tape.

'She is upstairs. She is still in her room. If you go upstairs you will see her. Your mother.' The words danced across the television screen, intermingling with the limbs of dancers, issuing like spume out of the mouths of comedians and crooners, they took on the rhythm of the drums and the double basses.

'Upstairs. In her room. Upstairs. In her room.

Your mother. Your mother. Your mother.

Upstairs . . .'

She jabbed at the push button on top of the set and the picture shrank and died, there was silence, and then she heard her own heart beating and the breath coming out of her in little gasps. She scolded herself for being morbid, neurotic. Very well then, she said, go upstairs and see for yourself.

Very deliberately and calmly she went out of the room and climbed the stairs, and went into her mother's bedroom. The light from the street lamp immediately outside the window shone a pale triangle of light down onto the white runner on the dressing table, the white lining of the curtains and the smooth white cover of the bed. Everything had gone. Her mother might never have been here. Esme had been very anxious not to hoard reminders and so, the very day after the funeral, she had cleared out and packed up clothes, linen, medicine, papers, spectacles, she had ruthlessly emptied the room of her mother.

Now, standing in the doorway, smelling lavender polish and dust, she felt ashamed, as though she wanted to be rid of all memory, as though she had wanted her mother to die. She said, but that is what I did want, to be rid of the person who bound me to her for fifty years. She spoke aloud into the bedroom, 'I wanted you dead.' She felt her hands trembling and held them tightly together, she thought, I am a wicked woman. But the sherry she had drunk began to have some effect now, her heart was beating more quietly, and she was able to walk out into the room and draw the curtains, even though it was now unnecessary to scold herself for being so hysterical.

In the living room, she sat beside the fire reading a historical biography until eleven o'clock – when her mother was alive she had always been in bed by ten – and the fears had quite left her, she felt entirely calm. She thought, it is only natural, you have had a shock, you are bound to be affected. That night she slept extremely well.

★

When she answered the front doorbell at eleven fifteen the following morning and found Mr Amos Curry, hat in hand, upon the step, inquiring about a room, she remembered a remark her Uncle Cecil had made to her on the day of the funeral. 'You will surely not want to be here all on your own, Esme, in this great house. You should take a lodger.'

Mr Amos Curry rubbed his left eyebrow with a nervous finger, a gesture of his because he was habitually shy. 'A room to let,' he said, and she noticed that he wore gold cuff links and very well-polished shoes. 'I understand from the agency . . . a room to let with breakfast.'

'I know nothing of any agency. I think you have the wrong address.'

He took out a small loose-leaf notebook. 'Number 23, Park Close.'

'Oh no, I'm so sorry, we are . . .' she corrected herself, 'I am twenty-three Park *Walk*.'

A flush of embarrassment began to seep up over his face and neck like an ink stain, he loosened his collar a little until she felt quite sorry for him, quite upset.

'An easy mistake, a perfectly understandable mistake. Mr . . . Please do not feel at all . . .'

'. . . Curry. Amos Curry.'

'. . . embarrassed.'

'I am looking for a quiet room with breakfast. It seemed so hopeful. Park Close. Such a comfortable address.'

She thought, he is a very clean man, very neat and spruce, he has a gold incisor tooth and he wears gloves. Her mother had always approved of men who wore gloves. 'So few do, nowadays. Gloves and hats. It is easy to pick out a gentleman.'

Mr Curry also wore a hat.

'I do apologize, Madam, I feel so . . . I would not have troubled . . .'

'No . . . no, please . . .'

'I must look for Park Close, Number 23.'

'It is just around the bend, to the left, a few hundred yards. A very secluded road.'

'Like this. This road is secluded. I thought as I approached this house, how suitable, I should . . . I feel one can tell, a house has a certain . . . But I am so sorry.'

He settled his hat upon his neat grey hair, and then raised it again politely, turning away.

She took in a quick breath. She said, 'What exactly . . . that is to say, if you are looking for a room with breakfast, I wonder if I . . .'

Mr Amos Curry turned back.

He held a small pickled onion delicately on the end of his fork. 'There is,' he said, 'the question of my equipment.'

Esme Fanshaw heard his voice as though it issued from the wireless – there was a distortion about it, a curious echo. She shook her head. He is not real, she thought . . . But he was here, Mr Amos Curry, in a navy-blue pin stripe suit and with a small neat darn just below his shirt collar. He was sitting at her kitchen table – for she had hesitated to ask him into the dining-room, which in any case was rarely used, the kitchen had seemed a proper compromise. He was here. She had made a pot of coffee, and then, after an hour, a cold snack of beef and pickles, bread and butter, her hands were a little moist with excitement. She thought again how rash she had been, she said, he is a total stranger, someone from the street, a casual caller, I know nothing at all about him. But she recognized the voice of her mother, then, and rebelled against it. Besides, it was not true, for Mr Curry had told her a great deal. She thought, this is how life should be, I should be daring, I should allow myself to be constantly surprised. Each day I should be ready for some new encounter. That is how to stay young. She was most anxious to stay young.

In his youth, Mr Curry had been abroad a great deal, had lived, he said, in Ceylon, Singapore and India. 'I always keep an open mind, Miss Fanshaw, I believe in the principle of tolerance, live and let live. Nation shall speak peace unto nation.'

'Oh, I do agree.'

'I have seen the world and its ways. I have no prejudices. The customs of others may be quite different from our own but human beings are human beings the world over. We learn from one another every day. By keeping an open mind, Miss Fanshaw.'

'Oh yes.'

'You have travelled?'

'I – I have visited Europe. Not too far afield, I'm afraid.'

'I have journeyed on foot through most of the European countries, I have earned my passage at all times.'

She did not like to ask how, but she was impressed, having only been abroad once herself, to France.

Mr Curry had been an orphan, he said, life for him had begun in a children's home. 'But it was a more than adequate start, Miss Fanshaw, we were all happy together. I do not think memory deceives me. We were one big family. Never let it be said that the Society did not do its best by me. I see how lucky I am. Well, you have only to look about you, Miss Fanshaw – how many people do you see from broken families, unhappy homes? I know nothing of that: I count myself fortunate. I like to think I have made the best of my circumstances.'

His education, he said, had been rather elementary, he had a good brain which had never been taxed to the full.

'Untapped resources,' he said, pointing to his forehead.

They talked so easily, she thought she had never found conversation flowing along with any other stranger, any other man. Mr Curry had exactly the right amount of formal politeness, mixed with informal ease, and she decided that he was destined to live here, he had style and he seemed so much at home.

He had an ordinary face, for which she was grateful, but there was something slightly unreal about it, as though she were seeing it on a cinema screen. All the same, it was very easy to picture him sitting in this kitchen, eating breakfast, before putting on his hat, which had a small feather in the band, each morning and going off to work.

'I do have some rather bulky equipment.'

'What exactly . . .'

'I have two jobs, Miss Fanshaw, two strings to my bow, as it were. That surprises you? But I have always been anxious to fill up every hour of the day, I have boundless energy.'

She noticed that he had some tufts of pepper coloured hair sprouting from his ears and nostrils and wondered if, when he visited the barber for a haircut, he also had these trimmed. She knew nothing about the habits of men.

'Of course, it is to some extent seasonal work.'

'Seasonal?'

'Yes. For those odd wet and windy days which always come upon us at the English seaside, and of course during the winter, I travel in cleaning utensils.'

He looked around him quickly, as though to see where she kept her polish and dusters and brooms, to make note of any requirements.

'Perhaps you would require some extra storage space? Other than the room itself.'

Mr Curry got up from the table and began to clear away dishes, she watched him in astonishment. The man on the doorstep with a note of the wrong address had become the luncheon visitor, the friend who helped with the washing up.

'There is quite a large loft.'

'Inaccessible.'

'Oh.'

'And I do have to be a little careful. No strain on the back. Not that I am a sick man, Miss Fanshaw, I hasten to reassure you, you will not have an invalid on your hands. Oh no. I am extremely healthy for my age. It is because I lead such an active life.'

She thought of him, knocking upon all the doors, walking back down so many front paths. Though this was not what he did in the summer.

'Sound in wind and limb, as you might say.'

She thought of racehorses, and tried to decide whether he had ever been married. She said, 'Or else, perhaps, the large cupboard under the stairs, where the gas meter . . .'

'Perfect.'

He poured just the right amount of washing up liquid into the bowl; his sleeves were already unbuttoned and rolled up to the elbows, his jacket hung on the hook behind the back door. She saw the hairs lying like thatch on his sinewy arms, and a dozen questions sprang up into her mind, then, for although he seemed to have told her a great deal about himself, there were many gaps.

He had visited the town previously, he told her, in the course of his work, and fell for it. 'I never forgot it, Miss Fanshaw. I should be very happy here, I told myself. It is my kind of place. Do you see?'

'And so you came back.'

'Certainly. I know when I am meant to do something. I never ignore that feeling. I was intended to return here.'

'It is rather a small town.'

'But select.'

'I was only wondering – we do have a very short season, really only July and August . . .'

'Yes?'

'Perhaps it would not be suitable for your – er – summer work?'

'Oh, I think it would, Miss Fanshaw, I think so, I size these things up rather carefully, you know, rather carefully.'

She did not question him further, only said, 'Well, it is winter now.'

'Indeed. I shall, to coin a phrase, be plying my other trade. In a town like this, full of ladies such as yourself, in nice houses with comfortable circumstances, the possibilities are endless, endless.'

'For – er – cleaning materials?'

'Quite so.'

'I do see that.'

'Now you take a pride, don't you? Anyone can see that for himself.'

He waved a hand around the small kitchen, scattering little drops of foamy water, and she saw the room through his eyes, the clean windows, the shining taps, the immaculate sinks. Yes, she took a pride, that was true. Her mother had insisted upon it. Now, she heard herself saying, 'My mother died only a fortnight ago,' forgetting that she had told him already and the shock of the fact overcame her again, she could not believe in the empty room, which she was planning to give to Mr Curry, and her eyes filled up with tears of guilt. And what would her mother have said about a strange man washing up in their kitchen, about this new, daring friendship.

'You should have consulted me, Esme, you take far too much on trust. You never think. You should have consulted me.'

Two days after her mother's funeral, Mrs Bickerdike, from The Lilacs, had met her in the pharmacy, and mentioned, in lowered voice, that she 'did work for the bereaved', which, Esme gathered, meant that she conducted seances. She implied that contact might be established with the deceased Mrs Fanshaw. Esme had been shocked, most of all by the thought of that contact, and a continuing relationship with her mother, though she had only said that she believed in letting the dead have their rest. 'I think, if you will forgive me, and with respect, that we are not meant to inquire about them, or to follow them on.'

Now, she heard her mother talking about Mr Curry. 'You should always take particular notice of the eyes, Esme, never trust anyone with eyes set too closely together.'

She tried to see his eyes, but he was turned sideways to her.

'Or else too widely apart. That indicates idleness.'

She was ashamed of what she had just said about her mother's recent death, for she did not at all wish to embarrass him, or to appear hysterical. Mr Curry had finished washing up and was resting his reddened wet hands upon the rim of the sink. When he spoke, his voice was a little changed and rather solemn. 'I do not believe in shutting away the dead, Miss Fanshaw, I believe in the sacredness of memory. I am only glad that you feel able to talk to me about the good lady.'

She felt suddenly glad to have him here in the kitchen, for his presence took the edge off the emptiness and silence which lately had seemed to fill up every corner of the house.

She said, 'It was not always easy . . . My mother was a very . . . forthright woman.'

'Say no more. I understand only too well. The older generation believed in speaking their minds.'

She thought, he is obviously a very sensitive man, he can read between the lines: and she wanted to laugh with relief, for there was no need to go into details about how dominating her mother had been and how taxing were the last years of her illness – he knew, he understood.

Mr Curry dried his hands, smoothing the towel down one finger at a time, as though he were drawing on gloves. He rolled down his shirt-sleeves and fastened them and put on his jacket. His movements were neat and deliberate. He coughed. 'Regarding the room – there is just the question of payment, Miss Fanshaw, I believe in having these matters out at once. There is nothing to be embarrassed about in speaking of money, I hope you agree.'

'Oh no, certainly, I . . .'

'Shall we say four pounds a week?'

Her head swam. She had no idea at all how much a lodger should pay, how much his breakfasts would cost, and she was anxious to be both business-like and fair. Well, he had suggested what seemed to him a most suitable sum, he was more experienced in these matters than herself.

'For the time being I am staying at a commercial guest house in Cedars Road. I have only linoleum covering the floor of my room, there is nothing cooked at breakfast. I am not accustomed to luxury, Miss Fanshaw, you will understand that from what I have told you of my life, but I think I am entitled to comfort at the end of the working day.'

'Oh, you will be more than comfortable here, I shall see to that, I shall do my very best. I feel . . .'

'Yes?'

She was suddenly nervous of how she appeared in his eyes.

'I do feel that the mistake you made in the address was somehow . . .'

'Fortuitous.'

'Yes, oh yes.'

Mr Curry gave a little bow.

'When would you wish to move in, Mr Curry? There are one or two things . . .'

'Tomorrow evening, say?'

'Tomorrow is Friday.'

'Perhaps that is inconvenient.'

'No . . . no . . . certainly . . . our week could begin on a Friday, as it were.'

'I shall greatly look forward to having you as a landlady, Miss Fanshaw.'

Landlady. She wanted to say, 'I hope I shall be a friend, Mr Curry,' but it sounded presumptuous.

When he had gone she made herself a pot of tea, and sat quietly at the kitchen table, a little dazed. She thought, this is a new phase of my life. But she was still a little alarmed. She had acted out of character and against what she would normally have called her better judgement. Her mother would have warned her against inviting strangers into the house, just as, when she was a child, she had warned her about speaking to them in the street. 'You can never be sure, Esme, there are some very peculiar people about.' For she was a great reader of the crime reports in her newspapers, and of books about famous trials. The life of Doctor Crippen had particularly impressed her.

Esme shook her head. Now, all the plans she had made for selling the house and moving to London and going abroad were necessarily curtailed, and for the moment she felt depressed, as though the old life were going to continue, and she wondered, too, what neighbours and friends might say, and whether anyone had seen Mr Curry standing on her doorstep, paper in hand, whether, when he went from house to house selling cleaning utensils, they would recognize him as Miss Fanshaw's lodger and disapprove. There was no doubt that her mother would have disapproved, and not only because he was a 'stranger off the streets'.

'He is a salesman, Esme, a doorstep pedlar, and you do not *know* what his employment in the summer months may turn out to be.'

'He has impeccable manners, mother, quite old-fashioned ones, and a most genteel way of speaking.' She remembered the gloves and the raised hat, the little bow, and also the way he had quietly and confidently done the washing up, as though he were already living here.

'How do you know where things will lead, Esme?'

'I am prepared to take a risk. I have taken too few risks in my life so far.'

She saw her mother purse her lips and fold her hands together, refusing to argue further, only certain that she was in the right. Well, it was her own life now, and she was mistress of it, she would follow her instincts for once. And she went and got a sheet of paper, on which to write a list of things that were needed to make her mother's old bedroom quite comfortable for him. After that, she would buy cereal and bacon and kidneys for the week's breakfasts.

★

She was surprised at how little time it took for her to grow quite accustomed to having Mr Curry in the house. It helped, of course, that he was a man of very regular habits and neat, too, when she had first gone into his room to clean it, she could have believed that no one was using it at all. The bed was neatly made, clothes hung out of sight in drawers – he had locked the wardrobe, she discovered, and taken away the key. Only two pairs of shoes side by side, below the washbasin, and a shaving brush and razor on the shelf above it, gave the lodger away.

Mr Curry got up promptly at eight – she heard his alarm clock and then the pips of the radio news. At eight twenty he came down to the kitchen for his breakfast, smelling of shaving soap and shoe polish. Always, he said, 'Ah, good morning, Miss Fan-shaw, good morning to you,' and then commented briefly upon the weather. It was 'a bit nippy' or 'a touch of sunshine, I see' or 'bleak'. He ate a cooked breakfast, followed by toast and two cups of strong tea.

Esme took a pride in her breakfasts, in the neat way she laid the table and the freshness of the cloth, she warmed his plate under the grill and waited until the last minute before doing the toast so that it should still be crisp and hot. She thought, it is a very bad thing for a woman such as myself to live alone and become entirely selfish. I am the sort of person who needs to give service.

At ten minutes to nine, Mr Curry got his suitcase from the downstairs cupboard, wished her good morning again, and left the house. After that she was free for the rest of the day, to live as she had always lived, or else to make changes – though much of her time was taken up with cleaning the house and especially Mr Curry's room, and shopping for something unusual for Mr Curry's breakfasts.

She had hoped to enrol for lampshade-making classes at the evening institute but it was too late for that year, they had told her she must apply again after the summer, so she borrowed a book upon the subject from the public library and bought frames and card and fringing, and taught herself. She went to one or two bring-and-buy sales and planned to hold a coffee morning and do a little voluntary work for old people. Her life was full. She enjoyed having Mr Curry in the house. Easter came, and she began to wonder when he would change to his summer work, and what that work might be. He never spoke of it.

To begin with he had come in between five thirty and six every evening, and gone straight to his room. Sometimes he went out again for an hour, she presumed to buy a meal some-where and perhaps drink a glass of beer, but more often he stayed in, and Esme did not see him again until the following morning. Once or twice she heard music coming from his room – presum-ably from the radio, and she thought how nice it was to hear that the house was alive, a home for someone else.

One Friday evening, Mr Curry came down into the kitchen to give her the four pounds rent, just as she was serving up lamb casserole, and when she invited him to stay and share it with her, he accepted so quickly that she felt guilty, for perhaps, he went without an evening meal altogether. She decided to offer him the use of the kitchen, when a moment should arise which seemed suitable.

But a moment did not arise. Instead, Mr Curry came down two or three evenings a week and shared her meal, she got used to shopping for two, and when he offered her an extra pound a week, she accepted, it was so nice to have company, though she felt a little daring, a little carefree. She heard her mother telling her that the meals cost more than a pound a week. 'Well, I do not mind, they give me pleasure, it is worth it for that.'

One evening, Mr Curry asked her if she were good at figures, and when she told him that she had studied book-keeping, asked her help with the accounts for the kitchen utensil customers. After that, two or three times a month, she helped him regularly, they set up a temporary office on the dining-room table, and she remembered how good she had been at this kind of work, she began to feel useful, to enjoy herself.

He said, 'Well, it will not be for much longer, Miss Fanshaw, the summer is almost upon us, and in the summer, of course, I am self-employed.'

But when she opened her mouth to question him more closely, he changed the subject. Nor did she like to inquire whether the firm who supplied him with the cleaning utensils to sell, objected to the dearth of summer orders.

Mr Curry was an avid reader, 'in the winter', he said, when he had the time. He read not novels or biographies or war memoirs, but his encyclopedia, of which he had a handsome set, bound in cream mock-leather and paid for by monthly instalments. In the evenings, he took to bringing a volume down to the sitting-room, at her invitation, and keeping her company, she grew used to the sight of him in the opposite armchair. From time to time he would read out to her some curious or entertaining piece of information. His mind soaked up everything, but particularly of a zoological, geographical or anthropological nature, he said that he never forgot a fact, and that you never knew when something might prove of use. And Esme Fanshaw listened, her hands deftly fringing a lampshade – it was a skill she had acquired easily – and continued her education.

'One is never too old to learn, Mr Curry.'

'How splendid that we are of like mind! How nice!'

She thought, yes, it is nice, as she was washing up the dishes the next morning, and she flushed a little with pleasure and a curious kind of excitement. She wished that she had some woman friend whom she could telephone and invite round for coffee, in order to say, 'How nice it is to have a man about the house, really, I had no idea what a difference it could make.' But she had no close friends, she and her mother had always kept themselves to themselves. She would have said, 'I feel younger, and it is all thanks to Mr Curry. I see now that I was only half-alive.'

Then, it was summer. Mr Curry was out until half past nine or ten o'clock at night, the suitcase full of brooms and brushes and polish was put away under the stairs and he had changed his clothing. He wore a cream linen jacket and a straw hat with a black band, a rose or carnation in his button hole. He looked very dapper, very smart, and she had no idea at all what work he was doing. Each morning he left the house carrying a black case, quite large and square. She thought, I shall follow him. But she did not do so. Then, one evening in July, she decided to explore, to discover what she could from other people in the town, for someone must know Mr Curry, he was a distinctive sight, now, in the fresh summer clothes. She had, at the back of her mind, some idea that he might be a beach photographer.

She herself put on a quite different outfit – a white piqué dress she had bought fifteen years ago, but which still not only fitted, but suited her, and a straw boater, edged with ribbon, not unlike Mr Curry's own hat. When she went smartly down the front path, she hardly dared to look about her, certain that she was observed and spoken about by the neighbours. For it was well known now that Miss Fanshaw had a lodger.

She almost never went on to the promenade in the summer. She had told Mr Curry so. 'I keep to the residential streets, to the shops near home, I do so dislike the summer crowds.' And besides, her mother had impressed on her that the summer visitors were 'quite common'. But tonight walking along in the warm evening air, smelling the sea, she felt ashamed of that opinion, she would not like anyone to think that she had been brought up a snob – live and let live, as Mr Curry would tell her. And the people sitting in the deckchairs and walking in couples along the seafront looked perfectly nice, perfectly respectable, there were a number of older women and families with well-behaved children, this was a small, select resort, and charabancs were discouraged.

But Mr Curry was not to be seen. There were no beach photographers. She walked quite slowly along the promenade, looking all about her. There was a pool, in which children could sail boats, beside the War Memorial, and a putting green alongside the gardens of the Raincliffe Hotel. Really, she thought, I should come out more often, really it is very pleasant here in the summer, I have been missing a good deal.

When she reached the putting green she paused, not wanting to go back, for her sitting-room was rather dark, and she had no real inclination to make lampshades in the middle of July. She was going to sit down, next to an elderly couple on one of the green benches, she was going to enjoy the balm of the evening. Then, she heard music. After a moment, she recognized it. The tune had come quite often through the closed door of Mr Curry's bedroom.

And there, on a corner opposite the hotel, and the putting green, she saw Mr Curry. The black case contained a portable gramophone, the old-fashioned kind, with a horn, and this was set on the pavement. Beside it was Mr Curry, straw hat tipped a little to one side, cane beneath his arm, buttonhole in place. He was singing, in a tuneful, but rather cracked voice, and doing an elaborate little tap dance on the spot, his rather small feet moving swiftly and daintily in time with the music.

Esme Fanshaw put her hand to her face, feeling herself flush, and wishing to conceal herself from him: she turned her head away and looked out to sea, her ears full of the sentimental music. But Mr Curry was paying attention only to the small crowd which had gathered about him. One or two passers by, on the opposite side of the road, crossed over to watch, as Mr Curry danced, a fixed smile on his elderly face. At his feet was an upturned bowler hat, into which people dropped coins, and when the record ended, he bent down, turned it over neatly, and began to dance again. At the end of the second tune, he packed the gramophone up and moved on, farther down the promenade, to begin his performance all over again.

She sat on the green bench feeling a little faint and giddy, her heart pounding. She thought of her mother, and what she would have said, she thought of how foolish she had been made to look, for surely someone knew, surely half the town had seen Mr Curry? The strains of his music drifted up the promenade on the evening air. It was almost dark now, the sea was creeping back up the shingle.

She thought of going home, of turning the contents of Mr Curry's room out onto the pavement and locking the front door, she thought of calling the police, or her Uncle Cecil, of going to a neighbour. She had been humiliated, taken in, disgraced, and almost wept for the shame of it.

And then, presently, she wondered what it was she had meant by 'shame'. Mr Curry was not dishonest. He had not told her what he did in the summer months, he had not lied. Perhaps he had simply kept it from her because she might disapprove. It was his own business. And certainly there was no doubt at all that in the winter months he sold cleaning utensils from door to door. He paid his rent. He was neat and tidy and a pleasant companion. What was there to fear?

All at once, then, she felt sorry for him, and at the same time, he became a romantic figure in her eyes, for he had danced well and his singing had not been without a certain style, perhaps he had a fascinating past as a music hall performer, and who was she, Esme Fanshaw, to despise him, what talent had she? Did she earn her living by giving entertainment to others?

'I told you so, Esme. What did I tell you?'

'Told me what, mother? What is it you have to say to me? Why do you not leave me alone?'

Her mother was silent.

Quietly then, she picked up her handbag and left the green bench and the promenade and walked up through the dark residential streets, past the gardens sweet with stocks and roses, past open windows, towards Park Walk, and when she reached her own house, she put away the straw hat, though she kept on the dress of white piqué, because it was such a warm night. She went down into the kitchen and made coffee and set it, with a plate of sandwiches and a plate of biscuits, on a tray, and presently Mr Curry came in, and she called out to him, she said, 'Do come and have a little snack with me, I am quite sure you can do with it, I'm quite sure you are tired.'

And she saw from his face that he knew that she knew.

But nothing was said that evening, or until some weeks later, when Mr Curry was sitting opposite her, on a cold, windy August night, reading from the volume COW to DIN. Esme Fanshaw said, looking at him, 'My mother used to say, Mr Curry, "I always like a bit of singing and dancing, some variety. It takes you out of yourself, singing and dancing."'

Mr Curry gave a little bow.

The Peacock

'Left or right?'

'Oh dear.'

He tapped his foot impatiently. And then conscientiously refrained from tapping it, not wishing to annoy her.

It was quite dark. It was raining. The lane was overhung with trees.

'Didn't you follow the last signpost, dear?'

'I'm sorry, I thought that you . . . I'm so sorry.'

'The point is you have been here before, you see, I'm the one who's in the dark.'

But it is over twenty years, Daisy Buckingham thought, I surely cannot be expected to . . . Oh but then, she was the one who had wanted to come here, she had first put the idea forward, made the arrangements, she . . . So it was her fault. It must be her fault.

She saw that he was trying hard not to tap his foot.

'We cannot stay here at a cross-roads all night, dear, that's all I'm thinking, we should make some decision. Right or left? I did think you knew.'

'I'm so sorry.'

The Bradney Court Hotel had once been a manor house, it was secluded, with a lawn at the back sloping down to the river. In front it was approached by a long drive, but the drive was lined with trees and in the dark, the hotel sign was half screened by hedges, so that in the end, it was another quarter of an hour before they accidentally took the correct turning.

She wondered if he were not being a little unfair. For twenty years was a long time, and even then, she had been driven here by her father, there had been no need for her to pay detailed attention to the route. Twenty years ago she and Humphrey had not met, twenty years ago she was Miss Poulteney, wearing a grey and white print dress, her father's companion. And now, she panicked, sitting next to her husband in the dark Rover car. Would he like the place at all? Perhaps her memories of it were rather unclear. Would it suit him? She wondered how she could know. For he would speak approvingly, he never complained, he was a good man. She did not always know where she stood with him.

Humphrey Buckingham liked his wife to have a mind of her own, he did not wish to do her thinking for her. But she had somehow become uncertain, she shrank away from herself more, since they left Africa, England was too subtle for her, life here had too many nuances. In Africa, where the contrasts had been simple and striking, she had been able to walk a straight, clearly defined course, she had been happier. Well, they had both been happier there, that was a truth he acknowledged daily.

So, he was glad when she had begun to persuade him to come to this hotel. She and her father had spent a very peaceful holiday, she said, there were such lovely walks and the people were so nice, she thought that Humphrey would find it very much to his taste.

They had no children, though sometimes, now, they called one another Mummy and Daddy, because her own parents had done so, it seemed the right, married thing to do. They had not made quite so many friends as they had hoped, now that they were back in England. They were rather dependent upon one another.

He switched off the car engine. She thought, now he will rub his hands together and say, 'Well, here we are,' and how his habits irritate me, I wish he did not have such habits. And was at once ashamed of herself. He was a good husband, a good man.

'Well, here we are.'

When they left Africa two years ago, he had shaved off his moustache. He had said, 'A new life, dear, the symbol of a new person.' And besides, he would not allow himself to slip into the image of an ex-Colonial. He had smiled to himself proudly, wielding the razor.

Now, she glanced at him and started again with surprise, for she no longer recognized him, his upper lip shelved down so abruptly towards the mouth, and there was not the dark line of bristle to add distinction. He looked younger and less decisive, his face was oddly crumpled, as though he were perpetually about to cry.

'Well now?' he had asked, his eyes narrowed anxiously, awaiting her approval, the moustache gone, and she had approved and would not have let him suspect how much his new appearance shocked her.

A little thing.

But he was not the same man she had married.

'Here we are.' He opened the car door and they stumbled through the rain across the hotel driveway.

Humphrey Buckingham thought, perhaps she did not notice. For he could not believe that she had actually looked about her carefully and approved of this place, and he wondered what kind of life she had led, how it had been, during those ten years with her widowed father. Perhaps the Bradney Court Hotel had been his choice and she was being loyal to him. Though she scarcely talked about him now. Yet she had said, 'I should like to go back there, I should like you to see it. We had such a happy holiday at Bradney, father and I.'

He looked around him, looked for something which he could wholeheartedly praise. Found nothing. He cleared his throat.

She said, 'Well, it is not *quite* the type of room I expected.' It was very cramped and the furnishings were not those antiques she had remembered. She walked over to the window. It was still raining, spattering down through the trees. She thought, it is my fault, I should have checked more carefully before making the arrangements.

'Wait for the daylight, dear, you can never tell anything before daylight.'

'It's only that I *had* thought we were to overlook the river, I'm sure . . .'

She ran her fingers uneasily over the nylon plush curtains. 'Of course, I had a single room then, things were rather different, I didn't see the double accommodation.'

'It was twenty years ago.'

'Father had a very nice view of the river, I'm sure he did. Yes. I'm quite sure I remember that.'

He went on with his unpacking. He was a careful man. His suitcase was neatly arrayed.

'We had such a happy holiday here.' But her voice faded a little into doubt at the end of the sentence. And when they walked through the lounge towards the dining-room later she remembered, everything came back to her as she breathed in the smell of the place, and her shoulders drooped under the burden of it.

The lounge was badly lit, from small, parchment-shaded brackets high up on the walls. There were circular tables with copies of *Country Life* and a row of pewter jugs above the fireplace. She had sat here in the evenings, sewing, while her father read detective novels, she had longed for young people, for some noise and cheerfulness to break in, for hope and opportunity.

It was late May now and cold but the central heating was off and the electric-coal fire did not quite take the chill off the dining-room. She thought of how her father had sucked his soup through clenched teeth and scraped the knife around the gravy on his plate, she thought of how she had sat opposite him and wished him dead.

Humphrey Buckingham rubbed his hands together. 'Well now,' and he picked up the menu briskly and again she noticed the limp, naked upper lip. Who is he? I do not know him, who is this man at the other side of the table? And she raised her own menu quickly, leaning her elbow on the table to stop her hand trembling.

'Restful,' Vernon Thackeray said, at the other end of the dining-room.

'Restful,' and sighed, for they did not allow themselves too much rest, nowadays it was too easy a habit to slip into, Elspeth said, too self-indulgent. 'We are going to be *active* in our retirement.' But after the Amateur Photographic Conference and before the Choral Society concert and the Summer Painting School, he had persuaded her to spend five days more quietly, they would simply stretch their legs and enjoy the countryside around Bradney. Though she had also brought a briefcase with her, full of the papers from her correspondence course on Creative Writing, and she had been justified, too, it had rained since Wednesday.

'Restful.'

After a moment, Elspeth Thackeray turned her eyes away from the Buckinghams. Retired, she had decided, like us, though perhaps a little younger – he might be sixty. But it was the woman she noticed, the woman, now leaning back for the waitress to put a bowl of soup before her. Mrs Thackeray was developing her powers of Observation, making herself aware of every detail. 'Look around you,' last week's lesson had advised. 'Look at your own, everyday world. You do not have to live an exotic life to glean material for Writing. Your material is there at your own fingertips, in the stuff of yesterday, today and tomorrow. No one else sees the world precisely as you see it. You and your life are unique. So take your time and pay attention to it. Really *look* at it. Become fully aware of the colour and shape and texture of everything, breathe in the atmosphere of the different places you visit regularly. You are training yourself, even as you go about your daily business, you are filling your own storehouse of ideas from the first moment you open your eyes each morning.' And it had gone on to suggest how, after observing people carefully, you could then take a step farther on, you might invent a background for them, imagine them in their home environment, or at their place of work. This was Step One to Creating a Character. She read each lesson through until she knew it by heart, so that little sections of it would come back to her during the day. She believed in following it very conscientiously. And so, now, she looked across the dining-room to where Daisy Buckingham sat on the wheel-backed chair.

'Nice. Sweet face. But – dowdy? Faded, anyway. That salt and pepper hair, in a loose bun, not very flattering to her neck and old-fashioned too. There's something . . .' She stopped, hovered a moment over the character she was building up, and then decided swiftly. 'No children. That's it. She is not a mother.' Then, she was proud of herself. The roast beef was very thinly cut and perhaps twice-cooked, but she folded a large piece carefully on to her fork, she said, 'I do not let my mind idle, I make use of every moment, and I shall never allow myself to stagnate.'

But she half wondered, later, whether her assessment of Mrs Buckingham was not such a one as any other woman might make.

There were plums and custard, cream crackers and cheddar cheese, to follow the beef. As each course was brought to them, Daisy Buckingham's heart sank, and because he said nothing, because he did not blame her, only ate what came, she felt more than ever at fault, and humiliated too. Well, why did he not say what he thought? Why did he not at least complain about the dullness of the cooking, for he was a man who enjoyed good food, in Africa, he had made her give a dinner party for ten or twelve people each week, and he himself helped to choose the menu. Of course, it had been easier there, with so much fresh fruit and the servants to help. And thinking of Africa made this worse than ever, this poorly lit, old-fashioned hotel, there was such an air of repression here, repression and restraint. She thought, surely this is not our place, surely we do not fit into these surroundings, we have come from Africa, and the marks of it are still upon our faces, we are trailing colour and light and gaiety. For they had been gay, hadn't they, in their bungalow in Nigeria, they had entertained, there was always conversation and laughter echoing down the garden towards the paddock, they had been part of such a lively, dominating crowd.

But this hotel received them now and its inspissated atmosphere, its plainness and lack of style absorbed them and rubbed away the last of their African bloom, until they seemed to belong, to merge into the background of chintz armchairs and fringed standard lamps, of foxed sporting prints and lukewarm beef. So it had been when she came here with her father, she had looked about her at elderly women who wore special, wide-fitting shoes and carried knitting or crochet around with them in little drawstring bags, and whose men, if they had them, had been drained of all strength and independence, so that they, too, were somehow female, their skin had taken on the same powdery softness, their mouths were filled with the same sexless artificial teeth. Then she had felt frustration and anger and misery welling up within her like a boil, she had thought, I am only thirty-four years old, I am still young, I have surely hope and fulfilment before me, why should I be in this place, why should I be still tied to my father, how can I bear it? She had almost cried out loud, but instead, had gone to walk along the river bank alone, looking for something to erupt before her eyes, praying to meet someone, to have an earthquake in her life. But the days had only passed by, her father had demanded attention, it had been another two and a half years before he died and she met Humphrey Buckingham, within the same month. He was a widower, he seemed genuinely to like her, so that she had repented of her anger and thanked God for understanding her, after all.

But now she was here again, and how could she have forgotten about this place, how could she have buried so much misery? They drank their coffee in the lounge, and, catching sight of herself in the heavy mirror, she saw grey hair and a thickened waistline, she thought, now we are almost old, and was shocked and afraid, suddenly, afraid of those whose company it seemed they must keep. For the other guests, sitting in the chintz arm-chairs, might have been those who had been here when she came with her father, they too were becoming a little blind, a little deaf, a little slow.

Humphrey read the gardening articles in *Country Life*. In Africa, the gardens had been kept up for them, and in any case it had only been necessary to hold back the profusion. Here they had bought a bungalow, and it was new, the garden had to be started, and so he had set himself to learn. She wondered if it was because he truly enjoyed it. She assumed so. But he did not tell her, she did not know.

She had noticed the other couple at dinner and now they were gathering up their things before leaving the lounge and she watched them and saw that they were quite different, they were younger and there was an alertness and confidence about them, they seemed to have a good deal with them in the way of books and papers and coloured pamphlets. The husband made some joke and they laughed aloud together, Daisy Buckingham felt herself flush faintly, for it seemed so out of place in this room, they had a vitality which the others would no longer be able to cope with.

And she is very smart, she said, very fashionable, she wears good clothes. Though perhaps the skirt was a fraction short for a woman of middle years: there was a veneer, which came from a flattering hairstyle and careful make-up, and perhaps Daisy Buckingham did not altogether approve. But she watched them and felt less depressed, and when they nodded to her so cheerfully and murmured good night, she answered, after glancing at Humphrey, she felt oddly flattered and hopeful – perhaps the Bradney Court Hotel was suitable for them after all. Humphrey read on about the soil constitution best suited to rhododendrons.

They went to bed rather early, mainly because they felt uncomfortable, left alone in the lounge after the other, older guests had retired. Well, she thought, we should do what is fitting, we should slip into this way of life. In any case, there was little to do; she would have liked to watch television but the set was in a smaller, even less welcoming lounge, and she shrank from trying to find someone who would switch it on, she simply sat and waited until Humphrey put down his magazine.

But she was still restless, still unhappy in this place, she tried to pin down what she wanted, what was really wrong, as they undressed in the awkward spaces beside their beds. It was not Humphrey, it could not be Humphrey, for he had come as the answer to her prayer, he was a good man and he had taken her out of the old life. He was not an exciting man, but it had not, in the end, been excitement that she had longed for, she had been very content to settle for something else, for the status of a wife, for security from the shame of spinsterhood. Humphrey was her companion. He had taken her to Africa, and had she not been happy there?

She lay down. The still air of the room, pressing in around her, smelled faintly of mothballs. Outside, it was still raining. Humphrey did not stir.

And then, feeling entirely alone, she knew what was wrong. She had no friends, no one with whom she could simply chat, no one who knew her and took the acquaintance entirely for granted. She was not needed, except by Humphrey, and even he, now they were in England, seemed to need her less, he did not talk a great deal, and there was a weariness about him.

Then, remembering all the nights she had lain awake, because of the heat, in Africa, she wished very much to be back there, for she had never felt alone, there had always been the servants, the sound of their voices as they called across the garden and the kitchens. And they had had such a social life, too, someone was always coming for drinks or tea or dinner, or else they themselves were getting ready to go out. And if she asked herself, momentarily, whether she had any true friends there, she was at once puzzled, for surely she must have done so. Certainly she had known where her place was and had tried to fit into it correctly, certainly she had never been *lonely*, as she seemed so often to be now. In Africa, it had never been quite silent outside the bungalow at night, there were always odd sounds, the darkness was always full of hidden movements, of secrets. She supposed that she missed the colour and the sunshine – there had been something dramatic and purposeful about their everyday life. Now we have come here, she thought, to a dull hotel in the English countryside, memory tricked me, I had forgotten the unhappiness of the past. Well, here we are, and so we had better accept that we are to grow old, we had better do things the way it is expected of us. She slept, trying to picture this woman she was to be.

'So what shall we do, dear?'

'Whatever you would like to do.'

'No please, you say, I am quite happy.'

'You would rather stay in?'

'I mean, I am happy to do anything at all, dear, whatever you prefer.'

'There are some rather nice walks. I do remember that.'

'Then we shall go out for a walk.'

'But if you would prefer to stay and rest – I should so hate to make you do something you did not like – it is your holiday, too, Humphrey.'

'It is a holiday for both of us.'

'It *has* stopped raining though it is rather grey still, perhaps . . .'

He had half-risen from his armchair, and now he looked at her and she thought that he was impatient or even angry, she felt again that it was her fault, he was not happy here, he was bored and irritable. If only he would say so, if only he would tell her quite plainly what he was really feeling. But he was so considerate, he was a good husband.

'Yes,' she said, for one of them must make a decision, 'I think that fresh air will really do us good.'

Though the air was not so fresh as she had expected, it was a damp, close day and a thin mist hung over the river. The grass sucked under their feet. No one else seemed to have come out, but the lounge had been almost empty, people were resting, she supposed, after their dull lunch. In a few years' time she and Humphrey would do that too, the day would overtire them. She wondered how long she would live.

There was not quite room for them to walk side by side along the path and so Humphrey went a pace or two in front. He was very upright, she thought, he made the most of his height. Humphrey. She mouthed his name, for she was still surprised, even now, that he should be with her, it seemed as if it was most natural to her to be alone. Though in fact she had never been truly so, there had been her parents and then her father by himself, and now there was Humphrey. Yet it was as if this man who accompanied her belonged to someone else and might at any moment return to them, she was still, even after seventeen years, unused to him.

The river curved a little but although they walked for over a mile alongside it, the outlook was much the same at any point. Water dripped on to their heads now and then from the trees and the clumps of long grass bordering the path were cold and clammy as they brushed against her legs. This was the countryside, then, this was what he had so often felt homesick for in Africa. This.

Humphrey walked steadily ahead, his hands in his pockets, as though he had a destination. But the path only led on, through fields and beneath trees, following the water. After a while a light rain began to fall again. She wore a headscarf and a sensible tweed coat. But perhaps Humphrey would not want to go on.

'Just whatever you like, dear, I really don't mind.'

'It is only a drizzle, it might not come to anything.'

'You would be happy to go on?'

'But you haven't a hat, I should not like to think you were going to catch cold.'

'No, no. If you want to go back, though, then of course we will.'

They stood uncertainly as usual, looking at the surface of the river, broken up by pin pricks of rain. Where are we going, she asked suddenly, what is life for? Is it this? A walk in the rain and the thought of tea, dry cakes and raisin biscuits, the lack of conversation in a draughty lounge. Almost in despair, then, she asked him what he truly wanted, begged him to make a decision, to suggest some purpose for them.

'Well, it may come on to rain harder, we may be better advised to go back now.'

'Yes, dear, I do think, if you're . . .'

He was impatient, he turned abruptly and began to walk away from her, retracing the path, so that she fidgeted with the knot of her headscarf, wondering how she had annoyed him, how she might . . .

Then they heard the voices. Humphrey hesitated, as the smart woman and her husband appeared. It was raining harder.

'Oh . . .'

'Good afternoon . . .'

'Really, I don't think much of this.'

'We did see you last night in the lounge . . .'

'I doubt if we're going to get far. My husband wants . . .'

'Yes awful weather, awful . . .'

They became somehow entangled with one another on the

narrow path, they were all laughing a little with embarrassment. Daisy Buckingham found herself next to the smart woman, who was suggesting tea, who said, 'Now, why should we not have it together?' so that they seemed to have taken an abrupt step towards acquaintanceship, two couples of similar age, sharing a similar holiday. She felt flattered but uncomfortable too, beside the fashionable woman, she tried to think out what she might say that would be interesting, and would keep their attention, keep them near her, for she felt very confined sometimes, alone with Humphrey, they seemed to have nothing new to say to one another.

When she mentioned that they had lived in Africa, she saw interest at once in the other woman's face, and she felt a sudden surge of confidence in herself, felt unusual. And Elspeth Thackeray was indeed interested, because of the sentence in last week's lesson about the new and exciting worlds to be found through conversation with even the most unlikely people. She would not have suspected Daisy Buckingham of having lived an adventurous and colourful life in Africa, and so she prompted her with questions and listened eagerly, storing away the answers in her memory, knowing that you could never tell just how useful they might be later for some article or story. Ahead of them, their husbands, too, spoke of Africa, and by the time the hotel was reached they were becoming friends. They met again, after going upstairs to discard their wet clothes, and had tea.

The lounge seemed bright, Daisy Buckingham thought, and the cakes had more flavour than she had expected, and Mrs Thackeray was still listening quite carefully to her stories about Africa. She had been quite right then, this was all they needed, some company and conversation, some new faces to take them out of themselves.

But was Humphrey happy, was this what *he* had needed? He had always been so sociable when they were in Africa, yet now he spent most of his time in her company – though once or twice he had gone off by himself for the day to London. She watched his face carefully as he talked to Vernon Thackeray, she thought, I should be able to tell what he is feeling, I am his wife. Certainly there would be no other clue, he said so little and always hid from her any displeasure or boredom. She could never be sure.

Vernon Thackeray told them of his life in retirement and really, it was most interesting and challenging, too, it struck Daisy Buckingham as she listened, with hope for their own future, she wondered if, after all, they might delay growing old. The Thackerays *did* so much.

'It is so very important, we feel, to keep ourselves up to the mark, to retain our curiosity.'

'What I say is, whatever our age, we can still learn. Oh, I have learned so much since our retirement, whole new worlds have been opened to me, I feel quite excited when I wake up each morning.'

Then how did they also belong here, in the lounge of the Bradney Court Hotel, among the elderly, those who had lost all their inquisitiveness about life?

Daisy Buckingham looked at them, at Mrs Thackeray's long, slim fingers with the two diamond rings and nails tastefully polished, and at her husband's rather wide floral tie, she tried to work out the answer. She was puzzled by them both. But heartened too, because it made their own presence here seem less of a mistake. A hotel, like home, could be what you made it.

Tea merged into drinks before dinner – whisky and sweet sherries – and after dinner they took coffee together too, so that by the end of the evening, they each of them felt they knew the others very well, there was a general easiness between them. When an excursion was suggested, therefore – it was not clear who first suggested it – they all agreed quickly, and then it was only a question of finding a suitable place. That night Daisy Buckingham slept at once and woke once, feeling oddly happy, though it was some time before she realized that it was because she had something to look forward to.

Afterwards, she came to believe that it was somehow her own ineptitude which brought the accident about. It was a nightmare. She had never been so afraid.

They had walked all around the castle, admiring furniture and tapestries and portraits, an Adam fireplace and a painted ceiling, and they continued to enjoy one another's company too, the afternoon was altogether a success. Daisy Buckingham felt younger and wished that she too had a way with clothes, for perhaps she did not make the best of herself. Well, possibly Elspeth Thackeray would take charge of her, teach her how to dress.

She said suddenly, 'Oh, I am so glad we met, how lucky that was!' and then felt slightly foolish, they all looked at her in such surprise, and she thought that Humphrey disapproved, there was a strange expression on his face. But why should she not say what she meant, just because he did not do so, why should their new friends not know how much they pleased her? She felt that she had awakened, that someone had tapped her on the shoulder, had given her new hope.

And so they made their way out into the gardens, and because it was a rather chilly day and early in the season, few other visitors were there, they could walk quite freely around the perimeter of the lake and down between the box hedges, admiring the pergola and the doric arch, the imposing façade of the castle viewed from the other side of the water. Humphrey and Vernon Thackeray strolled a little way ahead, and he was still talking about Africa. Vernon Thackeray had taken a photograph of them all, smiling a little self-consciously beside a garden statue of Venus. He had won prizes for his photographs, Elspeth said, a new tripod and a silver medal, even though he had not taken up the hobby until his retirement. He was specializing now in landscape and child portraits.

'He applies himself so wholeheartedly to a thing, once he has decided upon it, he does so much believe in using these years to the full.'

So the photograph of their outing would be something else to look forward to.

Then, it all happened rather quickly, and in some confusion. Humphrey had gone to sit down on a stone bench not far away, apparently to rest, and Elspeth Thackeray was walking forward to join him. Then Daisy Buckingham saw the small summerhouse, with its domed roof, and at once it reminded her of a similar one in their vice-consul's park in Africa, she went over to look and at that moment the sun came out, breaking through a gap in the heavy clouds and filling the summerhouse with warm light, she went inside, hoping to find . . .

She did not exactly know what she had hoped to find, she was simply curious. But the summerhouse was quite empty. A slatted bench ran around the inside walls, and cobwebs were stranded across it here and there. The floor was very dusty. She turned to leave, disappointed, to rejoin the others, and then somehow caught her arm against the door, so that it slipped off the hook and slammed shut, and when she turned the handle she found that it had locked itself. She banged and called out. The windows were high up and inaccessible, and when the sun went in again, the place was rather dark. It smelled dry and musty and there was another smell, as though someone had once kept hens here. She called again, feeling not so much frightened as foolish. The men would have to come and wrench the door down, people would laugh at her. But it seemed that they could not hear her, their voices were some way off.

Then she heard a sound inside the close, dark space, a scratching noise underneath the slatted bench. She looked down. A peacock was there, cornered and bright-eyed. When she took a step towards it, a low, hostile noise came from its throat like a cat hissing.

Her mother would never have peacocks' feathers in the house, they were unlucky, she said, they brought sickness and death, and it was the same with lilac. Once, as a small child, she had been given a peacock's feather by an aunt, and the evil eye of it had watched her, she had been very frightened of the bright colours.

Now, she shrank back against the summerhouse door. But the bird did not move. She began to sweat. And called out again. But almost at once she heard Elspeth's voice on the other side of the door.

'Can you not try to push the door really hard? Perhaps . . . What has happened to the lock? Listen, dear, there is something the matter with Humphrey, he . . . I think he is not very well . . . we must get someone, we shall get help, but can you not try and pull the door, pull it really hard?'

'It's locked. I'm so sorry. How silly this is. Perhaps Humphrey could . . . but you say there is something wrong with Humphrey?'

'Just a moment, dear, can you wait a moment?'

And she went away again. The summerhouse was silent.

Daisy Buckingham felt a little faint now, trapped with the terrifying bird. She heard it shift about softly, the claws scratching on the stone floor, and at once imagined it flying forward, the wings beating into her face and the bright eyes staring, staring. Oh why ever did they not try and push the door from the outside, for surely it could only be sticking a little, they had only to work at it for a few minutes?

'Elspeth, please come here . . . Can you not . . .'

But it was quite a long time before anybody came. The sun filled the summerhouse again and the feathers of the peacock glinted where the light fell onto its beautiful tail through the slatted bench. It was hot and rather stuffy. She wanted to sit down, her legs felt weak and the palms of her hands were damp, she wiped them over and over again nervously on her dress. She wondered why the bird had come in here. Perhaps it was ill, and had come for seclusion in which to die. She dared not look at it again.

And then she realized what the smell reminded her of. It was the close, hot, animal smell of Africa. There was the scent of danger, of fear, and she remembered how afraid she had always been there, afraid of the strangeness of it all, of the black servants with their soft, silent movements and the cries of animals from far away, afraid of something threatening which seemed to hover permanently on the air. Their life had been lived as though on a skin, and below that membraneous surface, everything was pressed together and simmered, and might at any time erupt into some form of violence and death. When it rained, it rained violently, and when the sun shone it was with a concentrated, angry heat.

She had hated Africa. That was the whole truth. She had walked in dread of everything there. And all the time, too, had felt her own life to be out of place with the lives of the others, to have no real meaning. She had gone there because Humphrey had taken her. But she had felt a stranger in his company, he was a man she had married for fear that there might prove to be no alternative, a secretive man, a man she did not know. Humphrey.

She was shocked, now, remembering so much truth, admitting to it. For while she had told Elspeth Thackeray the stories of Africa she herself had fully believed them, there had been no uneasiness. She had tried to forget, as she had forgotten her own loneliness and misery all those years ago at the Bradney Court Hotel. She was trembling and almost in tears, she had turned her back upon the silent, menacing peacock and its bright eyes. Oh come, oh please come, oh help me, where have you gone, why have you left me? She wanted to scream, to claw and hammer at the closed door. Oh help me.

In the end, naturally, they came. They had gone for a castle official and he had fetched a workman who prised open the door.

But they had of necessity been delayed while an ambulance was fetched for Humphrey, who had suffered a heart attack, lying upon the grass.

They were shocked at the sight of Daisy Buckingham's face, crumpled and white with fear, they noticed that she was crying a little, and trembling, and did not know how to break this other news to her, they felt in some way to blame.

But things were done, Humphrey was taken to hospital, the sun went in again behind banks of iron-grey cloud. No one knew about the peacock. This is drama, Elspeth Thackeray thought, this is the stuff of literature, this is Life. And was at once excited, though also a little ashamed.

He will die. Daisy Buckingham said, looking down at her husband's face, ashen and dry, on the high pillow. He will surely die. And a thrill went through her, for she realized that it was what she wanted. She knew nothing about him, felt nothing. He had never given her any of his true self, they had not been close. She had been ill with unhappiness and guilt at the death of her father, whom she had so much resented and, after all, so much loved. It had startled her to discover how much she loved him and now, she found that she did not love Humphrey. Though certainly she did not hate or even dislike him. There was nothing. A dullness.

As soon as she understood that, she could not bear it and reproached herself bitterly, for he was a good man, a good husband, it was her plain duty to love him, to feel distress. So she began to do so. She sat at his bedside, not knowing if he would live or die, trying to forget her own true feelings.

At the Bradney Court Hotel, Vernon and Elspeth Thackeray drank small glasses of brandy and found that for once they had nothing to say to one another, they had been stilled and silenced by the events of the day.

Death, Vernon Thackeray said to himself at last, death. And

was suddenly chilled, looking down at the backs of his own hands, realizing he was growing old.

I shall be a widow, she thought, I shall be left alone, and I should prepare for it now, make some plans. I must learn from the Thackerays about how to be busy, how to keep up a real interest in life. Her mind turned over various ideas, about courses of study she could follow, hobbies to take up, places to visit. She would entertain, she would learn a foreign language. She would fulfil herself. She said, I am over fifty and I have never known myself, never tested myself, I have never truly lived. She felt suddenly hopeful and sorry for her husband, the man she did not know, who lay so stilly in the narrow hospital bed. She tried to imagine everyday life without him, and it was easy, she could not remember what place he had filled.

He did not die, and after a while, he came home, although he must be rather careful about his diet and exercise, just as her father had been. Daisy Buckingham prepared to devote herself to him. And Humphrey was very good, she told Elspeth Thackeray – for they kept in touch, they remained friends – he was so considerate, never complained, he was a good husband, a good man. But for some years afterwards, she found it hard to forget the peacock, and the black brightness of its eyes looking at her across the summerhouse.

Missy

'There you are, Mrs Ebbs, hold the cup steady. Can you manage, dear? Whoops! That's it. Now sit up properly, you'll slip down in the bed again, sit up against your pillows. That's it. Don't nod off again, will you? Now careful, Mrs Ebbs, I haven't got all day, dear. That's it, good girl.'

The voice came roaring towards her. The face was bland as suet. The face was a cow's face. An ox.

'Ox-face,' she said. But she had not said it.

She tipped the spoon and sucked in her soup, little bits of carrot and soft lentil sieving through the spaces between her teeth.

'All right now, Mrs Ebbs?'

Ox-face.

'I'm not *deaf*.'

Was she?

'Drink plenty, Mrs Pender, we want to get your waterworks right again, don't we? Drink up.'

Then the screech of trolley wheels on the polished linoleum. Birds chattered outside the window.

She said, When they come back I shall tell them, 'I had a mother who loved me.' My mother once said, 'Bless me, you've got a touch of sunstroke, you'll have to go and lie down on your bed.' That was not in India, though, but in England and because of going across Daker's field without a bonnet. She had been in her bed in the middle of the day.

A little sticky ball of soup dissolved against her tongue and inside it was powder, so they used things out of packets then, it tasted of salt, in spite of fifty guineas a week.

Her mother had said, 'Is that cool on your head? Is that better now?'

The handkerchief had been soaked in iced cologne, cold as metal.

'I had a mother who loved me.'

But in the end, she never said anything to them.

Later on, she let herself slip sideways down in the bed, so that the soup, what was left of it, pale and congealed, trickled out and stained the counterpane. Then they scolded her, told her they'd have to put her in the corner, and the others gloated in their beds, their bones shiny through the skin, because this time it was not them, they were in favour. 'Dirty, messy girl, how many times have I told you, Mrs Ebbs? You don't try, dear. Now sit yourself up, that's it. Here's the bedpan. Pull up your nightie.'

For once they drew the curtains around her bed, dragging them roughly along the rail.

'My own little corner.'

Whenever she could she used to sneak into the dining-room and crawl beneath the chenille cloth hanging down from the table, and in there it was dark and quite stuffy, her own corner, only that sometimes it smelled of dog, after Bruce had been lying there during dinner. She was afraid of Bruce, with the slavering mouth.

'A man's dog,' her father said, flourishing the carving knife and fork about in the air as he talked, for he was master, he liked all to see that he was there, to pay attention to him. Sometimes Bruce nuzzled up to her legs beneath the table, and she drew them back as far as possible, for fear of his saliva, though she never dared to complain.

Her father and mother did not, as people said, 'get on'. He was a man without understanding, though he spoke four languages and made a good enough income for them to have the seaside house for the whole of August and two pianos, a grand and an upright, in London.

Nesta said that their mother was a silly woman, and vain. Tactless, anyway, that was true. She compared the ways of this house unfavourably with those of her family home, and her husband, she always said, was not half the man her father had been. She played the piano and sang, wearing a kingfisher satin dress, showing off her arms and shoulders, and her hair was done in little, round curls clustered together at the back of her neck, like a bunch of black grapes. She sought compliments, turning her head from side to side of the room as she played, though there might only be the children there, and Bruce, nevertheless, she sought admiration with her eyes, so perhaps Nesta was right, she was vain, for certainly she was not very musical. 'I had a mother who loved me.'

Ox-face was there, pulling away the bedpan.

'Come on, Mrs Ebbs, wake up, dear, forever nodding off, it's not good for you, you know, you should take more of an interest. Come on, we'll have you out in the chair a bit later, shall we, do you good, you give in too easily, dear. There's no sense in giving in too easily.'

'Nobody comes to see me.'

'What? Oh, I never heard such nonsense! That nice Mrs Whatsername comes, she comes every other Thursday.'

Mrs Whatsername. Her cardigans smelled of stale cupboards and old, dried-up egg.

'I'll have you know that some people here never have anyone, not a soul do they see from the outside world, month in, month out. You're one of the lucky ones. Where are your teeth, Mrs Ebbs? It isn't nice for other people, dear, you sitting there without your teeth. Here you are, put them in there's a good girl, you'll feel better – we mustn't let *go*, Mrs Ebbs, must we?'

The teeth were like plastic bricks slithering into her mouth. Her gums were sore where they rubbed along the edges.

They're not *my* teeth, in any case. I had my own teeth. I had perfect teeth, as a child, perfect teeth and perfect eyesight. The others wore a brace or spectacles, but I never did.

Sometimes, it was very hard to remember things, they floated in the air just out of reach, she needed somehow to free them. But now there was the smell of cow-pats suddenly thick in her nostrils, and she saw them, yellow-green and pock-marked where the flies had settled. The summers smelled of cow-pats. Brother Royston had caught diphtheria and died, in the summer. Then they had gone to the sea.

'Have you been, Mrs Pender? You should have been by now, dear, are you trying? You don't want to sit all day on the bedpan like that, I'm sure. Well, better have a glass of barley water and try you again later, otherwise we'll have to be sending for the doctor to look at the plumbing. Pull your nightie down, dear, that's it. *Can you hear me?*'

Then it was night and she touched her hands to her face, felt it all over, for she was afraid of losing herself, of death.

For two years they had lived in India, but what did she remember of it now? An old woman with dark-skinned, wrinkled arms carrying something in a bowl and pausing to spit down on to the grass at the edge of the path.

In India there had been a horse lying dead on a roadway, its eyes sticky and swarming with flies, and the houseboy had lain down one afternoon and died in the heat, moaning and drawing up his legs. She had been hurried away.

She had an English friend, Agnes, who came to lessons and tea.

'The houseboy is dead.'

'Well that's all right.' Agnes had little fat shiny lips.

'Only the natives die.'

'But I saw a dead horse.'

'Oh well, and animals die.'

'Shall I die?'

'I told you, we're different, it's only the natives and the animals.'

'How do you know?'

'I just *know*.'

In India she had changed her frock and petticoat and stockings twice a day.

'*We won't die.*'

But then her brother Royston died the summer they returned to England and after that she had something like a germ growing inside her, of which she was afraid.

Her hands moved over the side of her face, down to the jaw.

'Is it falling into a dark pit and then nothing, or is it something that will last forever, like it or not?'

They gave her a blue capsule at night, which blurred the edges of her mind, soaking into them like water into blotting paper, crumbling them away, but in the centre she was there, not asleep, waiting to die.

When her husband died, she had been afraid to look into his coffin. Now, she could not remember his name.

'Why didn't you ask before, Mrs Pender? Disturbing everybody with the bell. You must have known you wanted to go. Have you been drinking too much? Move over then dear, you'll have to help yourself a bit. Next time try and remember to ask earlier, won't you? All right. *Can you hear me?*'

I am not like that. I will not be like that, helpless. I have two arms and legs.

She felt herself in panic, touched her hands to her legs beneath the bedclothes. But she was there.

It isn't like it used to be. Nothing is. I want to remember everything.

She remembered how he had once had to slap her, slap her

arms, during an air raid in the war. They had moved back to London then and there was a wedge of cupboard under the back stairs. The planes had whined, the bombs had whined, her head sang with the noises. She had screamed to drown them and he had said think, think of the servants, what will the servants make of you? And slapped her. One night, a house was bombed on the opposite side of the street, and all the china had been shattered in their front sitting-room, all the Dresden figurines which had belonged to his mother, and the Royal Worcester, all gone with the blown-out windows, and she was glad, she had hated it but she had been quite calm, an example to the servants.

The servants were Mrs Bondy and a girl. But he had been accustomed to a full household and old habits died hard. Once, she had begun to tell him about the number they had had in India but he had waved at her impatiently, not wanting to know.

They never talked.

Mrs Pender snored, long, greedy snores.

Some time ago, some weeks or months, a woman had died in the opposite bed, where Mrs Pender was now, there had been lights and voices and footsteps all through the night and the terrible sound of breathing. She had thought then, dying is a private thing, like using the toilet and bathing, dying is . . . But she did not know what it was. All her life she had been a fastidious woman about personal matters. But if death came to her here in this room with the green linoleum, how could she escape?

Mrs Whatsername sat in the chair beside her bed and the smell of the cardigan came to her every now and then. Mrs Whatsername had greasy hair. She had lived three – or was it five? – doors away, and was Chapel. Not the sort of friend she would have chosen.

'My daughter has a budgie now, did I tell you? For the children.

She believes in bringing them up along with the pets, you see, they've the dog already, Tinker, *and* he is.'

In India they had scarlet and green and golden birds flying about freely in the garden. She remembered the smell of the kitchen in their Indian house, the rancid smell of ghee and the sweat smell of the cook as she lifted her arms to take a great brown pot down from the shelf. They had called her Missy, and given her aniseed-flavoured water to drink out of a blue cup. Missy. She was only allowed in the kitchen occasionally. Why had she forgotten all the other things? Missy.

'He always has been very pernickety about the children, my son-in-law has, he wants them brought up really nice, you know – not that he could expect anything else from my Jean. But of course, now he's manager he does have a position to keep up. The children have to wash their hands before every meal and wipe their mouths on serviettes, he's very particular. Of course the boy, our Clive, he'll be going to the private school. You get what you pay for, my son-in-law says. He had his tonsils out privately.'

'How many slices of bread, Mrs Ebbs?'

'Four.'

'What? Goodness gracious, I don't think you could manage *four*, dear, what about your waistline? Have two and come back for more if you really need them. Cup of tea, Mrs . . . ? Now sit up, Mrs Ebbs, lean right up on your pillows, there's your tray. Don't you think she's looking perky, Mrs . . . with her new bedjacket on, fit for a party, isn't she?'

'Did I tell you they had a man try to set fire to the cinema last week? Tried to leave a burning firework, one of those rocket things, under the seats. Of course, my son-in-law was on to him, they're prosecuting. Well, you can't let that sort of thing go on, can you? He's his reputation as manager to think of. What kind of a person would do a thing like that?'

Horse-face, she thought. That's it. She's ox-face and you're horse-face. Mrs Whatsername had long teeth and wide nostrils you could look right up, half-way to her brain. Horse-face. She choked on her bread and butter, laughing, they had to take the cup from her and pat her on the back.

'Gone the wrong way, has it? You want to be careful, Mrs Ebbs, you must chew it properly, dear.'

But she didn't chew it, she held it in her mouth and sucked in the sweet warm tea and let the bread soak.

Horse-face.

'You're in the best place today, dear, I can tell you, it's really nasty out, cold and blowy and nasty. We'll have more snow yet, I know, wouldn't be surprised if we didn't have snow for Easter. I wouldn't mind being tucked up there in bed and waited on.'

Later, though, they sat her out in the chair in her dressing-gown. She looked down at her own hands and the joints were knotted and shiny, she did not recognize them any longer.

She said loudly, 'They're opening my letters and reading them.'

Mrs Pender stared, across the space of green linoleum. Outside the tall windows, it rained like needles.

'I think she wants something, she was asking for something, I thought I'd better ring.'

'What was it, Mrs Ebbs? Are you all right? It's nice for you being out of bed, it's a nice change.'

'They're opening my letters.'

'Does that Ebbs have anyone write to her?'

'There was a letter from a solicitor, once – oh, last year it must be, she had me read it to her. That's all I know of.'

'I thought . . .'

Now she remembered something. The truth was that she had been afraid of India. The black people were strange, looking so different, their eyeballs yellowish and always moving about in their thin faces, and their hands were thin, too, sinewy and with palms looking as though they had been stained. Once, her father's servant had passed her in the corridor and started to laugh, showing the pink inside of his mouth and shaking his head at her, he had said, 'Here's Missy' and though she had burst into tears, he would not speak to her, or tell her why.

She had been afraid of the chattering noise the people made when they came together and the quickness of their movements and the brightness of their clothes, afraid of their smell. And at night there were always sudden sounds in the darkness, sudden calls and cries, and then the peculiar, wailing music.

And then there had been all those nights with sirens and bombs, and now nights here, and the snoring of Mrs Pender, or the terrible dying breathing. She could not remember ever having been happy at night. The darkness put out soft feelers towards her.

Now, the days were grey. Days used to have colours. Monday white, Saturday green, Thursday blue – no, Thursday purple – Friday brown – though she could never remember the colour of Sunday, and the seasons of the year, too, spring green, summer yellow, autumn brown, winter white, you slipped down a slope towards Christmas and then rose slowly up again on the other side. Now, everything had changed, and nothing changed, all the days were grey.

For her honeymoon, she had been taken to Venice. She had woken in the mahogany and plush wagon-lit and drawn up the blind and seen dawn just spreading over Montreux, though the lake was still dark, dark blue. She had longed to get out alone, and walk from the strange station, to smell the foreign air at five o'clock in the morning. But now she was married.

They had breakfast while the train went past Stresa and the farmhouses of Italy were rose-red in the sun. He had eaten two eggs, boiled so softly that she had to turn her eyes away as he spooned up the yolk with stringy white threads hanging from it. Now, every day she must sit opposite him while he ate eggs at breakfast.

But she liked the world of the railway train, and when Venice came she was unhappy, with the heat and the foetid canals, the endless, dark churches. She had asked if they could go elsewhere or go home, and he had stared at her, told her she was married now and could not always be spoiled.

'I had a mother who loved me.'

'Did you say something, dear?'

She jumped. They were there with the hot drinks, so it was night again. She could have wept.

'Was there something you wanted, Mrs Ebbs?'

She let her mind wander to and fro, wondering what she had said.

'I want sugar in it.'

'No, you never take sugar.'

'I want sugar now.'

'Well you are contrary, dear, I must say. Now are you quite sure you want sugar? You don't generally want sugar.'

'I want sugar.'

But the drink was thick and sweet, it clung to the roof of her mouth and she left it to go cold on the bedside locker.

If she laid one hand over the wrist of the other, she could feel her own pulse jumping. It soothed her. She wished she could remember, some things but not others.

It was winter now, the nights were longer. The pills did not make her sleep and besides, she did not want to sleep, she did not want the confusing dreams, or the swirling sensation as sleep filled her head. She kept awake and jerked herself up when she dozed, she kept watch upon herself.

'You're in the best place there, dear.'

★

The truth was that he had been very unkind to her, the truth was that she was glad when he had died. He had spoken sarcastically or scolded her in front of the servants. The truth was that she had lain awake at nights and thought of ways to kill him, she had planned everything in her head.

She said, 'They want to kill me. They want me dead.'

'Lie down again, Mrs Ebbs, lie right down, that's it, I'm going to tuck you in properly this time.' And the sheets were tight as bandages.

'They want to kill me.'

'You'll have to do something about that Ebbs, she's on now about someone wanting to do away with her. You can't have her going on like that all the time, upsetting everyone.'

'Last week it was her letters being opened.'

'She never gets a letter.'

'Next thing, her food'll be poisoned.'

'I'm not eating it, it tastes peculiar. They've put something in it.'

'Well, what a thing to say!'

'I'm not eating it.'

And, after a time, she found that she no longer wanted food, the sight of lumps of it on the plates repelled her, she was no longer hungry.

She felt sure there ought to be more to it than this, that something was hovering, like the memories, just out of her reach. All the ties of blood and friendship, all the time spent on mother and father, brother and sister and husband, all these seemed, now, to count for very little. Now she lay for hour after hour and looked out of the tall window at the grey sky.

They tried to make her drink soup from an invalid cup. She would not drink. So that now, when she looked down at her arms, she did not recognize them because they were so thin, the skin hung off the bones in folds.

'You're not doing yourself any good, dear, are you? I don't like to see you like this. We're doing our best for you, you know, but you're just letting yourself go.'

Mrs Whatsername leaned over the bed and she wanted to reach out and push her away, for why should she be here in bed with the face of a woman she disliked so close to her and the smell of the cardigans filling her nostrils. She was the person she had always been, she had a right to choose.

Then, in the night, she thought of it. All her life she had let others decide, father and husband, she had been as helpless as she was now, in this bed.

She would like to be in another place, a warm country with hard, bright flowers and a lot of water in streams and rivers and lakes, she would like to smell the air of that place. She tried to remember if it was India, but then all she could think of was the deception Agnes had practised upon her.

Why was there no sun now, never any sun?

But it was in the night that she thought of it, and she held a hand on to her chest over the heart, feeling how fast it was beating, because of what she had thought. Now, she did not mind the darkness.

'Now, Mrs Ebbs, lean forward, I want to straighten your pillows.'

'I haven't had my breakfast.'

'Well of course you haven't, our food's not been good enough for you the last few days, has it?'

'I want my breakfast now.'

'Changed your tune have you? I'm glad about that, I must say. I told them, leave her alone, I said, she's got some bee in her bonnet. Well, I'm glad it's buzzed off somewhere else.'

'I'll have toast and bacon.'

'You'll have a bit of bread and butter and a lightly boiled egg to start off with, I'm not having you with an upset tummy and indigestion after starving yourself.'

'I'll have a pot of tea.'

'We'll just see what there is.'

But now, it did not matter, now she had decided. She turned to look out of the window again. They brought the egg, which she spooned into her mouth with her eyes closed, it reminded her so strongly of all those breakfasts in the past and washed the taste of it away with sweet, warm tea.

She wanted to know where they kept her clothes. When she came in here, everything had been put away. She thought of the houses she had lived in, crammed full of furniture, thought of all the things she had owned during her lifetime. When she was eight, her godmother died and left her the silver-backed hairbrushes and a gold locket, and that had begun it all, the love of what she owned. Before that there had been only clothes to which she was indifferent and toys which she shared. The brushes were her own. After that there had been books and a cat, and when she married, a cornelian brooch and an aqua-marine brooch, though the other presents were cut glass and silver for the house, and she had never felt that any of it truly belonged to her until he died and it was in writing in the will.

Now, she had a locker with two pairs of spectacles and a glass for her teeth, only the glass was theirs, and her handbag with wrist watch and purse inside, but the books were from a library. Where had they put her outdoor clothes?

She could not remember how long she had been here, the days and nights slid into one another. She jerked her head up suddenly. Was it morning or afternoon? Outside it was grey. There was nothing in the room to tell her, no clock, no trays of food. Mrs Pender was dozing, back against the pillows. It was evening then? She would not have to wait very long. She dozed herself, and woke and dozed again, and then there was Ox-face with a tray, soup and minced meat in gravy.

'Can you manage, Mrs Ebbs? I hope you're going to eat all

that, it's been done specially for you, I hope you're not going to be silly again. All that's over and done with, I'm sure.'

So it was still daytime.

'Where are my clothes? I want my clothes.'

'Bless me, whatever do you want to worry your head about clothes for? You don't need your clothes for anything.'

'Where are my clothes?'

'Well they're put away, aren't they, with all the others, they're quite safe. Nobody wants to take your clothes away.'

When she woke the next time, Mrs Pender's visitor had come, the brother-in-law with hair like a hedgehog's back.

'I want you to get my clothes for me. I want you to go and see where my outdoor clothes are.'

He looked from one to the other of them uneasily, and the skin of his face looked hard and shiny, as though it had been boiled, he said, 'Well,' and coughed.

'My clothes . . .'

She felt very tired, suddenly, weak and giddy with tiredness, her head seemed to touch the pillow and sink down and down, she could not keep it on her shoulders. Her dreams were full of noises.

But when she woke in the darkness, everything was clear, she remembered at once what she had to do.

The linoleum was oddly warm under her feet, but she went very slowly, very carefully, she said, 'They thought I couldn't walk.' And all at once she wanted to laugh and shout, standing there, she had deceived them and now there was nothing that she could not do.

Once, as a child, she had come downstairs in the night and opened the front door. The gravel drive had gleamed, white as bone, under the moon and there were great black shapes between the fir trees. She had closed her eyes and breathed in the smell of night. She thought. Nobody ever knew. And they had not known, she had gone back to her bed and kept the secret from them forever, though it made her uneasy, it was like a faint nausea, always present inside her. Now, there was no one to tell.

It was very cold, she shivered, trying to unbolt the big front door, and there was no moon. It was windy. She waited, held herself very stiff, sniffing like a cat at the night. Then she told herself that she need not be afraid, for he was dead, they were all of them safely dead, and even Bruce the slavering dog could not find her out, she could do as she pleased.

There was no feeling in her legs, she had to look down and say, 'Left Right, Left Right,' to help herself along, she watched each foot move in front of the other.

In the house, the door swung wide open and the wind was sucked up the well of the stairs.

She thought, now they cannot do anything to me, and she hugged her arms tightly round her body. Her head sang. They had all left her alone.

So that when the car slowed down for her, she gave the driver careful directions and then sat back, unwilling to talk, for he had always frowned upon chatter to the servants and old habits died hard, she had taken on so many of his standards, she did not know, now, where he left off and her own true self began.

But then, because she did not wish to appear unfriendly, she told him that she had once lived in India and all the colours and smells and cries of that bright, hot, seething country filled her head, and she said 'Missy' to herself, savouring the importance the word had always had for her. 'They called me Missy.'

It no longer mattered, then, that he took her to the wrong place and they put her back to bed, and in another room this time, a room by herself, for everything she wanted was there right in front of her, she had only to look, and she lay, dazed by the freshness and beauty of her memories. Nothing evaded her any more. The yelping of street dogs and the thud of the feet of great, grey, swaying elephants and the sound of the brass dinner gong in their own house were all in the room with her, she was overwhelmed by them. She ate and drank little, and impatiently, and ignored them when they talked to her, indifferent now to Ox-face and Mrs Whatsername, and anxious to get back, now that she knew none of them could touch her, that she was entirely free.

The Badness Within Him

The night before, he had knelt beside his bed and prayed for a storm, an urgent, hysterical prayer. But even while he prayed he had known that there could be no answer, because of the badness within him, a badness which was living and growing like a cancer. So that he was not surprised to draw back the curtains and see the pale, glittering mist of another hot day. But he was angry. He did not want the sun and the endless stillness and brightness, the hard-edged shadows and the steely gleam of the sea. They came to this place every summer, they had been here, now, since the first of August, and they had one week more left. The sun had shone from the beginning. He wondered how he would bear it.

At the breakfast table, Jess sat opposite to him and her hand kept moving up to rub at the sunburned skin which was peeling off her nose.

'Stop *doing* that.'

Jess looked up slowly. This year, for the first time, Col felt the difference in age between them, he saw that Jess was changing, moving away from him to join the adults. She was almost fourteen.

'What if the skin doesn't grow again? What then? You look awful enough now.'

She did not reply, only considered him for a long time, before returning her attention to the cereal plate. After a moment, her hand went up again to the peeling skin.

Col thought, I hate it here. I hate it. *I hate it*. And he clenched his fist under cover of the table until the fingernails hurt him, digging into his palm. He had suddenly come to hate it, and the emotion frightened him. It was the reason why he had prayed for the storm, to break the pattern of long, hot, still days and waken the others out of their contentment, to change things. Now, everything was as it had always been in the past and he did not want the past, he wanted the future.

But the others were happy here, they slipped into the gentle, lazy routine of summer as their feet slipped into sandals, they never grew bored or angry or irritable, never quarrelled with one another. For days now Col had wanted to quarrel.

How had he ever been able to bear it? And he cast about, in his frustration, for some terrible event, as he felt the misery welling up inside him at the beginning of another day.

I hate it here. He hated the house itself, the chintz curtains and covers bleached by the glare of the sun, and the crunch of sand like sugar spilled in the hall and along the tiled passages, the windows with peeling paint always open on to the garden, and the porch cluttered with sandshoes and buckets and deckchairs, the muddle and shabbiness of it all.

They all came down to breakfast at different times, and ate slowly and talked of nothing, made no plans, for that was what the holiday was for, a respite from plans and time-tables.

Fay pulled out the high chair and sat her baby down next to Col.

'You can help him with his egg.'

'Do I have to?'

Fay stared at him, shocked that anyone should not find her child desirable.

'Do help, Col, you know the baby can't manage by himself.'

'Col's got a black dog on his shoulder.'

'Shut up.'

'A perfectly enormous, coal black, monster of a dog!'

He kicked out viciously at his sister under the table. Jess began to cry.

'Now, Col, you are to apologize please.' His mother looked

paler than ever, exhausted. Fay's baby dug fingers of toast down deeper and deeper into the yolk of egg.

'You hurt me, you hurt me.'

He looked out of the window. The sea was a thin, glistening line. Nothing moved. Today would be the same as yesterday and all the other days – nothing would happen, nothing would change. He felt himself itching beneath his skin.

They had first come here when he was three years old. He remembered how great the distance had seemed as he jumped from rock to rock on the beach, how he had scarcely been able to stretch his leg across and balance. Then, he had stood for minute after minute feeling the damp ribs of sand under his feet. He had been enchanted with everything. He and Jess had collected buckets full of sea creatures from the rock pools and put them into a glass aquarium in the scullery, though always the starfish and anemones and limpets died after a few, captive days. They had taken jam jars up on to West Cliff and walked along, at the hottest part of the day, looking for chrysalis on the grass stalks. The salt had dried in white tide marks around their brown legs, and Col had reached down and rubbed some off with his finger and then licked it. In the sun lounge the moths and butterflies had swollen and cracked open their frail, papery coverings and crept out like babies from the womb, and he and Jess had sat up half the night by the light of moon or candle, watching them.

And so it had been every year and often, in winter or windy spring in London, he remembered it all, the smell of the sunlit house and the feeling of the warm sea lapping against his thighs and the line of damp woollen bathing shorts outside the open back door. It was another world, but it was still there, and when every summer came they would return to it, things would be the same.

Yet now, he wanted to do some violence in this house, he wanted an end to everything. He was afraid of himself.

'Col's got a black dog on his shoulder!'

So he left them and went for a walk on his own, over the track beside the gorse bushes and up on to the coarse grass of the sheep field behind West Cliff. The mist was rolling away, the sea was white-gold at the edges, creaming back. On the far side of the field there were poppies.

He lay down and pressed his face and hands into the warm turf until he could smell the soil beneath and gradually, he felt the warmth of the sun on his back and it soothed him.

In the house, his mother and sisters left the breakfast table and wandered upstairs to find towels and sunhats and books, content that this day should be the same as all the other days, wanting the summer to last. And later, his father would join them for the weekend, coming down on the train from London, he would discard the blue city suit and emerge, hairy and thickly fleshed to lie on a rug and snore and play with Fay's baby, rounding off the family circle.

By eleven it was hotter than it had been all summer, the dust rose in soft clouds when a car passed down the lane to the village, and did not settle again, and the leaves of the hedges were mottled and dark, the birds went quiet. Col felt his own anger like a pain tightening around his head. He went up to the house and lay on his bed trying to read, but the room was airless and the sunlight fell in a straight, hard beam across his bed and on to the printed page, making his eyes hurt.

When he was younger he had liked this room, he had sometimes dreamed of it when he was in London. He had collected shells and small pebbles and laid them out in careful piles and hung up a bladder-wrack on a nail by the open window, had brought books from home about fossils and shipwrecks and propped them on top of the painted wooden chest. But now it felt too small, it stifled him, it was a childish room, a pale, dead room in which nothing ever happened and nothing would change.

After a while he heard his father's taxi come up the drive.

'Col, do watch what you're doing near the baby, you'll get sand in his eyes.'

'Col, if you want to play this game with us, do, but otherwise go away, if you can't keep still, you're just spoiling it.'

'Col, why don't you build a sandcastle or something?'

He stood looking down at them all, at his mother and Fay playing cards in the shade of the green parasol, and his father lying on his back, his bare, black-haired chest shiny with oil and his nostrils flaring in and out as he breathed, at Jess, who had begun to build the sandcastle for the baby, instead of him. She had her hair tied back in bunches and the freckles had come out even more thickly across her cheekbones, she might have been eleven years old. But she was almost fourteen, she had gone away from him.

'Col, don't kick the sand like that, it's flying everywhere. Why don't you go and have a swim? Why can't you find something to do? I do so dislike you just hovering over us like that.'

Jess had filled a small bucket with water from the rock pool, and now she bent down and began to pour it carefully into the moat. It splashed on to her bare feet and she wriggled her toes. Fay's baby bounced up and down with interest and pleasure in the stream of water and the crenellated golden castle.

Col kicked again more forcefully. The clods of sand hit the tower of the castle sideways, and, as it fell, crumbled the edges off the other towers and broke open the surrounding wall, so that everything toppled into the moat, clouding the water.

Jess got to her feet, scarlet in the face, ready to hit out at him.

'I hate you. *I hate you.*'

'Jess . . .'

'He wants to spoil everything, look at him, he doesn't want anyone else to enjoy themselves, he just wants to sulk and . . . I hate him.'

Col thought, I am filled with evil, there is no hope for me. For he felt himself completely taken over by the badness within him.

'*I hate you.*'

He turned away from his sister's wild face and her mouth which opened and shut over and over again to shout her rejection of him, turned away from them all and began to walk towards the caves at the far side of the cove. Above them were the cliffs.

Three-quarters of the way up there was a ledge around which the gannets and kittiwakes nested. He had never climbed up as high as this before. There were tussocks of grass, dried and bleached bone-pale by the sea winds, and he clung on to them and to the bumps of chalky rock. Flowers grew, pale wild scabious and cliff buttercups, and when he rested, he touched his face to them. Above his head, the sky was enamel blue. The sea birds watched him with eyes like beads. As he climbed higher, the wash of the sea and the voices of those on the beach receded. When he reached the ledge, he got his breath and then sat down cautiously, legs dangling over the edge. There was just enough room for him. The surface of the cliff was hot on his back. He was not at all afraid.

His family were like insects down on the sand, little shapes of colour dotted about at random. Jess was a pink shape, the parasol was bottle-glass green, Fay and Fay's baby were yellow. For most of the time they were still, but once they all clustered around the parasol to look at something and then broke away again, so that it was like a dance. The other people on the beach were quite separate, each family kept itself to itself. Out beyond the curve of the cliff the beach lay like a ribbon bounded by the tide, which did not reach as far as the cove except in the storms of winter. They had never been here during the winter.

When Col opened his eyes again his head swam for a moment. Everything was the same. The sky was thin and clear. The sun shone. If he had gone to sleep he might have tipped over and fallen forwards. The thought did not frighten him.

But all was not the same, for now he saw his father had left the family group and was padding down towards the sea. The black hairs curled up the backs of his legs and the soles of his feet were brownish pink as they turned up one after the other.

Col said, do I like my father? And thought about it. And did not know.

Fay's baby was crawling after him, its lemon-coloured behind stuck up in the air.

Now, Col half-closed his eyes, so that air and sea and sand shimmered, merging together.

Now, he felt rested, no longer angry, he felt above it all.

Now, he opened his eyes again and saw his father striding into the water, until it reached up to his chest: then he flopped onto his belly and floated for a moment, before beginning to swim.

Col thought, perhaps I am ill and *that* is the badness within me.

But if he had changed, the others had changed too. Since Fay had married and had the baby and gone to live in Berkshire, she was different, she fussed more, was concerned with the details of things, she spoke to them all a trifle impatiently. And his mother was so languid. And Jess – Jess did not want his company.

Now he saw his father's dark head bobbing up and down quite a long way out to sea, but as he watched, sitting on the high cliff ledge in the sun, the bobbing stopped – began again – an arm came up and waved, though as if it were uncertain of its direction.

Col waved back.

The sun was burning the top of his head.

Fay and Fay's baby and Jess had moved in around the parasol again, their heads were bent together. Col thought, we will never be the same with one another, the ties of blood make no difference, we are separate people now. And then he felt afraid of such truth. Father's waving stopped abruptly, he bobbed and disappeared, bobbed up again.

The sea was still as glass.

Col saw that his father was drowning.

In the end, a man from the other side of the beach went running down to the water's edge and another to where the family were grouped around the parasol. Col looked at the cliff, falling away at his feet. He closed his eyes and turned around slowly and then got down on his hands and knees and began to feel for a foothold, though not daring to look. His head was hot and throbbing.

By the time he reached the bottom, they were bringing his father's body. Col stood in the shadow of the cliff and shivered and smelled the dank, cave smell behind him. His mother and Fay and Jess stood in a line, very erect, like Royalty at the Cenotaph, and in Fay's arms the baby was still as a doll.

Everyone else kept away, though Col could see that they made half-gestures, raised an arm or turned a head, occasionally took an uncertain step forward, before retreating again.

Eventually he wondered if they had forgotten about him. The men dripped water off their arms and shoulders as they walked and the sea ran off the body, too, in a thin, steady stream.

Nobody spoke to him about the cliff climb. People only spoke of baths and hot drinks and telephone messages, scarcely looking at one another as they did so, and the house was full of strangers moving from room to room.

In bed, he lay stiffly under the tight sheets and looked towards the window where the moon shone. He thought, it is my fault. I prayed for some terrible happening and the badness within me made it come about. I am punished. For this was a change greater than any he could have imagined.

When he slept he dreamed of drowning, and woke early, just at dawn. Outside the window, a dove grey mist muffled everything. He felt the cold linoleum under his feet and the dampness in his nostrils. When he reached the bottom of the stairs he saw at once that the door of the sun parlour was closed.

He stood for a moment outside, listening to the creaking of the house, imagining all of them in their beds, his mother lying alone. He was afraid. He turned the brass doorknob and went slowly in.

There were windows on three sides of the room, long and uncurtained, with a view of the sea, but now there was only the fog pressing up against the panes, the curious stillness. The floor was polished and partly covered with rush matting and in the ruts of this the sand of all the summer past had gathered and lay, soft and gritty, the room smelled of seaweed. On the walls, the sepia photographs of his great-grandfather the Captain, and his naval friends and their ships. He had always liked this room. When he was small, he had sat here with his mother on warm, August evenings, drinking his mug of milk, and the smell of stocks came in to them from the open windows. The deckchairs had always been in a row outside on the terrace, empty at the end of the day. He stepped forward.

They had put his father's body on the trestle, dressed in a shirt and covered with a sheet and a rug. His head was bare and lay on a cushion, and the hands, with the black hair over their backs, were folded together. Now, he was not afraid. His father's skin was oddly pale and shiny. He stared, trying to feel some sense of loss and sorrow. He had watched his father drown, though for a long time he had not believed it, the water had been so entirely calm. Later, he had heard them talking of a heart attack, and then he had understood better why this strong barrel of a man, down that day from the City, should have been so suddenly sinking, sinking.

The fog horn sounded outside. Then, he knew that the change had come, knew that the long, hot summer was at an end, and that his childhood had ended too, that they would never come to this house again. He knew, finally, the power of the badness within him and because of that, standing close to his father's body, he wept.

Red and Green Beads

All afternoon the Curé had been walking and it was after five o'clock as he came down the slope towards the village and met Albert Piguet. A hundred years ago all the land on both sides of the valley had belonged to the Piguets. The Curé remembered the old man sitting on a walnut stump outside his back door, his head nodding forward and a thin trickle of rheum wetting the grey stubbled chin. The dog had always been lying at his feet – Lascar, a thin, vulpine creature with the pointed head and arched back of a greyhound. Nobody dared to touch it save the old man.

But that was fifty years ago, when he had come here to his first parish. Then, he used to stride the length and breadth of it, feeling a kind of boundless excitement, for in those days he knew what he believed, what life was all about, he had been both devout and ambitious. For many years, the parishioners had been suspicious of him.

Old man Piguet had remembered three of his predecessors and talked a great deal about them, so that when Curé Begnac looked up their names in the register he felt close to them. Often, he walked in the graveyard opposite the church and stood for a moment before each of their small, plain headstones.

The Piguet land was broken up now, they had had misfortune – sickness and accident and death, since before the old man died, and gradually they had to sell off this and that field to the other farmers around. Now they owned only two, together with a few vines and an orchard. And they continued to be unlucky, both in the business and in the family. They had sold the red-tiled farmhouse and moved to a cottage which had once been let out to a man they employed. Albert's elder brother was killed falling off a cart, and Albert himself was bent and grey before his time, his eyes weary in the sallow face. He was not yet fifty.

The Curé stopped and watched him mending two of the bird scarers. Very early that morning, as he was going up the church path to say mass, he had seen Albert's youngest boy slipping up towards the wood, where he would search for the big Cèpe mushrooms for an hour, before going to school. As soon as Piguets walked, they must work. All except Marcel, who only counted his string of red and green beads.

Now, Albert saw the Curé, and stood up, putting a hand round for a moment to his aching back. The sky was clear, bright blue, with streaks of mulberry cloud over to the west. The gnats were gathering.

'Curé.' Albert watched the old man make his way along the field track. He is old, he thought – well, we are all old. But the priest seemed to have shrivelled and dried out like a branch without sap, the shape of his skull was revealed under the thin coating of flesh.

They stood together beside the hedge and talked about the harvest and the weather, and the illness of Madame Curveillers at the Château.

'I married them,' Curé Begnac said reflectively, for all that day the past had been shadowing him.

'So you did. I was a boy but I remember it all right – I climbed the church wall and threw a handful of petals. They'd gone damp and brown, I'd clutched them so long but I threw them just the same. That was a day!'

'How's Amélie?'

'The same. Her leg troubles her. She dreads the bad weather coming. And her father is worse, madder than ever. We'll have to try and get him here for the winter, somehow or other, he can't be left in that hovel of his, though Lord knows there's little enough room with us.'

'I must go and see him, but . . .'

'But he won't thank you, I know. He's a rude old devil.'

There was a silence then, during which the Curé might have asked about Marcel. He had not seen the boy for several days. He wondered if he had been told about Madame Curveillers' illness, and if he understood. She was the only person who took any notice of Marcel – she talked to him sometimes as they came out of mass. To him and to no one else.

But what was Albert to say? 'The same. Always the same.' When he returned home, that was time enough to be reminded of the boy. The Curé had tried to bring him round to a change of attitude, but he knew now that he had tried in the wrong way. He was ashamed to remember how he had been, raw and tactless and over-confident. It had taken fifty years for him to learn something about acceptance and silence.

Piguet said, 'Everything's the same,' and scratched his leg with a mud-caked boot.

And so it was. And yet, not the same at all. Little by little the character of the soil altered, trees grew and were felled, changing the contours of the woodland. Last winter the river had over-flowed into a field which had never been fully drained since, so that a pasture was now a marsh. One of Piguet's cows had been drowned. That was the kind of thing which happened to them. The Curé listened to his confessions of resentment and grievance against God. Why does this happen to us? Why always to us? And could not answer. On the night his small daughter died, Albert had stood in the presbytery path and cursed, and then wept, beating his fist again and again upon the crumbling stone wall.

The parish register was full of births and marriages and deaths. Nothing changed, everything changed. But one thing which did not was the distance they set between themselves and the Curé. So, Piguet stood now, waiting for him to speak again, or to shake hands and go. The priest, like the blind, the dumb and the mad, inhabited some special place, was somehow different. The Curé wished it was not so, he did not want to be cut off from the people among whom he had lived for so long. He looked at them when they took the communion wafer, when he held the infants for baptism and stood over the coffins of the dead, and felt nothing but loneliness, a desire to throw out his arms and cry to them. But when they asked him questions, he could no longer answer.

He patted Albert on the shoulder and walked away.

That night. Madame Curveillers died. Robert's boy came to the presbytery at ten o'clock with an urgent message for the Curé. He wished that he could mourn her, if only because no one else would – she was widowed fifteen years, and childless. One-eyed Gaston and his wife, the housekeeper, stood together in the shadowy hall, waiting for news, but when it came they did not weep. And to Curé Begnac, death now seemed a more natural condition than life.

'Are you distressed?' asked the doctor, who was young, and suspicious of the church.

'She was very old.'

'Certainly. With respect, you are old. But I asked if you were distressed.'

'Why do you ask?'

'She was an old friend of yours. There can't be so many left.'

Friend? No. For how much had he and Madame Curveillers known of one another, below the surface politeness? He had heard her confession every week for forty years, but she had not been his friend. None of them were.

'Was she a good woman?'

The Curé stopped in the middle of the stone stairs. He realized that he could not answer because he no longer knew – perhaps he had never known – what 'good' was. If they asked him to point it out, he could not.

'I daresay she was like the rest of us,' Doctor Domecq said. 'The usual mixture.'

'Perhaps.'

He left the house. But in the middle of the path, still a mile from home, he stopped again and heard the night sounds, the faint, cool rush of air through his ears, the creak of cherry and chestnut trees.

What was 'good'? He did not know. He felt suddenly afraid.

Marie had left him some cold supper and he drank a glass of wine because he was shivering. The fire glowed still, and sparked up when he threw on another log.

So, Madame was dead. But it was not this which had so upset and confused him. He tried to read his breviary, but his eyes smarted, tried to pray, but could think only that he did not know the answer to the question. He slept. And dreamed of the night he had been fetched to the Piguet cottage, after the birth of Marcel.

The great bed looked out of place in this poky, low-ceilinged room. A fire burned, and Albert Piguet had sat beside it, the little girl on his knee. Amélie lay in the bed, her hair streaked dark with sweat and her eyes feverish. The Curé went over and touched her hand.

'Amélie . . .'

The fire hissed as Albert spat into it disgustedly. Amélie had given him a look of exhaustion, misery – and anger. She was a proud, rather hard woman, daughter of Nouvert who trapped and skinned animals.

Now, she gestured to the cot, standing in the shadow of the bed. She did not look at it herself.

'You have a son?'

Silence, except for the shifting of the fire, and the small girl murmuring something to her father.

The Curé touched the baby's face. Then Albert raised his voice across the cramped room.

'Pull back the covers, go on, Curé – see it for yourself. Look.'

The small body was twisted oddly to one side. There was a

lump on the back and both legs ended just below the knee.

'Have a good look – see what we are blessed with!'

The man's voice seemed to be sounding, now, through the room. The Curé opened his eyes suddenly.

'See what we are blessed with!'

And that winter the small girl died. 'Why not him?' Albert had shouted. 'Why couldn't he be the one to die?'

To Curé Begnac, for the first time in his life, there was no sense in things, as there was sense tonight in the death of Madame Curveillers, who was old and lonely.

The fire was out. He moved his cramped limbs and went slowly to bed. At the back of his mind still was the question he could not answer.

Madame Curveillers' funeral was on the Tuesday. The weather was grey and dank and there were few mourners. The Curé felt old, and ill, confused, for his life seemed to have been lived in complete ignorance of truth.

The next morning was colder. If the weather continued like this the grapes would rot before they were ready to be picked, and men like Piguet would lose the money which was to see them through the winter.

At the entrance to the graveyard, he stopped. Someone was there, but it was too early for Madame Machaut, who cared for the graves and swept the paths clear of leaves. The Curé went through the gateway.

Marcel Piguet was squatting beside Madame Curveillers' grave, and scrabbling gently in the soil with his hands. The hunch on his back had grown with him, and his head had sunk down. He wore two wooden half-legs, the leather straps going over his shoulders, and he walked in a cumbersome fashion, on crutches. He was twenty now, a large boy but with a child's soft-skinned, hairless face. In the village some were afraid of him, and the children ran after him shouting, they imitated him, hopping on one leg. Marcel never minded, he watched them and clapped when he thought they had got it right.

When he heard the footsteps he turned, but only smiled his open-mouthed, sheepish smile and went on digging.

'Marcel? What are you doing? That is Madame Curveillers' grave.'

But the boy got up then, patted the soil back into place, and took the old man's hand, pulling him away. They walked together all the way back to the cottage.

'Well, he goes,' Amélie said, shrugging, 'I don't know where – I can't be forever watching him. He's old enough, isn't he? I suppose he'll come to no harm.'

Marcel smiled and tried to embrace her.

When Curé Begnac got back to the grave, he uncovered the pile of soil, and found the string of bright red and green beads. Marcel always had them somewhere about him, in his hand or pocket, they seemed to be a comfort. He would finger them and count them, and sometimes touch them to his face, smiling. What he would never do was let them go. Until now, when he had brought them to the grave of Madame Curveillers.

The Curé bent down and reburied them and for a moment did not know how he would get up again, his legs were so stiff and painful. But he managed it and walked home. It was raining. He was glad to reach his chair. Marie had only just lit the fire, the room was cold. He sat there alone for a long time, thinking about Madame Curveillers and Marcel, and Marcel's gift of the red and green beads which had given him the answer to his questions.

He outlived the old lady by less than a couple of weeks.

Ossie

As soon as I saw that the man shaking hands with the chaplain outside the English church in Venice was Ossie Lawton, I realized that I had also seen him the previous day, selling clockwork toys out of a suitcase on the Rialto Bridge.

But really, nothing about Ossie would ever have surprised me. It was about twelve years since we last met, in equally unpredictable but, knowing Ossie, entirely likely circumstances and that had been in Italy too.

I had been chasing a picture and was due at an auction in Cologne the following day. An airport ground staff strike had obliged me, at the last minute, to take the night sleeper from Milan, and it was in the first-class waiting hall on the station there that I came across Ossie.

The hall has always reminded me of some London club rather down on its luck. It is gloomy and it has huge writing desks of dark polished wood set against the walls, and the high-backed seats, studded and covered in dark red leather, are like so many papal thrones. And Ossie was sitting like a Pope, his arms stretched out along those of the seat, head back and slightly uplifted, his eyes closed. I thought he might be ill – he often used to be, and his skin had a peculiar, curded look, there were purplish stains beneath the eyes. We were exact contemporaries but even in those days at school when we had been so close, Ossie had always looked several years older than me. There was something exhausted and worldly wise about his long face which had probably been there from birth.

I was pleased to see him that night, perhaps because we had not met since the end of the war and so there had been time for

the memory of what a liability he could be to fade. I watched
him for a moment, studying the disdainful expression on his face,
and then I touched his arm. The oddly smooth, freckled eyelids
slid up like blinds. Nothing else moved.

'Ossie . . .'

It was unnerving. He simply sat there, his lead-grey eyes fixed
upon me, giving no indication of surprise or even of recognition.
His hair still thick though going grey, was longer than men –
even men like Ossie – usually wore it at that time, little fronds
of it curled around behind his ears and hung over his brow.

'It's Terence Halliday.'

He was motionless for another few seconds, and then he gave
a tremendous sigh, which seemed to come from somewhere way
down inside him, and to rise like a wave, gathering momentum,
through every part of his body, until he shuddered as it finally
escaped his mouth.

'I know *that*, dear boy, of course I know.'

He had always affected that drawl, but now it was much more
pronounced, and he moved a hand in the familiar, impatient little
gesture as he spoke.

'Well – what a surprise! What are you doing in Milan, Ossie?'

Though I was uncomfortably aware that I sounded false – too
full of heartiness and enthusiasm, both of which Ossie had always
loathed.

'I'm waiting for a train. I've been here for five hours.'

'Five *hours*? You missed one?'

'I did not. You know perfectly well what a horror I have of
missing trains.'

I did.

'The only safe way is to arrive at the station in plenty of
time.'

'Yes, but five hours, Ossie!'

He shook his head impatiently. 'It was a question of connec-
tions. There were two trains available, one of which gave me

only half an hour to spare and the other five hours. Naturally I took the latter.'

'But what on earth have you been doing?'

'Sitting here. It's perfectly comfortable.'

'Why don't we have a drink? I've got time and it'll help pass some for you.'

'You know I don't drink.'

I knew nothing of the kind. The weekend I had spent with him in Cambridge in 1945, he had been drinking, and drunk, the entire time. But I felt too embarrassed to refer to it. Nor could I think of a reply when Ossie said, 'I'm on my way to a monastery.' I suggested that we at least have coffee. 'It's long enough since we saw one another, there's plenty to talk about.'

But I found, when we were seated at a café table, that there was not. Ossie sat, staring languidly down at the black coffee, one arm resting on a vacant chair, one leg crossed over the other, and said absolutely nothing.

'Really,' I began in the end, a little desperately, 'one could almost live on Milan station – I mean one would want for nothing at all, food – full meals or snacks – every kind of drink, toilet facilities, books, newspapers, a parade of people to watch. You could sleep quite comfortably on those leather benches and the place is long enough to give you exercise walking from one end to the other. There's a chemist's shop and a barber.'

'Quite.' Ossie said, and sipped his coffee in little, delicate sips. 'Oh, quite.'

I felt foolish. 'Well – what are you doing with yourself these days, Ossie?'

'This and that,' he replied after a pause. 'Do you have an English cigarette?'

I gave him one and he fitted it carefully into an ivory holder. It was entirely characteristic of him to tell me nothing about his life. He had always been secretive, though for most of the time when I knew him well there had been precious little to be secret about. But, at school, he would quickly fold up a letter he might be reading and hide it in his pocket if one went near him, and he always kept one drawer of his study desk firmly locked. He would refer, in the course of conversation, to some friend, and if I asked a question, would say, 'Oh, nothing to do with you, no one *you* know.'

I wonder, in fact, why I ever put up with Ossie's rudeness. Because, excuse it as I might, as 'character' or 'mannerism', I knew that it was rudeness, though perhaps in a fairly innocuous form. Ossie was my friend, my first and best friend, and the truth was that I was flattered by him at that time, amazed that he had chosen me and too afraid of losing his favour ever to challenge the cavalier way in which he so often treated me.

And yet that is only part of the truth. For there was a great deal more to Ossie than affectation or self-opinion or rudeness, though it was well concealed. When we were both fourteen, he astounded me, I had never met anyone like him, he seemed to me the most glamorous person in the world. I was the son of a middle-class doctor in Solihull. Ossie had been born in Russia, though of English parents. When he was only seven, he had travelled alone by train from Moscow to Turkey. He had lived for a year in Persia, where he had learned to do needlework in gold and silver thread, from a woman of ninety-seven. By the time we met, at school in Sussex, his father was dead and his mother was remarried to an Israeli concert pianist. They travelled constantly so that Ossie had no real home. His holidays were spent either moving around the cities of Europe or else with an aunt who lived alone by the sea in Suffolk. To amuse himself, he once told me, during these latter rather dull holidays, he used to dress up in some of his aunt's mother's old clothes, which were preserved in an attic trunk, and go busking at the far end of the little town, singing and doing elaborate tap dances on street corners, his face powdered with flour and painted with wax crayons in various shades of lemon or turquoise. He collected, he said, 'no end of money' and was constantly just a few yards ahead of the pursuing police. At the time I did not believe him.

He had some bizarre possessions, a selection of which he brought back to school at the beginning of every term. I suppose he had been given them by friends of his adoring, rather inefficient mother or of his stepfather, whom he always called the Albino, because he had immensely pale hair and skin. I particularly remember a tiny, faded brocade shoe into which some poor Chinese woman had once had to squeeze her misshapen foot. Ossie used to measure it from time to time against his own, very long, though slender feet. He had a box of some blond wood, inlaid with ivory strips on which were traced erotic Indian pictures. Ossie took no interest in them, telling me, in the blasé way of his, that he 'knew all there was to know about that kind of thing'. I, who was passionately desirous of examining the pictures closely, had to adopt an equally blasé air, and dared not show any interest in the box, even – so much was I in awe of him – when Ossie was out of the room. There was a tiny Japanese puppet from the bunraku – a very, very old man with a wizened face and violet robes, curiously unfaded; a heavy seal ring with the initials QQR – I remember Ossie telling me that it stood for Quentin Quenington Royce, an ancestor of his. He also had a miniature Russian scent bottle, oval in shape, quite heavy and covered in tiny enamel flowers, most delicately executed – I think it must have been valuable. Perhaps everything in his collection was and I used to wonder at his being allowed to bring them away with him to school. Once, the disloyal thought came to me that they did not belong to Ossie at all, but that he had filched them from his mother or the Albino, or – though less likely – from the house of the Suffolk aunt. But I was ashamed of the thought and dismissed it.

Ossie and I were close friends from the day we went to that school until the day, three and a half years later, that he left – or rather, on which he did not come back after a Christmas holiday.

I remember now the shock I received and the sensation I had of the world – which was especially beautiful just then, because there was snow – turning sour and grey, losing light and somehow curling at the edges.

After a couple of weeks, Ossie sent me a note from Israel, where the family had gone to live, and which, he said, promised 'extraordinarily well'. I was sick with jealousy of Israel, of his mother and the Albino, of anyone with whom Ossie would come into contact, any friends he might make. I knew how my own image would fade, how poorly I would measure up to the fine, brilliant personalities he was likely to meet, and I wrote him long, desperate letters.

He did not answer, and although the following Christmas I received an exotic card made of some richly textured, handmade paper, by then my misery had lifted and jealousy had worn away, my life was filling up again with new activities, new people. I found that I scarcely missed Ossie.

But we were to meet again the year I left school, and to resume our acquaintance, if not our friendship. Ossie had abandoned Israel as 'too provincial' and come to London, where he was like a juggler scattering the tense, post-Munich atmosphere with light and gaiety and brilliant colours, entertaining a huge, cosmopolitan circle of people to parties, river jaunts, afternoon theatre matinées, cocktails at the Ritz – heaven knows that else. It was the life of a wealthy young man of talent and charm. Except that Ossie had no talent for anything in particular, was too rude to be very charming, and had, so far as I knew, no money, apart from an allowance from his mother, who was now in New York, nursing the Albino in the early stages of multiple sclerosis. Ossie was 'working' part time as secretary to a rich and famous playwright, a poisonous man called Sherwin. Sherwin brought out the worst in Ossie. He had become vain and supercilious, and also remarkably silly. It was now that he began to make a full-time job of cultivating those affectations with which he had first begun to divert himself when we were at school. He dressed foppishly, ate too much, he minced and lisped and drawled and I could not, after a short while, stand any of it.

I was fond of him, in spite of everything, I knew that he had value. I went to one or two parties and tried, always fruitlessly, to get him into a half-way sensible conversation. But he did not want that, and it was quite clear I would never fit into his world. I was working with one of the large fine-art auctioneers and in my spare time studying the history of painting, and visiting galleries. All of which made me, in the eyes of Ossie and his set, altogether too much like a serious man.

'Terence is in *art*,' he once said, introducing me to a girl in a backless silver dress, 'but it's turning him into such a *bore*.'

After that I began refusing his invitations, which soon petered out and we lost touch. When I came out of the Navy after the war, I got a job with one of the best London galleries – the same of which I am now senior partner. From that year, when he turned up and dragged me off to the drunken weekend in Cambridge – Ossie flitted occasionally, like a colourful and distracting butterfly, in and out of my life. As on that night when he sat looking bored and unwell, at the table in Milan railway station.

The only thing I found out about his life that night was that he had been living for some time in Paris. Whether he was there still, I did not know. But certainly I got the impression, from the way he looked more than anything else, that the old, gay, frivolous life was at an end. Ossie seemed to have sunk down into himself, though I doubted if it resulted in any very deep and profitable thinking. He was morose and clearly indifferent to company. We drank our coffee and I went for my train, rather earlier than was necessary, because I found it curiously embarrassing to sit there struggling for something to say.

As we reached the gate to my platform, Ossie said, looking at a point over my left shoulder, 'Would you lend me five pounds?'

This was not like him – he had always had a great distaste for borrowing, even small things – ink, envelopes, and for lending, too. He kept a tight hand on his possessions, as though they were his only security. It did not seem likely that I would ever get the money back. We had met by chance and he had offered me no address. I did not mind that. There was something between Ossie and me, some closeness, which had not been lost, in spite of the change in our ages and circumstances, the rarity of our meetings. Even though he had been so off-hand that night, I felt that we were still friends, that I could resume an easy, happy relationship with him at any time, in any place, we would simply pick up the threads and there was no need for letters or any sort of formal contact, for months or years. I have often wondered whether this sort of tie – rather like that between siblings – is common or at all remarkable. Certainly I had no explanation for it. I still have not. There were many other people to whom I had been much closer for longer periods of time but yet with whom I did not have this bond of – what? Affection? Responsibility?

I gave Ossie five pounds in Italian lire and he scarcely thanked me, only tucked the notes casually into his top pocket and wandered off to return to his bench in the waiting hall. He appeared to have no luggage. I wondered what monastery he might possibly be going to, and why, I felt anxious on his behalf. Indeed, so strong was this feeling that I almost followed him, to try and discover more, to satisfy myself that he would be all right. He had not seemed particularly happy, and if he had not met me, what would he have done for money? How badly did he really want it? It was only in the middle of that night that I woke on the train and felt a spasm of irritation that Ossie should have taken five pounds off me in such a lordly way, should once again have snapped his fingers and had me dance to his tune, as I had always, so gladly, so subserviently, danced, at school. But I was not a boy now, I was a man of fifty.

He had vanished from my life again and now, here he was in Venice, leaning forward to catch what the chaplain was saying, an ingratiating expression on his face. As he turned away he saw me, raised his eyebrows, though only fractionally, and held up a hand. He did not seem particularly surprised to see me, and, typically, he did not come over to me, but waited for me to go to him.

'I didn't know you were a churchgoer, Ossie.'

'Well, of *course* I'm not, dear boy, not in the slightest, but I find it so useful, socially speaking. I mean, at least one knows they're going to speak *English*.'

He took my arm and began to walk me rapidly away, in the direction of the Accademia. 'You can buy me an aperitif,' he said, 'but not just here. I like to tuck myself out of sight rather, you know how it is.'

I did not, and wanted to. I said, 'You don't seem surprised to see me.'

'Oh, my dear, people are always turning up in Venice, you can't imagine, and besides, you and I do seem to have a way of bumping into one another like a couple of punts every so often.'

I suppose he was right, and perhaps I had not been specially startled to see him. But I was startled at my recollection of him on the Rialto Bridge the previous day, and by his appearance now. Indeed I might easily not have recognized him.

He was a middle-aged man and looked an old one. His hair was bone white now, and even longer than before – it curled onto his collar and flopped over his face, which was blotched with red veins, meshing over the cheekbones. His hands, which had always been very fine, long-fingered and well-shaped, were very thin and twisted at the joints with rheumatism. But it was his clothes which shocked me, and which contributed most to the overall effect of seediness and genteel decay. He wore grey trousers so baggy that they must have been made for someone else, and a black velvet jacket of which the pile had worn away in patches around the collar and cuffs – it was, in any case, a jacket for evening, not for day wear. Under this was a checked shirt, also considerably frayed and stained, and a yellowish-white silk cravat. I looked at him closely as we sat at a café in the Campo San Barnaba. The sun shone on his long hair, and the worn, ill-assorted clothes, making him look like a clown or a music hall tramp come out into the daylight. Certainly he was unwell – the skin beneath his eyes was chalky as tissue paper and he had difficulty in holding the glass of campari steady. I felt, at that moment, a great upsurge of misery on Ossie's behalf, and it was prompted by something like love – he was my friend, he had always been my friend, a colourful misfit, entertaining, devious, high-handed, altogether extraordinary.

The picture of him sitting on the steps of the Rialto flashed across my mind. He had been winding up three or four little tin monkeys on bicycles, which circled round and round jerkily, the keys turning in their backs like knives. The feet of the people crossing the bridge were dangerously close to treading on them several times, but few people stopped and none bought.

Because Ossie was silent again, I talked about myself – about the gallery, and the book I was writing on Guardi, which was my reason for being in Venice, and about a mutual school friend of ours, a fat, adenoidal boy who was now a Cabinet Minister. Ossie appeared to be listening. He leaned his head on one side and tapped his hand upon the glass, but he said nothing about himself, and I was feeling, as I had felt on Milan railway station, that he was trying to forestall any attempt of mine to find out about his own life.

But then, as though changing his mind abruptly, he rose to his feet and extended an arm in one of those dramatic, endearing gestures of his. I followed him out of the square, and he strode a pace ahead of me, his head held up in a defiant way, as though he were challenging everyone who passed us to look him in the eye. We went towards the Zattere, and it was very quiet here, ours were the only footsteps on the flat, sunlit stones. A bony, biscuit-coloured cat watched us from a doorway. We went over a small bridge, into a dark, narrow passageway between high houses. The smell of canal and dank walls was thick in my nostrils. Ossie stopped half-way down.

'The point is, my dear, it's just a little too pricey if you want a *view*.' I could understand that, but all the same, I was shocked by the gloomy, dingy house, and by his room at the top of it. There was a smell of sour milk, and the window looked onto a wall, so that he was obliged to keep the light on the whole time – a muddy, low-watt bulb. He had plenty of furniture – huge, dark oak furniture, cluttered into the small space.

On the table was a brown suitcase, and a woman's blonde, curly wig. I had no idea what to say, whether to express the depression I felt in the room, or to sit down somewhere and pretend to ignore it.

'Venice suits me,' he said jauntily, 'because it's not a place where you can ever be yourself, don't you see? You have to put on some kind of disguise – look at how it always used to be, in those pictures of yours – masked balls, elaborate costumes, double identity, deception. That's what I need, my dear.' He turned to the table, and touched his hand gently to the blonde wig, as though it were the hair on the head of some beautiful, living woman.

I wanted urgently to get out of that cell-like room. 'Come on, Ossie, let me take you to lunch.'

I needed sunshine and wine, and a light breeze blowing off the water, needed to see ordinary faces about me, chatting, eating, laughing, not faces so grotesque as Ossie's was now, as he stood under the centre light which gave such a waxen cast to his flesh.

'Are you rich, Terence? I suppose you are.'

'I wouldn't say that, but I'm not poor, I live well and I've only myself to please. Do you want some money?'

For a moment, he did not reply. He had opened the suitcase and taken out one of the clockwork bicyclists, and now it was running, making its grating, mechanical noise as it circled round

and round. Ossie was staring at it in fascination. 'Pretty things!
Pretty things!' He changed its direction with one finger. 'I could
do with twenty pounds.'

'I'll go to the bank tomorrow. You can have fifty, if it will
help.'

'What I need,' he said, in a distant voice, 'is some fun, my
dear. I can pay the rent, all that sort of dreary business. I just
need to have some *fun*.'

I did not know what sort or how far fifty pounds would go
towards providing it for him. But it did not matter. I wanted to
help Ossie in any way that he chose.

We went and lunched on fat shellfish, veal and white peaches
at the Taverna, and Ossie drank more than a bottle of wine to
himself, becoming more and more gay in that expansive, camp,
rather sinister way of his, But I felt happy for him, for perhaps I
was providing a little 'fun'.

Afterwards we strolled with the crowds of tourists and
Venetians into the Piazza, and sat over Quadri's costly coffee,
listening to The Gold and Silver Waltz.

'There really is nowhere like Venice,' I said, comfortably full
of food and wine and nostalgia. 'Nowhere at all.'

And then Ossie began to weep, noiselessly at first, and later in
great, racking sobs, the tears coursing down his old cheeks and
onto the white cravat. In the end he put his head in his hands. I
could say nothing at all, do nothing to help him. People at the
other tables began to stare at us and I wanted to strike them, so
furiously protective did I feel towards him.

'It's none of it right,' he said after a time, 'none of it any good.
You know what I mean, don't you, Terence? It's no *good*.'

He had drunk too much of course, but what of that? It had
only served to bring up the truth, that Ossie was, for some
terrible accumulation of reasons, bitterly unhappy, lonely,
depressed, poor. He had never been a clever man certainly, but
what was he doing here in Venice, selling clockwork toys to

tourists and dressing up in a blonde wig to walk about that shadowy, duplicious town at night?

'It's no good your just having money from me,' I said. 'I can do better than that for God's sake. I've got to stay here for another week, there's some work I must do, but after that you'd better come back to London with me. We'll find you a flat there. At least you'll be among friends, someone will keep an eye on you.'

He looked up at me, and his face was crumpled and stained with tears, his eyes bloodshot. 'I hate it,' he said quietly, 'God knows how I hate this fucking place.'

The expletive was so unlike him, that it carried, for once, a full charge of meaning – of misery, loathing, despair. Venice is beautiful, is enchanting, is cruelly so to anyone as alone and ill and unlucky as Ossie. I felt hatred for it too, at that moment, for that graceful Piazza, those extravagances in gold and stone, those elegant, painted palaces.

'We'll get you back to London.'

Ossie wiped his eyes carefully. 'My dear boy, I really do need a drink. Can't you see how I need one?'

I ordered a cognac, and watched the mask of sarcasm and lordly amusement once again overlay his own true face.

By September, Ossie was back in England and as soon as he was settled in a couple of rooms in Earls Court, he went to ground. I didn't blame him. He was enormously proud and seeing me reminded him too clearly of that desperate time in Venice. Several times, I invited him to a meal, but he never replied and I let the matter drop. I felt better now that he was in London – he knew where to find me, and other old friends if he wanted them.

During the next year, I only saw him twice. Each time, the change in his appearance and circumstances was typically dramatic. One evening, I was coming out of Covent Garden theatre with a woman friend, after a performance of *Eugene Onegin*. It was not a first night, not even a Saturday night, and so the audience had been for the most part smartly but not formally dressed. Suddenly, Eleanor touched my arm. 'I'm glad to see some people still make the effort!' She looked amused. In front of us were two men, an old one and a young one, in full evening dress, with midnight-blue jackets, ruffled shirt-fronts and silk-lined opera cloaks. They might have stepped out of nineteenth-century Paris. The face of the young man was vaguely familiar – I think he was a peer – he was rather florid, thick-lipped and already balding. The man with him, white hair flowing, was Ossie. As we reached the doors of the foyer he glanced over his shoulder and saw me. For a second, he looked me full in the face, then half-closed his eyes and, giving no sign of recognition, moved away.

More than anything else, I felt hurt. Surely Ossie knew me well enough to be sure I didn't in the least care who he was with, and would never disapprove of his change of fortune. Later, I was irritated, too. Wasn't I good enough for him now? Though I knew that this, too, had been nothing but pride. I wished him well.

The following November, I was studying the X-ray photographs of a seventeenth-century Dutch portrait one evening, when the telephone rang. It was a police station near Notting Hill: Ossie was there and had given them my name.

I arrived to find him sitting on a bench in one of the interrogation rooms, a place with scuffed green and cream paint and an overhead light which reminded me of the room in Venice. Ossie had been given a cup of tea but he could scarcely hold it, the spoon rattled in the saucer, his hands were shaking so much. He looked appalling, haggard, shocked, terribly old. He was unshaven, his clothes might have belonged to a tramp. But there was something of the old, imperious look about him still, as he waved to me to sit down.

'They've been perfectly *civil*, but one can't help but loathe them all the same. I'm not used to this kind of thing.'

'What are you charged with?'

Ossie waved a hand dismissively. 'I really don't understand. Some nonsense.'

Certainly he wasn't drunk. I asked him where he was living.

'Terence, if you could just see to all this business, I'll simply go home and *collapse* on my bed, I feel quite drained.' He looked down at the cup in his hand. 'My dear, it's perfectly filthy. You know I can't stand Indian tea.'

I went out and saw the Inspector. Ossie was charged with soliciting and obstructing the police. I stood surety for him – he would appear in court the following morning – and took him home.

If the room in Venice had been depressing, this was worse – a cramped bedsitter in a crumbling Victorian block. He shared a gas ring with four people, lavatory and bathroom with ten. The floor and windows were filthy, the table and bed were littered with clothes, half-eaten bits of food, unwashed cups, newspapers. The brown suitcase was on the table, open and full of clockwork toys, different ones, now, bright yellow ducks on mechanical feet.

I found a flask of whisky half full on the window ledge.

'There doesn't seem to be a clean glass, you'd better drink it out of the bottle.'

'I generally do.'

Absently, he took out one of the ducks and set it going, its splayed feet jerked left right, left right, across the table.

'It's so tiresome here, you can't imagine, my dear, it was so much better in Venice. The English police are such a nuisance. I was in Oxford Street – really, with the Christmas crowds I stood to do rather well out of these little things, but they moved me on. They do *harass* one so.'

'Have you any money?'

'Oh my dear, you needn't worry your head about *that*, I'm going after a job. I was going tomorrow. Well, perhaps I will when that other silly business is sorted out.'

I picked up the newspaper to which he pointed. A large department store was advertising for a Father Christmas.

'Well, it would be rather *fun*, don't you think? That lovely red costume!'

I looked across at him and he tossed his head, taking another drink of whisky. He knew, as I knew, that no store would employ him, looking as he did.

'What happened to the Earls Court flat?'

'Oh, my dear, I gave that up simply ages ago, I moved in with a friend, you know, and then, oh, this and that – young people are really so *fickle*, have you discovered that? There was a little fracas. Besides, I never really cared for that place – so full of Colonials.'

I frowned.

'My dear, I don't mean blacks, there are plenty of blacks here. I'm perfectly happy with them. No, I mean Australians. So boorish, you can't believe.'

I suppose I should have done more for Ossie that night. I blame myself now, every day I think of him and blame myself. I should have taken him away from that foetid room, kept him with me, pulled him together. Certainly, he must already have been ill, and certainly proper food, decent clothing, and care, simple, attentive care, would have helped him, if only to self-respect. But I could not face it. I could not face Ossie in his dirt, full, as he was, of those grandiose, self-deceiving sentences. I left him all the money I had on me, with the promise of more the following day. How easy it is to give money! I went into court with him the following day, and paid his fine, and I could have wept at the expression on his face as the magistrate told him what he thought of him, in that bleak, open, daylit room. Ossie was Ossie, I cared for him.

There is not a great deal more to tell. For various personal reasons, and because we were exceptionally busy at the gallery, I did not see Ossie again for almost a month. I told myself that at least he had enough money to buy food, and comfort himself with whisky. When I had the time, I would see about moving him out of that terrible room into somewhere cleaner and less dispiriting. But of course that was not what Ossie really wanted, I know that now – I knew it then – he wanted friendship, company – and fun. They were all he had ever wanted.

When eventually I got up to Notting Hill, he had been ill for several days and no one had been near him. I felt bitterly ashamed. In the hospital, he had a stroke, and rallied a little, and then another, which left him speechless and unable to move anything but his eyes and his hands. I sat with him, late one afternoon. Outside it was raining, the sky was full and muddy with cloud. The ward was quite small, and full of old, dying men. I think that Ossie did not notice them. He lay still, and one side of his handsome face was twisted and pulled down by the paralysis, so that more than ever he looked as though he wore a mask over his own features.

Then, he began to make a gargling noise, and to twitch his hand several times towards the bedside cabinet, he moved his eyes to the mirror which stood there. I held it up to his face, though I was dubious about letting him see how he looked now. But he seemed only puzzled. For several minutes, he stared into the glass, and then he bowed his head gravely, as though he were greeting some stranger. And when he glanced up at me, I saw that there was no recognition in his eyes. He bowed to me, too.

Two days later, he died. After I had made arrangements for his funeral, I went back to the bed-sitting-room.

In full daylight, it was in a worse state than I had remembered, dirtier, shabbier. Among his things, I found a suitcase full of extravagant, old-fashioned women's clothes – perhaps those which used to belong to the mother of the Suffolk aunt – evening dresses, chiffon scarves, silk stockings. There were two wigs, besides the original blonde one. In another case, there were clothes of his own, the velvet jacket, the white silk cravat and more besides, evening shirts and silk day shirts, a cummerbund, a cashmere dressing-gown, handmade shoes. I wondered if he had bought them in a jumble sale, or if they were cast-offs from one of his recent, fair-weather friends. They smelled faintly of must and old sweat.

In three cardboard boxes were the clockwork toys, dozens of them, monkeys and the ducks, and others, too, dancing bears, grey mice, circus jugglers, seals balancing balls on their noses. As I touched them, a few, with some momentum left, started to grind and clatter, wheels went round, tin legs and arms jerked.

Months later, when it was found that Ossie had no relatives at all left, the property came to me. I threw most of the clothes away, they were of no use to anyone now, and the clockwork toys went to a children's hospital. But I kept one of the bicycling monkeys, and it is here on my desk. I wind it up and it circles round and round, as it circled on the steps of the Rialto Bridge in Venice. It has a grotesque, grinning face and bright pink feet. It is hideous. It reminds me constantly of Ossie.

The Elephant Man

It was on the same day that they drained the Round Pond, for the first time in forty years, that Nanny Fawcett met her Friend. And in all the time the three of them spent together afterwards, she never gave him any name in front of the child, he was always My Friend.

William had asked anxiously about the Pond, what it would look like, how big it would be now?

'The same size as always, won't it? *That's* a silly question.'

'Just with no water in it?'

'We don't say "with no" we say "without any".'

'Yes. How big will the pit be?'

'What pit? There won't be any *pit*, will there? Lift your arms up.'

The stream of lather came trickling around both sides of his neck and down his pale chest. At the edges of the bath, the scum was grey, when the water moved. He struggled to imagine the Round Pond, to which he went every day, empty of its expanse of water, rippled across the centre by the wind, but he failed, he could not picture it and was alarmed by his ignorance of how it might be.

'If there won't be a pit, what *will* there be, then?'

A grip fell down into the bath out of Nanny Fawcett's coiled-up red hair, as she bent over him.

'Mud,' she said sharply. 'Stand up.' There was a line of sweat-beads along her upper lip. She retrieved the grip impatiently. Wary of her moods, which came unpredictably, and then hung about her, thickening and tainting the atmosphere of rooms, he did not ask what would have happened to the ducks. He imagined them, kept in individual, waterless cages, and fed by keepers with broken bread, and later, hung in rows by their webbed, pink feet along the steel rail at Murchison's, Butcher and Poulterer.

Nanny Fawcett began to rub him with a very dry towel.

At the beginning, there had been another Nanny, about whom he now remembered only a smell, and an air of weariness and loss of hope. 'I was trained in the old school,' she had said, on arrival, 'I am only used to the best type of home.' And she had been firm in her demands for Sole Charge and no sweets of any kind and the sacking of the cleaning woman who used bad language. 'But then she is so reliable and decided,' William's mother had said, sipping a Manhattan in the oyster-grey drawing-room, 'everything is so nice for me, so straightforward.' Though, in truth, she felt a little guilty that this was so, believed obscurely that it was not altogether natural to have a nanny who gave simply no trouble. So that it had been almost a salve to her conscience when that Nanny had, abruptly, died, and the problems of finding someone new and suitable began. William was three and a half.

He could not now imagine how it had been before Nanny Fawcett came to the house, he saw the world entirely through her eyes, all his experience of life reached him filtered through her. Nanny Fawcett was Irish, she was in her middle thirties, she came from a good, Protestant family in Dublin, she was moody. Her breasts were too large and concealed a heart filled with prejudice, most markedly against men, and against the Republic of Eire.

William's mother had some weeks of anxiety. 'I do hope we have done the right thing, she did *seem* the most suitable, though it is clear to us all that Nannies are not what they were. But I am afraid that I suspect Nanny Fawcett of dying her hair. That red is so unnatural.' She spoke as one of some distant generation, but she was not old-fashioned, merely true to her breeding. She spoke in a high-pitched, nasal, slightly whining voice. But she felt, too, a little more comfortable with Nanny Fawcett, felt secure in her own position as mistress of both house and child. It was only what one expected, to have to put up with some quirks, in a Nanny.

When they visited the house in Cadogan Square, William's maternal grandmother sat among the fringed sofas from Peter Jones, the skin beneath her eyes most carefully powdered, and asked, 'What about this Nanny Fawcett?' 'But I think, you know,' said William's mother, when they had discussed it, 'that she is *all right*, I think that everything is as it should be, on the whole. Of course, I would never entrust William to just anybody.'

They could feel their duty done, then, and dismiss the child's welfare under Nanny Fawcett from their minds.

To William, the only realities of which he could be certain, the only truths he knew, came to him through Nanny Fawcett. Everywhere else was the territory of strangers, the ground upon which he walked, in company with his mother and father and the Cadogan Square grandmother, was insubstantial. He sensed that he could never have survived, permanently, in their atmosphere. From Nanny Fawcett he learned that there were 'Irish *and* Irish', and that the Protestants of good family living in Dublin kept themselves very much to themselves, they had their own clubs and dances and private schools.

'A trained Nanny,' she said, over and over again, 'is not a servant. This is a profession. I am not a *maid*, you know, nothing of that kind.'

He learned about the spoliation of Dublin's Georgian buildings and about the low character of the feckless Southern Irish, Roman Catholics and working class, who came over to England and gave their country a bad name. He learned about the winning ways and loose morals of the colleens who worked as waitresses in Lyons Corner House and conductresses on buses of the Green Line. He learned about the integrity of the Unionist party and the reign of terror by bigoted priests among the peasants of Eire.

He learned that Nanny Fawcett's grandmother bred Irish setter dogs, and that her family had always been 'proud'. Above all, he learned that most of the trouble in the world, and all the troubles of women, could be laid at the door of men.

'You'll be a man,' she said, laying his checked Viyella shirt out on the chair. 'You'll be as bad as all the rest.' And he had felt suddenly ashamed, knowing that his days were strictly numbered with her. He wished that he might do something to change his sex, to grow up or in some other way escape from the general mantle of male guilt. He was uncertain how he stood with Nanny Fawcett, what she truly thought of him. Her eyes, upturned slightly at the corners like those of an Oriental, flitted over him and gave him no reassurance, nothing more than a casual, spasmodic approval for some point of manners remembered or temptation not succumbed to. He planned ways to ingratiate himself with her, so that he might perceive some definite sign that her commendation would last for ever. But always, the eyes swept quickly over him, and he despaired. There was only the immediate chance of an hour, or day, of favour to cling to, he learned to live his life in these small snatches. They were like stepping stones, below which ran the dark river of her moods.

And so, he was surprised, the first day they met the Friend. It was January, slate-grey, a cold wind cutting across between the trees at their legs. He began to trail behind Nanny Fawcett up the slope, anxious about how the Round Pond would look, of how he might cope with getting to know it all over again, the unfamiliar.

'Don't scrape your shoes, you've only just this week had a new pair.'

Today, her hair shone redder than before, and the coils were more elaborate, gripped under the navy-blue hat. She had said, 'You're to behave yourself very nicely and not to be a nuisance, you're to make a good impression.'

'Why?'

'Because we might be going to meet someone, that's why. And you're having a jumper on under that coat, the wind's enough to cut you in half.'

He wondered who it was that they might see, if it was not the other Nannies, beside whom she would sometimes sit, on the green bench. Though, more often than not, she ignored them, neither sat nor talked, preferring to keep herself apart. The others, she had told him, had nothing of interest to say, or else they gave themselves airs, or were in charge of unsuitable children.

'Who might we see?'

'Never you mind, you'll find out in good time – and that's something else, you're to be quiet and not to go pestering with questions like you do, and "I want this, I want that", every five minutes. *We* want a bit of peace and quiet to ourselves, my friend and I.'

He gave up trying to imagine what kind of friend Nanny Fawcett might have. At the top of the slope, he walked forwards a little, and then stopped. The Pond was huge, it had spread and spread, with the exit of the water it seemed to him that he would never be able to walk as far as the opposite edge, he could barely see it. It was mud, thick and stiff and sculptured into lines of thin waves, towards the rim, as though the water had coagulated. He noticed the boats, beached on the mud and larded with it, so that their shape was disguised. They had been there for years, he thought, since before he was born, they had been there forever.

'Don't stand staring at that, it's only a basinful of mud, and thick with germs, I shouldn't wonder, there's nothing to see.'

But he could not take his eyes off the landscape of the pond, the craters and pits, the branches of trees and the abandoned boats picked out on it, he wanted to step down and walk across, poking and digging, to get into the centre where no one could reach him, not even the men with long grappling hooks, who sometimes had to bring the boats in, when the wind dropped.

Nanny Fawcett caught his hand. 'Did you *hear* me?' He went

after her, away from the Pond and up towards the bandstand on the edge of the trees.

For a long time, nobody came. He went away from her and down between the horse-chestnut trees, mashing the old leaves with his feet. He found an almost straight stick and held it like a lance. No other children were here, only, some yards away, a woman in green with a dog. From the beginning the afternoon had been strangely different, this place was not like the gardens to which he usually came, to rush about and sail a boat, while Nanny Fawcett looked on. The whole landscape was changed, everything was coloured differently, and the trees were a new shape. The Pond was dry. They might have been in another country. He was excited by it, and a little alarmed.

From far away, down the pleached walk came the shouts of boys, high and thin in the wind. He began to poke about in the leaves again with his straight stick.

When he looked up, he saw that Nanny Fawcett's friend had arrived, they were sitting together beside the empty bandstand. Nanny Fawcett touched her hand now and again to the coils of hair underneath the navy-blue hat. After a moment or two, William went nearer. The fact that her friend was a man completed his sense of strangeness, everything was suddenly out of joint in his view of the world and of people, if Nanny Fawcett, who despised men, could be so publicly friendly with one, nodding and smiling on the green bench.

He looked, William thought, as though his clothes did not belong to him, as though he were used to wearing something quite different. Though they were ordinary, a grey tweed overcoat, rather long, over grey trousers, and an egg-yellow scarf. And his face, the shape of his head and the set of his flesh across the bones, seemed not to fit with the rest of him, he was like a figure out of the Crazy Men game, where you moved a row of heads along, fitting them in turn to a row of different bodies underneath, and none of them seemed exactly to belong. Something in the man's features was constantly changing, as though he were trying on new expressions, toying with them and then discarding them, he smiled and grimaced and frowned and formed his mouth into a little, soft, pursed shape, and the flesh of his forehead slipped up and down somehow, under the shelf of thinning hair, the skin of his neck was loose.

William thought that he was old – and then not so old, it was hard to tell. He had a lot of very long teeth, and a tiny chin, and very pale, gloveless hands.

He moved the stick about on the grass at his feet, and Nanny Fawcett saw him.

'Come here now, you're not to go off too far into those trees by yourself – come right here. This is him, this is William – stand up properly, child – Now, *here* is the person I told you we might be going to meet.' She was talking much faster than usual, and every now and then, her hand went up to the coils of hair. William took a step nearer the bench, and the man leaned down and put out one of the pale hands, smiling with all his teeth, as though it were a joke, that they should be so formally introduced. William thought, he is not a very old man, but he is older than my father. He said, 'They've emptied the water out of the Round Pond. It's just mud now.'

'Ah!' said Nanny Fawcett's friend, and the expression on his face slipped and changed again, and now he looked secretive, he put a tongue inside his cheek and made it swell out a little, as though he were sucking a toffee. 'I daresay you wanted to sail a boat, didn't you? I daresay that's the trouble.'

'No, I didn't, I like it empty. I want it to stay like that. There are boats that have sunk, you can see them. And twigs. There are . . .'

'Off you go,' Nanny Fawcett said, suddenly impatient. 'Don't chatter so, about nothing, off you go and run about and don't wander too far off into those trees, do you hear me?'

He saw her turn a little on the bench, so that she was facing the Friend, saw a bright expression come into her face, as though everything he had said and would say were all that could interest her. The man turned his back, so that there was only the dark grey tweed and the line of yellow scarf below.

William moved away, chilled by the abrupt loss of their attention, and wandered about on the path by the trees. His hands were cold inside the woollen gloves. He wanted something to happen, for the day to become familiar again. Above his head, and stretching away into the distance, the sky was uniformly pale, and grey as brains. The woman in green, with the dog, had gone, everybody was going, out of the January wind.

Under one of the horse-chestnuts he found a conker, and although the green pulpy case had blemished, and the spines were soft and rotten, inside the nut was perfect, hard and polished like a mahogany table. He scooped it out and held it, feeling it slip, shiny, between his fingers. When he disturbed the leaves, the soil and moss beneath the trees sent up a cold, sweet stench.

He heard nothing, only saw the feet and legs in front of him. Very slowly he straightened up, holding the stick. It was another man. William glanced over to Nanny Fawcett, sitting with her friend on the park bench, wanting reassurance. Their faces were turned away from him.

'Nice,' the man said, 'that's nice.' His eyes were sharp and vacant at the same time, and he had a tall head. William stepped back.

'I could give you another. I could give you a lot.' And suddenly his hand shot out from under the mackintosh, and in the open palm lay eight or nine conkers, huge and glossy. 'I might give them all to you.'

'That's all right, I've got my own, thank you,' William was afraid of not being polite enough to the man, touched by the offer of the conkers, yet uneasy, not liking him to be there. When he looked again, the conkers had disappeared, and so had the man's hand, back into the pocket of the raincoat, so that he wondered whether he had seen them or not, and the man stood, smiling at him. The collar of his shirt was stiff, and shiny white.

'What's your name?'

'William.'

'That's nice. That's what I like.'

A gust of wind came knifing through the trees, stirring the dead leaves, and rattling down a loose branch. Abruptly, the man turned and began to move away, slipping round the grey trunks until he had vanished as quickly as the conkers had vanished. William stood, remembering the way he had come there. He dropped the conker into his coat pocket and kept his fingers tightly round it.

'Men,' Nanny Fawcett had said. 'There's always something that's not right about men, always something.' Now, he felt betrayed somehow, left alone among the trees with a stranger who offered him conkers, while she went on talking to her new friend.

On the way home, he asked if they would see him again.

'Oh, now, that all depends and don't little boys ask a lot of questions?'

They were walking very quickly, everyone was leaving the gardens and going off down the concrete slopes to tea, it was too cold for snow, she said, and he was out of breath now, with trying to keep up to her.

'But we might, and then again we might not, there might be treats in store, we might be seeing him somewhere else.'

'Where else? What sort of place?'

No answer.

'Doesn't he go to work?'

Nanny Fawcett rounded upon him alarmingly. 'Of course he goes to work, don't all honest men go to work, what do you take me for? I wouldn't have anything to do with any layabout, any idle man, you needn't imagine that I would.'

'No,' William said.

'But if we were to go and see him at work – well now, we might and that would be something!'

'What does he do?'

'Oh, something that would just surprise you.' Nanny Fawcett gripped his hand as they crossed the road at Kensington Gore. 'Something you'll never have heard of, and never would expect.'

'Tell me about it, *tell* me.'

'You'll find out soon enough, I daresay you will find out.'

Her face was flushed, set against the wind, and he dared not ask now, how her friend was different from all the rest, how he managed to escape her blanket condemnation of men. He had not looked any different. But perhaps he might learn the trick from him, if they met again, perhaps he could listen and watch, and discover the secret of Nanny Fawcett's favour.

He had tea in the oyster-grey drawing-room, with an apricot Danish pastry brought in by his grandmother from Cadogan Square.

'We're not going to the Park today, we're going somewhere different. It's to be a treat.'

He was being dressed in best trousers and a white shirt, his mother had gone out. 'Mum's the word,' Nanny Fawcett had said. He wondered what to expect, dared not ask.

Outside a hotel, they stopped. Nanny Fawcett bent down to him. 'You're to enjoy yourself,' she said, pumping his hand up and down to emphasize her words. 'You're not to be a trouble. You go with my friend and do as you're told, and remember just how lucky you are.'

He looked up at her, prepared for anything at all. Nanny Fawcett laughed. 'Cow's eyes!' she said. 'You'll be the death of me. It's a *party*, isn't it?'

They walked up the wide, white marble steps of the hotel and through the revolving doors, and inside everything was hushed and softly lit from chandeliers, the carpets were rose-red on the floor. Nanny Fawcett held hard on to his hand. It was some minutes before her friend came, looking more than ever strange, in shirt sleeves, and with his hair combed flat back, as though he had been disturbed from a sleep, or in the middle of some job, up a ladder. William wondered if he lived in the hotel. He made a curious face at him, screwing the flesh up around his eyes and nose, and then letting it collapse again like a pile of ash, looking blandly at Nanny Fawcett.

'Well,' he said. 'It's all fixed up, you see, all arranged.'

'I wouldn't like to think that it was not,' said Nanny Fawcett.

He brayed with laughter, showing the long teeth.

'*We* were not coming to the back entrance,' Nanny Fawcett said.

The friend's hand shot out and pinched William's cheek, and he danced a little, on the balls of his feet.

'Time presses,' he said. 'We'll do well to be getting off, getting this one settled and so forth. Well, now . . .' He winked.

'Get *along* . . .' Nanny Fawcett gave him a little push in the back, 'and you mind your manners, I'll be around to collect you later, won't I?'

The friend waved his arm in the direction of a deserted lounge, full of green and gold armchairs. 'What about getting settled,' he said, 'having a nice tray of tea, what about you going and putting your feet up, and I'll be down directly.'

He took William's hand.

He had thought that the upstairs corridors of hotels led only to bedrooms, but when they emerged from the left, there were tall cream-painted pillars, and huge, fronded plants, and gilt mirrors, and they walked towards another lounge.

'Going to enjoy yourself?' the friend said.

William frowned.

'Well, don't have a lot to say, do you? Don't have much of a tongue in your head.'

He leered down horribly, the rubber face contorting itself and seeming to flush and darken, until a grin broke it open like a wave, and everything was different again. William wondered if the face changed in sleep, too.

'Where am I going?'

They stopped. The friend banged him lightly on the back. 'Well, to a *party*, aren't you? You're going to a party.'

'Oh. Is it your party?'

'It is not.'

A door swung open ahead, letting out voices.

'All you've to do, you've to mind what you say, then you'll be nice and dandy, you see, and nothing to do but enjoy yourself.'

He did not explain further.

At Christmas, there had been four parties, and none of them was at a hotel and all of them had terrified him, each time he had prayed that there would never be another. Now, he stood back behind Nanny Fawcett's friend, looking upon the room full of strangers, other children, in ribbon and net and velvet and white shirts under tartan ties, and his stomach clenched with dread. He did not know why he had been brought here.

'Well now, how very nice!' said the woman in mauve, bending down to him, 'How nice, dear! We were expecting you.' And she turned to the other, beside her. 'Our entertainer's child!' she said, and both of them laughed a little, and looked about the room for someone to take charge of him. 'His name is William,' she said.

He had thought that always one met the same people at parties, his cousin Sophie and the Cressett twins and fat Michael, but he knew nobody here at all, their names confused him and he hung back on the edge of their games.

'We've been told to be nice to you,' a boy said.

William stood, thinking of Nanny Fawcett and the friend, far away down all the carpeted stairs, eating tea in the empty lounge.

As it went on, it became like all the other parties he had

known, the terrors were at least familiar, the awful taste of the tea and of trifles in little, waxed paper cases and the staring of the bigger girls. There were games which he did not win and dancing for which he had not brought his pumps. The woman in mauve clapped her hands and laughed a lot and changed the records on the gramophone, and from time to time, she took his hand and led him closer into the circle of the others. 'You are to look after this little boy, you are to be kind to William now, dear, try and remember.'

But then, suddenly, one of the hotel waiters had drawn the curtains and they were all made to sit tightly together on the carpeted floor, squealing a little with apprehension and excitement. Then the music began. Oh God, Oh God, make it not be a a conjuror or a Punch and Judy, William thought, pressing his nails deeply into the palms of his hands. But it was not, it was something he had never seen before, something worse.

The area ahead of them was lit like a stage, with a high stool placed there, and then a figure came lumbering out of the darkness. From the shoulders down it was a man, his costume all in one piece and wumbling as it moved, like the covering on a pantomime horse. But it stood upon only two legs and the legs were three times, ten times, as long as human legs, and oddly stiff at the joints. Above the shoulders, the huge head was not a man's head, but that of an elephant, nodding and bobbing and bending forward to the music and waving its disgusting trunk.

William sat and every so often closed his eyes, willing for it to be gone, for the curtains to be drawn again and the ordinary January daylight to flood the room. But he could still hear the music and when that stopped, the elephant man spoke and sang, the voice very deep, distorted and hollow, booming away inside the huge head. He opened his eyes and did not want to look, but he could not stop himself, the square of light and then the lurching animal man drew him. It was dancing, lifting its huge legs up and down stiffly, clapping its hands together, while the head nodded. From somewhere, it produced a vividly coloured stuffed parrot, which sat upon its shoulder and answered back to jokes, in a terrible rasping voice. Then the music started again.

'Now, children, now what about everybody doing a little dance with me, what about us all dancing together? Would you like that?'

'Yes,' they yelled. 'Yes, Yes!' and clapped and bounced up and down.

'And what about somebody coming up on my shoulder and being as high as the sky, what about that? Would you like to do that?'

'Yes,' they screamed. 'Yes, yes!' and rushed forwards, clamouring about the baggy legs, clutching and laughing.

From the gramophone came the music for a Conga, and the elephant man set off with everyone clinging on behind in a chain, prancing about the room, and first one, then another was lifted high up on to its great shoulders, swaying with delight, hands touching the ceiling, swinging the chandelier. William stood back against the wall in the darkness, praying not to be noticed, but when the line reached him, he was noticed, the woman in mauve clucked and took his hand, putting him in with the others, so that he was forced to trot on one leg and then the next to the music. And then, suddenly, he felt the elephant man behind him, and he was lifted up, the hands digging tightly into his sides, and he could neither scream nor protest, he could scarcely breathe, only dangle helplessly there, near to the cream-painted ceiling, and see, far below him, the upturned, mocking faces of the others, hear the blast of the music. Through the slits in the elephant head, he could see eyes, flickering like lanterns in a turnip, and he looked away dizzy, praying to be set down.

At the end, the lights did not go on immediately, he could slip out of the door and nobody noticed him.

The corridor was silent, everything closed and secret. The music faded away as he ran, and found a flight of stairs and climbed them, not daring to look back. Here the passages were narrower, the carpets dark grey and thick as felt, so that his feet made no sound. There might have been nobody else in the building.

He had thought that he would die of fear, high up in the clutch of the elephant man, but he had not died, and now he must remember it, he could still hear the music and the shrieking of the others, pounding in his ears. He came up to a long mirror at the end of the corridor, and was terrified by his own reflection, tense and white-faced. The elephant man could be following him, might be anywhere at all, and perhaps there were others. He began to run, back down the stairs, but on the lower corridor heard voices and imagined some punishment inflicted upon him by the elephant man, or else by the hotel porters and maids, and the woman in mauve. He pushed open one of the grey doors in his panic. When the voices and footsteps had gone away, he would run again down to the lounge where Nanny Fawcett was having tea with her friend, it would be all right.

'Well, now!'

He spun round. It was a bedroom, with draped curtains and a light switched on over the long dressing-table, and reflected in the mirror, he saw the elephant man, arms up on either side of his head. He could not move, only stare in terror as the hands lifted off the grey head, up and up, and then down again, until it rested on his knees.

'Master William the party-boy,' said Nanny Fawcett's friend, and the face creased in sudden, wicked mirth, trembling and quivering. On a chair, William saw Nanny Fawcett's navy-blue coat and hat, and the sensible handbag. 'All a bit of a romp and a treat,' said her friend, 'blowed if it isn't!' His face crumpled into sadness and mock-weeping. 'Poor old elephant!'

William saw the two images separately, the face of the man, and that of the elephant on his lap, and then the reflections of them in the glass, he was surrounded by the terrible faces. He gave a sob, and put up a hand to shield his eyes, groping for the door-handle. It would not yield, something pushed him back, and then there was Nanny Fawcett, straightening her skirt, he was forced to go back into the room, while her friend the elephant man laughed until the tears ran down his cheeks. Outside in the corridor, the voices of the others, leaving the party.

'You didn't collect your present,' Nanny Fawcett said.

Because it was raining and the hotel was not near home, they went on a bus.

'You never would have guessed it, I know, never in a million years,' Nanny Fawcett said, her face flushed with pleasure. 'He used to be in the pantomimes and circuses, my friend, he's a very high class entertainer.'

The lights of the cars swept down Piccadilly in a row, like an army advancing through the rain.

'You're the lucky one, aren't you, there's plenty that would envy you, I know. Going to a party and not even knowing the person! Well!'

He realized that he had not discovered for which child the party had been held.

'You've gone quiet,' she said, making him walk too quickly round the Square. 'If you ate too much, I shan't be very pleased, shall I, after what I told you?'

He thought of the dreams he would have that night.

'Mum's the word,' Nanny Fawcett said, turning her key in the latch. For he must say nothing about her friend and nothing about the party.

He woke in the darkness to find his pillow, and the well of the bed below his neck, filled with vomit.

'The *next* time, you learn to hold back,' said Nanny Fawcett, stripping off his pyjamas. Her hair was twisted into curious plaits about her head. 'Your eyes are bigger than your stomach, so they are. The next time you just curb your greed, thank you very much.'

He stared into her face, and did not dare ask about 'the next time'. 'He's a very nice type of man,' she said, rubbing the cold sponge briskly about his face. 'Not at all the sort you would commonly meet, so mind your P's and Q's in future and play your cards right and you'll be going to quite a number of parties, I shouldn't wonder.'

Lying in the dark again, between stiff, clean sheets, he knew that since the day they drained the Round Pond, everything had surely changed and would never be as it was, and felt afraid, wishing for the time past, when Nanny Fawcett had despised all men.

Friends of Miss Reece

'You're in the way,' Wetherby said, but quietly, hissing under her breath, in case Matron, who was also the boy's Aunt, should come in through the door.

'Nuisance . . . as if there weren't enough.'

She bent down and jabbed at the coals with a black poker, so that they burst hotly open like poppy pods, showering sparks for seeds. He watched her covertly, out of the sides of his eyes, feeling ashamed of being so disliked. The warmth from the fire came up into his face.

'You can drink your milk on the hearth stool, you won't get under everyone's feet,' his Aunt Spencer had said. But she was kind, beneath the sharp way of talking. He had always known her.

'*Which* room was I born in?'

'Number Six, next to the old nursery, down the corridor from Reece.'

It was familiar as a rhyme. When he asked, she answered, automatically, banging in and out of the swing doors with trays and pans and white enamel jugs of steaming water, always using the same words.

'Number Six, next to the old nursery, down the corridor from Reece.'

It was his mother who refused to comfort him in this way.

'*Which* room was I born in?'

'Oh, don't be silly, do try and remember, do stop asking the same questions, haven't I *told* you . . .'

Wetherby was dumping fresh coal on to the fire, in great chunks, darkening it. He felt the warmth go off his face, a sudden shadow. Wetherby held the starched white apron flat against her body, with her left hand, out of the way of the fire. The door swung in and out again, water glasses chinked on a loaded tray. One of the bells rang. He looked up at the little, glass-fronted box. There were rows of numbers, and rows of little scarlet flaps. When somebody rang their bell, the flap dropped down and up, down and up, down and up, under the number of their room. Six, he thought, let it be six. He closed his eyes, and opened them again. But it was not six, it was nine. Nobody ever rang from six, when he was here.

'Number Six, next to the old nursery, down the corridor from Reece.'

But Reece never rang her bell, either.

'Never wants anything,' Aunt Spencer had said. Yet Wetherby still hated her, still grumbled, just out of earshot of the Matron, about how much trouble she was given, by Reece.

He tipped the mug of cooling milk up to his face and allowed a very little to slide into his mouth. He did not want to finish it, Wetherby would notice. 'Upstairs with *you*, then, that's one thing out of the way, get along.'

Wetherby had always been here, in the Cedars Lawn Nursing Home, just as Reece had always been here, in Number Seven. He hated Wetherby, and he was a friend of Reece. '*Miss* Reece,' his mother made him say. And worried, vaguely, from time to time, about whether it did any harm to him, going so often to see her. But she supposed not.

He thought of how terrible it would be, if he were always in Number Seven, like Miss Reece, and always looked after and fed and woken and put to sleep and washed and chided, by Wetherby

'*Nurse* Wetherby, to you . . .'

Once, he thought that the very first face he had ever seen had been that of Wetherby, it was the thing he could remember quite clearly, from the day of his birth, in Number Six.

'What did I look like?'

'A good, healthy baby,' said his Aunt Spencer, holding a white china feeding cup to the light, looking for a crack.

'*Red*,' Wetherby had told him, coming behind him and whispering on the dark stairs. 'Red and ugly, that's what. You squalled.'

Her top teeth were very large, and yellow, with even gaps, and they stuck out below her lip, like a bow-window. He moved away quickly.

The milk was thickish, and sweet. He held it in his mouth and swirled his tongue around inside, comforted.

'We are going out until very late. It will be much nicer for you to sleep at the nursing home,' his mother had said. 'It will be a treat.'

He had looked away and out of the window, on to the garden, where the last of the melting snow lay, grubby as the stained linen that came down to Aunt Spencer's washroom in a hand-operated lift.

He would have said, I don't want to, I want to stay here, I don't like sleeping there all night, because of Wetherby. Once, he had half-spoken.

'*Nurse* Wetherby, to you, and you are very silly about her.'

'She's ugly.'

'Not everybody can be beautiful.'

'Her teeth are all yellow.'

'That is a nasty, *personal* remark, polite little boys do not say things like that.'

'She . . .'

But he could not have told. He kept his mind turned from the thought of the upstairs landings of the Cedars Lawn Nursing Home, and the attic where he must sleep, in the room next to Wetherby.

'Are you going to a ball?'

'No, dear,'

'To a dinner?'

For they were always putting on new clothes and getting into the warm car and driving off somewhere. The names of the people whose houses they visited were familiar as those of the streets and squares around which he walked, every afternoon, with the girl Shirley, who was paid to take him out, by the hour.

'Are you going to the Mayor's Banquet, then?'

'Oh, don't be *silly*, that is in the spring. It is November now.'

'*Where* are you going?'

'To play bridge with Mr and Mrs Templeton. There, now.'

He knew that bridge was a game played with cards, sitting at tables, yet whenever he heard the word, there was the same picture in his mind, of the bridge over the lake in Beecher's Park, and the railway bridge, and all the other bridges he had ever seen. He saw the people, too, his mother and father, and the Templetons and the Hoylakes and the Askew-Fishers, all rushing about on the bridges, playing some kind of elegant tag, in their evening clothes.

'Why do I have to go to Aunt Spencer's? Why can't I stay at home and be sat with?'

'Because I have told you, we shall be very late and it is altogether more convenient, that is all. Now, eat up your carrots, please.'

There was only a dribble of milk left at the bottom of the mug. He looked down into it and thought about his mother, in the palely floating chiffon dress. The Templetons owned the Park Royal Hotel, facing the Esplanade. It had a monkey puzzle tree, thick and dark as felt, in the garden.

'Just *playing* with that,' Wetherby said venomously, and leaned over, pushing her face close down towards him, to see the thin, liquid layer in the blue mug. He smelled her starched cotton material in the warmth from the fire, and the breath coming out from behind her yellow teeth, like the thick, stale fumes of tea.

Aunt Spencer banged through the swing doors, with Night Sister behind her, calling out that Eleven had been sick over the side of the bed and down on to the floor. He heard about it, and was unmoved, it seemed to him that the whole of adult life was about these things, the sickness and temperatures and bowels and dying, of the patients in nursing homes. He was not afraid. He had always come here.

'*Bed* . . .' said Aunt Spencer suddenly, but when he looked up, he felt safe, knowing her concern for him, behind the bustling about and the care of so many patients. He had been the last child born at the Cedars Lawn Home, before they 'gave up maternity'. In the evenings, she had nursed him, beside the fire in her private sitting-room, warding off the recognition of her own growing old.

'Bed . . .'

He got up from the hearth stool.

'*Which* room was I born in?'

'Number Six, next to the old nursery, down the corridor from Reece.'

He paused at the kitchen door, satisfied. 'I could go and see her.'

'Who, Reece? No. Wetherby's gone to put her on the commode.'

'But I could just wait and then say good night to her.'

'She doesn't want visitors at this time of night.'

'It's only . . .' He looked up at the clock, but his memory failed him again, he still could not work out what the hands said, unless it were very straightforward, midday or six o'clock.

His father said, 'He is very *stupid* over this matter of telling the time,' and stared down at him, leaning forward a little. 'I hope he is not going to be stupid in many other respects.'

The fire was beginning to spurt through the new coals, now, he did not want to leave it, and the warmth and light and smells of the kitchen, for the iron-framed bed, five flights of stairs up in the dark attics. Aunt Spencer said, 'I'm going up to Eleven now, I'll come and see to you as well.'

She pushed open the swing door and he followed, looking at the stiff folds of her matron's cap, streaming behind her, and the black matron's shoes, and thick, black stockings, over stout legs. He felt better, now that she was to supervise his undressing and washing and the saying of prayers. He was not going to be left to Wetherby.

Outside the door of Six, he hesitated, staring at the magic number, in gold on the brown paint, feeling the importance of it.

'Don't dawdle,' Aunt Spencer said, beginning to be out of breath. 'We're short-staffed tonight and Twelve is dying, I haven't time to wait about for you.'

He glanced down the short corridor that led to Number Seven.

'You can see Reece in the morning.'

They began to climb the next, steep flight.

Nurse Wetherby, red and puffy about the face, banged the tray on the kitchen table. He looked up and then down again, quickly, stirring his spoon through the porridge.

'Nothing but a filthy, dirty mess,' Wetherby said, under her breath, 'things slopped everywhere.'

He flushed with alarm, and looked at the table around his plate anxiously, and down the front of his Fair Isle jumper. But there was nothing, it was not him. Reece, he thought, Miss Reece.

'It's getting worse . . . slopping everything about . . . she's not fit to live.' The words came in spurts, from different parts of the kitchen, as Wetherby moved about. He knew that she was not talking to him.

Outside the window, he could see the sky, leaden with the new snow to come. He took another spoonful of sugar and tipped it slowly over the porridge, watching the brown grains spill and then sink into the soft mess, melting and leaving little stains. Aunt Spencer was upstairs with Nurse O'Keefe, laying out Number Twelve. He wondered what time his mother might come for him.

'*Dawdler*, you're as bad as that Reece, messing your food about, look at you. Huggitt's waiting to clear, I suppose you know.' He stiffened. It had been quite dark when she had woken him, coming into the attic. And then her thick fingers, fumbling with his pyjamas. He thought, when my mother comes, I shall tell her, or else I shall tell Aunt Spencer, and nobody will make me sleep here again. But he knew that he would say nothing, would not know the words to use. And he was afraid of Wetherby.

The door swung open. 'I thought you wanted to go and see Reece,' said Aunt Spencer.

Getting down from the table, he asked who had been Number Twelve. Aunt Spencer's arms were full of rubber hot water bottles, taken out, morning-cold, from the beds.

'Mr Perrott, poor old soul.' She turned to Wetherby. 'There's a brother-in-law, apparently,' she said, 'that's all. Never been here, you see, not interested. I shall have to ring. The undertaker's coming at three.'

He went out of the kitchen, and slowly up the first, linoleum-covered flight of stairs. After that, the polished wood began, and the ruby-red carpet, trodden by the shoes of the nurses and the doctors and the visitors of patients in Cedars Lawn. He thought about the dead Mr Perrott, in Number Twelve. Once he had been in to see him, but nothing was said, Mr Perrott had been asleep. He had been slightly relieved. There was always the one, bad moment, when they sent him to visit some new patient in a strange room. 'Go and cheer up Nine . . . Fifteen . . . Two . . . give the poor soul a bit of company, go on.' And he tapped upon the brown doors and pushed them open and went inside, and did not know what terrible things he might see.

Mr Perrott had been shrivelled, his skin and hair were the same, yellowish white. His mouth had been slightly open as he breathed. Twelve was the smallest room, facing on to the side of St Martin's Church. He had waited for a moment, politely, but Mr Perrott had not woken.

In the nursing home kitchen, Aunt Spencer had cut slice after slice of bread and said, 'Cancer', in passing, to his mother.

Now, Mr Perrott was dead.

He came to the door of Number Seven. Reece. She had been here when he was born – *before* he was born. There were those, like Mr Perrott, who came for a time and died and were replaced, and those, like Miss Reece, who stayed here forever. He knocked, but out of courtesy, because there would be no answer, and then opened the door.

'Rolling in money,' Wetherby said, 'everything it can buy. It means nothing to them, that family of hers, nothing at all.' For Miss Reece had the largest and most expensive room at the front of the Cedars Lawn Nursing Home, Miss Reece's bed overlooked the garden, and some of the furniture belonged to her family – the Sheraton dressing-table at which she would never sit, and the Persian carpet and the armchairs for visitors, and the large picture over the mantelpiece. Miss Reece lay in the high bed, and her rich family paid, the sister and the two married brothers, and an elderly aunt, and once a week, on Sunday afternoons, they visited her, by turns. They arrived in chauffeured cars, wearing coats with fur collars and doing their duty, eating tea and being bored.

He walked around the screen and crossed the Persian carpet and stood beside the high bed. It took a long time for Miss Reece to move her head on the pillow, so that she ceased to gaze out of the window, and could focus upon him, instead. He waited. Reece, about whom Wetherby always complained, rich Miss Reece, with the straight grey hair and very soft skin and the tremor in head and body, hands and legs. 'Parkinson's', Aunt Spencer had said once.

He saw the recognition of him, in the slight widening of her pale eyes. On the gold, quilted counterpane, her hands lay and shook. He said, 'I've just had my breakfast. I stayed here the night because my mother and father went out. They went to play bridge at the Park Royal Hotel.'

Once, Miss Reece had been able to nod, but now, he realized that he could no longer tell the difference between the nod of interest, and understanding, that was meant for him, and the helpless nodding which went on all the time.

'Did you have porridge as well? I had porridge.'

Like some small, individual animal, with a life of its own, the left hand of Miss Reece twitched slightly on the counterpane. The half-moons were sketched, white as chalk, on the oval nails.

'For Christmas, I'm going to have a puppy. It's going to be a spaniel. I could bring it to see you, couldn't I? You'd like that.'

The shaking continued.

He had thought that Reece was old, the oldest person in the world. She had been in her bed at the Cedars Lawn Nursing Home for eleven years. But when he had asked Aunt Spencer, she had said no, no, Reece wasn't old at all, was young, was not yet fifty, and that was the tragedy. She had had, Aunt Spencer said, 'no life'.

Now, he waited beside the bed, as the bell from St Martin's Church began to toll the hour. Eventually, Miss Reece would speak. He knew what she would say. It was always the same. He stood, rubbing the sole of his left sandal over the surface of his right, trying to be patient, for he must not say the words for her, must not be impolite. 'She isn't soft in the head,' Aunt Spencer had said. 'You needn't think that, just because her speech has gone. She's all there. You must show a decent respect no matter what.'

Only Wetherby muttered and grumbled, day after day, clashing the breakfast trays and the lunch trays and the trays with the visitors' teas, the jugs and bowls and bedpans, only Wetherby said, out of earshot of the Matron, that Reece was not fit to live.

He watched the small, flabby mouth begin to quiver, saw the tongue fumbling about wetly between palates, trying to grasp and form the words. There was a dribble of dried egg on one side of her chin. 'Messes,' Wetherby said, 'messes and dribbles her food like a baby. It's getting worse and worse. I know, I have to put up with it, nobody else, I can see the way she's going. Not fit to live.'

He wondered why Wetherby was a nurse, and then supposed that she could do nothing else, would not fit into any other world. He had watched her, shovelling spoonful after spoonful of liquid mess into Miss Reece's helpless mouth and never giving her enough time, making noises of impatience and irritation. But once, she had gone out of the room to answer a persistent bell, leaving the cup, and then, he had fetched a stool and stood upon it to reach the bed, and, very slowly and carefully, he had begun to put the food into Miss Reece's mouth. She had managed, there had been no dribble. But it had taken a long time. He dared not say anything to Wetherby. There would be the nights when he must sleep here, upstairs in the attic.

In the end, the words came. He understood them only because they were always the same.

'Would you like a sweet?'

It might have been some language spoken by one of a race whose mouths were shaped unlike human mouths, or else the noise of some animal, slurred and uncontrolled. He thought of what it must be like, to know the right words inside your head, to hear them there, and not to be able to bring them out, thought of words going around and around, all tangled together like washing inside a machine, trapped.

He said, 'Yes, I would. Thank you very much,' and waited again, for the hand to creep forwards, a little, over the gold counterpane, the forefinger to twitch, pointing as best it might, in the direction of the Sheraton dressing-table.

The box was made of tin, with a pattern painted on to it, to look like the stitchings of needlepoint, roses and leaves on a black ground. Where the lid opened and beside the hinges, the paint had been thumbed away. It had always been here, in the left-hand drawer. He knew every dent and mark upon it. It contained humbugs, striped brown and cream, in cellophane paper. Never any other kind of sweet. The humbugs were brought in by the rich relatives of Miss Reece, on their Sunday afternoon visits. She was not able to eat them herself.

He unwrapped the cellophane and put a humbug inside his mouth, and then he could say nothing, only suck at the tricklings of sweet saliva, and walk about the room, touching things lightly, looking at the picture of 'The Boxing Day Meet' and the Delights of Britain's Gardens Calendar. Miss Reece lay in the high bed and shook and looked out endlessly on to the dull lawn and the empty avenue. 'She likes me to go and see her,' he had said to Aunt Spencer. The visits were like the words she used to answer his question.

'*Which* room was I born in?'

'Number Six, next to the old nursery, down the corridor from Reece.'

Unchanging, familiar, a comfort. Miss Reece. He had always known her.

'You get along downstairs, your mother's here and waiting.' Wetherby banged the door, and went straight away to Reece, heaving her up the bed, down which she always slipped, little by little every hour, unable to stop herself. He watched for a moment, and remembered the feel of Wetherby's hands, and went quickly away, not looking again into the patient eyes of Miss Reece.

'Now we are going to stay with some people in Lincolnshire, for the weekend. It is nobody you know, and there will not be any children, you would find it so dull. It will be much nicer for you to spend the whole weekend at Aunt Spencer's.'

He ate the crust off a piece of toast, turning it round and round in his mouth. There had been more snow. It squeaked under the soles of his Wellington boots, as they walked to the nursing home. He was carrying his own case.

Aunt Spencer's private sitting-room smelled slightly sweet. There was a great deal of furniture, there were cushions of ruched silk and hand-embroidered pictures and firescreens and samplers and tray-cloths.

'I've cleared a space for you at my desk, you can do your drawing and painting on that,' she said. 'It will keep you out of everybody's way.'

And so he sat for a long time in the stuffy room, fiddling with a penknife and a new box of crayons, trying to draw horses, bored. He found Lincolnshire on a tray-cloth map of Britain, and wondered about his mother and father, trying to picture the house in which they were staying.

'What are the people called?'

'Now I have already told you, darling, you have never met them, they haven't been here, to this house.'

'I want to know their names. I like names.'

She gave him a curious look. 'How funny you are! Well, they are called Pountenay. Mr and Mrs Roger Pountenay. There!'

'Do they play bridge?'

'Oh dear, *I* don't know. Yes, I expect they do.'

'Why don't they have any children in their house?'

'That is not the sort of question you should *ever* ask.'

He did not know whether he would have wanted to go to the house in Lincolnshire, or not. On the wall, beside Aunt Spencer's small desk, was a carved crucifix, and a picture, in soft, blurred colours, of Jesus the Lamb of God.

He began to draw horses again.

When he heard the sound of the door opening, he woke up at once, sitting up in the bed. It was quite dark. A long way downstairs, in the kitchen, Night Nurse, with the lamp and the banked-up fire and the silent row of bells above the swing door. Nobody else. The floorboards creaked on the landing outside. Wetherby. He thought, I could do anything, shout or scream or anything, and nobody would ever hear me, and I cannot run away. He waited for the turning of the knob on his attic bedroom door. Nothing. Sounds, but going a different way, along the corridor and down the stairs.

He got out of bed and put his hands out in front of him, feeling for the door.

All the way down to the basement, the night lamps burned dimly on every landing, at the head of each flight of stairs. When he looked over the banister, he saw the back of Wetherby's head, saw her turn and go out of sight, down the corridor leading to Number Seven, the room of Miss Reece. For no reason, he felt afraid.

There was an ache in his bladder, but he dared not go down to the lavatory, on the first floor, not now. He went back into the attic and groped his way to the bed and lay, squeezing himself tightly between his legs, for fear of wetting the mattress. He did not go to sleep again. Wetherby came back. He waited, and wept with relief when her footsteps went on, past his door. It was all right, it was all right, nothing was going to happen to him. He thought about Reece.

When he woke again, he was still afraid, because he had dreamed and could not remember what he had dreamed, only felt certain that something was wrong. His pyjamas were damp, and there was a cold patch in the sheet. It was dark. There was no sound on the landing, or from downstairs. The night lights were still lit. He felt awake and not awake.

The door of Number Seven was closed. At first he did nothing, he stood outside shivering and feeling the wetness of his pyjamas. Last night, he had seen Miss Reece, he had stayed with her and eaten two sweets and talked about his mother and father in Lincolnshire and how he could not draw horses. 'Turn out her light,' Wetherby said, 'I don't want to go traipsing back up there again.' But he had not done so, it had seemed too early, too unkind, leaving Miss Reece in the dark.

Every morning, after breakfast, every afternoon, and every evening, Wetherby, and somebody helping her, stripped the bedclothes off and lifted up the shaking Miss Reece and placed her on the wooden commode. But yesterday, Wetherby had had to change everything, she said to Huggitt, sheets, blankets, the lot, it went straight through, she was filthy, she didn't try, didn't care, she couldn't bother to lift her finger and press the electric bell. She was getting worse. 'Filthy,' Wetherby said.

He thought, now, that by seeing Miss Reece, he might find comfort for himself.

The room was in darkness. He could hear nothing, until the door closed, and then the faint hissing of the gas.

He thought that she would be dead, and he had never seen a dead person, only the coffins being carried down the stairs by the overcoated men. But Miss Reece lay, propped on the two, full pillows, and he saw that she was not dead, she was breathing deeply, her face a little flushed and pink, in the light of the lamp.

After he had opened the window, he ran, holding his breath, and in the lavatory, on the next landing, was sick. He could not imagine what he might do, could not think of the words he could use to tell them, and be believed. Miss Reece was not dead. He must go back to bed, that was all.

On Saturdays, Wetherby did the early morning teas, and then went away, wearing a green woollen coat and hat, caught a bus to visit her married sister in the country, eleven miles away. She did not come back until very late at night. Tomorrow was Saturday. Nothing could happen to him.

As he closed his door, he heard Wetherby open hers. Downstairs, the clock struck six-thirty. At seven, the rattle of teacups would begin. He did not sleep again.

'Something's wrong with Reece,' Aunt Spencer said. He looked up quickly, from the moist centre of his boiled egg, and saw that Wetherby had come into the kitchen and was watching him, her eyes narrowed and angry, beneath the fleshy lids. He thought, she is dead after all, she is dead and it is my fault because I said nothing. Wetherby has killed her with the gas from the fire. He thought that he had done the right thing, because his father had taught him about gas, and about fires too, and fainting and deep cuts; he said, a boy should not flinch, he should learn to be prepared for any kind of accident from an early age.

'I took her tea up,' Wetherby said. 'She was right enough then.' Her eyes were still on his face.

'Her breathing's bad.' Aunt Spencer opened the enormous bottle of Dettol and began to pour.

So she was not dead, it was all right. He thought about how he could avoid having to sleep tonight in the attic room, how he might pretend to be ill, so that Aunt Spencer would let him stay on the couch in her own room. Tomorrow, his father and mother would come back from Lincolnshire, nothing would happen, nobody should know.

Aunt Spencer put a mug of hot milk down on the desk. He was trying again to draw horses. Wetherby had gone out, he had seen the movement of her green coat, past the window, and turned his head away. She knows, he thought, she watches me and knows.

'Your *bed* . . .' said Aunt Spencer.

He was silent, remembering the wet patch of mattress.

'You needn't look like that, I shan't tell your mother.'

'Oh.'

When she reached the door, he said, 'I want to go and see Miss Reece.'

'Not now you can't, Doctor Mackay's coming to her any minute?'

'What's the matter?'

'Nothing much, bit of a cold, I shouldn't wonder.' She went out. He remembered her saying. 'Her breathing's bad,' to

Wetherby, and he thought of the gas and the window he had opened, on to Miss Reece's head and chest. Outside, there was more snow. He could tell nobody, there was nothing he could say. He wondered how much of it had been his dream.

'If you wrap yourself up sensibly, you can go out and play,' Aunt Spencer said.

He was rolling the head of a snowman round and round the front lawn, enlarging it, when the navy-blue car of Doctor Mackay drew up, outside the nursing home. He thought, now it is all right, now Miss Reece will not die.

The snow had soaked through to his hands, matting the red woollen gloves, and making his flesh burn with cold, as though the fingers had been trapped in a door. He went on with the rolling of the snowman. A little while before lunch, Doctor Mackay came down the steps and got into his navy-blue car and drove carefully away.

In the kitchen, that afternoon, Huggitt and Nurse O'Keefe played Beggar My Neighbour with him for over an hour, banking up the fire with logs and great chunks of coal. He won four times.

'Have a cherry cough drop,' said Huggitt, sorting her cards, and the smell of them came up, sweet and sharp, into his nostrils. It was snowing again, beyond the window. He thought, this is the best place to be. And perhaps Wetherby's bus will not be able to get back.

At half-past four, Aunt Spencer and O'Keefe went up with the tea trays, and at twenty minutes to five, O'Keefe came down again to the kitchen.

'Reece is dead.'

He had forgotten to pretend that he was ill, and now it was too late for that. He sat on the hearth stool, drinking the hot milk.

'There's a chamber pot under your bed this time,' Aunt Spencer said. He looked away from her, and tried not to think about the dead body of Miss Reece, still for ever, in the high bed. The implications of there being someone else in Number Seven, of the words 'Down the corridor from Reece' ceasing to mean what they had always meant, were too much for him.

'I've telephoned to that sister of hers. Not that they care. They'll be glad to save the money, I daresay . . . mean as they're rich . . . poor soul.' But there seemed to be no alarm, no surprise among them.

At ten past seven, the kitchen door opened and there was Wetherby, shaking the snow from off the shoulders of her bottle-green coat.

'Reece is dead,' said O'Keefe at once.

He looked down into his milk. Wetherby went out into the hallway, in search of Aunt Spencer. Because of the bad weather, she had been shopping, just into the town, she had not tried to go as far as her married sister's.

The fire exploded and spat little slivers of coal out at him, like shell-shot. The flames were blue-green.

'Pneumonia,' he heard Aunt Spencer say, swinging the kitchen door. 'And Mackay's talking nonsense about the Coroner.'

He felt Wetherby come across the room towards him.

'I'll take this one upstairs,' she said, 'and that'll be one job out of the way.'

He saw her feet, misshapen and bumpy with corns, inside the black nurse's shoes. Beyond them, Aunt Spencer shook a thermometer.

'Yes,' she said, 'and there's a chamber pot for him, under the bed.'

He followed Nurse Wetherby out of the kitchen, and up the first flight of linoleum-covered stairs.

Cockles and Mussels

Both the lounge and dining-room of the Delacourt Guest House commanded a view of the sea.

'There is nothing at all gloomy *here*, nobody has to suffer some dark, poky bedroom with outlook on to a wall,' said Mrs Muriel Hennessy, the proprietress. Though she did not count the cook, Mrs Rourke.

There had been, until five years ago, a Mr Hennessy, dealer in fine wines and spirits. In the early days of their marriage, they had gone around the Châteaux of France together every spring, tasting, buying. But Mr Hennessy had begun to drink, two, and later three, bottles of sherry a day, the relationship had soured, his wife had put money aside, secretly, in a building society account.

After his death, she had waited six, decent months before leaving their bungalow in the home counties and travelling to the sea, to make her fresh start with the Delacourt Guest House.

'It has always been a little, private longing of mine,' she had told her friends, giving a small sherry party to say goodbye, 'to be of some service to others, give a few, retired people a very comfortable and happy home.' Though, in fairness she was forced to admit to prospective clients that her charges were somewhat higher for the larger, front bedrooms.

A year ago, Miss Avis Parson had come into money from a deceased aunt, and then she had been able to take one of these, to move from a pink room overlooking the garden, into a blue room, overlooking the sea.

Mrs Hennessy was fond of saying laughingly that Miss Parson had 'served her time', she deserved to come into her inheritance.

For she did not like to think of any of her residents pinching and scraping, anxious about where the next month's rent was coming from.

It was not the quietness, not the gentle slope of the Guest House garden, down towards the promenade, not the different moods of the sea, for which Miss Parson was grateful. They pleased her well enough, but nothing happened, it was all a little dull.

'I am sixty-nine,' she said, brushing her white hair, which was as long as it had ever been when she was a young girl, 'I am not like Old Mr Brotherton, who is fit only to doze and dream and remember little incidents of his naval past. I have my eyes open to modern life and what goes on about me.' For, from the side window of the blue bedroom, she could see towards the Lower Bay, and it was to the Lower Bay that the day trippers came. Mrs Muriel Hennessy, and, indeed, all the property owners and shopkeepers and residents of the upper town, held day trippers in the lowest possible esteem. 'They are not *real* visitors,' she would say, bringing the tea trolley with their late, hot drinks around the lounge, 'they come in charabancs and throw away their litter, they do nothing for the image of the town.'

And, along the foreshore and up and down the narrow streets of the Lower Bay were all the most common attractions, the souvenir gift shops full of rose-painted pottery and highly varnished shells, the ice cream and fish and chip parlours with tall stools set against eau-de-Nil marble counters, the rifle ranges and the five shilling photographers and the sellers of novelty balloons.

At the far end of the foreshore was the Fun Fair, and, opposite the Fun Fair, beside the lifeboat house, the shell-fish booths, where cockles and mussels and winkles and shrimps were shovelled into little paper cones and sprinkled with malt vinegar.

'Everything is so vulgar on the Lower Bay,' said Mrs Hennessy, 'everything is so cheap and nasty, it smells so, I wonder anyone at all can bear it.'

But, in her heart, Miss Avis Parson felt that life as it should be lived was lived along the foreshore of the Lower Bay. At night, she drew the curtains of her side window and sat, watching the flickering lights of the amusement arcade and the Fun Fair, saw the big wheel turn round in an arc of gold and mauve and the water chute cascade electric blue. If she opened her window, and the breeze was in the right direction, she could hear the shrieks and cries of girls as their skirts went about their heads on the swing-boats, the crack and pop of bullets on the rifle range. The hours between ten and midnight, when everything was abruptly doused and darkened, filled Miss Parson with excitement and little, sudden spurts of longing. I have lived too sheltered a life, she thought, I have never known enough about the truth of things, about what really goes on. For she had been companion to her father in his Rectory – Miss Parson the Parson's daughter, said the village children, though she did not mind – and later, to her unmarried brother in Wales, the years in which she had meant to do this and that had slipped too quickly by.

That summer, when she moved into her more expensive, blue front room at the Delacourt Guest House, the weather was almost always good, the days long and hot and the beaches bright and noisy with day trippers.

Mrs Hennessy turned away importunate families, evening after evening, at the door. 'I am not a hotel for passing visitors, I am entirely devoted to the care of the elderly, of my permanent residents,' she told them, smoothing down the skirts of her pastel linen dresses, watching them go off in their laden cars, hot and tired and disappointed down the drive.

In the afternoons, tea was served on the terrace and the deckchairs were occupied by old Mr Brotherton and Mrs de Vere and the Misses Phoebe and Ethel Haynes, sleeping under striped umbrellas to shade them from the glare of the sun.

Miss Parson took little solitary walks up Cliff Terrace, behind the Guest House, and the desire to venture along into the streets and shops and arcades of the Lower Bay became an obsession with her. Though she would have said nothing about it, and she was not, in any case, anxious to chat a great deal with any of her fellow guests, she saw herself as both younger than they were and somehow less permanent, for was she not entirely free, might she not suddenly choose to move on? She had money, she had her health, one day she might buy a flat in some quiet place abroad, might go on a cruise or pay an extended visit to her old school friend in Edinburgh. She reviewed her situation daily. And, meanwhile, she longed to mingle with the crowds who came in charabancs and private cars, to unmask the noisy secrets of the ghost train and eat shrimps and winkles with her fingers, sitting beside the sea.

It was only her sudden discovery of the drinking habits of Mrs Rourke which, for a short while, diverted her attention.

When the lights of the Fun Fair were switched out, Miss Parson left her chair by the window, after drawing the curtains again, and prepared herself for bed. As long as there had been something to watch and listen to, the attraction of roundabout music and the lights flickering in the sky, she was never tired, her mind was filled with pictures of the scene, couples arm-in-arm together and the mothers of grown-up families, ridiculous in cardboard hats, middle-aged romances brought to a point of decision among the dodgems. But later, in the abrupt darkness, she remembered that she was sixty-nine years old and knew nothing, was ready to climb a little stiffly into her divan bed. But before doing so, she went quietly along the corridor to the bathroom, and it was just outside the bathroom that Miss Parson first found the cook, Mrs Rourke, her eyes curiously glazed, unable to focus on Miss Parson's face, and her hand clutching at the bare wall. Mrs Rourke had been cook for seven months, at the Delacourt Guest House.

The following day, old Mr Brotherton complained again, loudly, about the quality of the mashed potato. 'There are lumps,' he said querulously, paddling them about in the serving dish with a spoon, 'there are more lumps at every meal, every day there are more.'

Rita, the daytime waitress, shot him an evil look, but in the kitchen she exaggerated the nature and number of the complaints to Mrs Hennessy.

'You needn't think the staff have never noticed,' she added, balancing four vegetable dishes along her outstretched arm, 'it isn't as if any of *us* are exactly satisfied.'

Mrs Hennessy lifted a fork out of the remaining potatoes, and peered into them. She could not see any lump, and had she not had trouble and worry enough over cooks, in years past? Was this not always the season for groundless complaints? The heat was proving too much for them. She decided to say nothing.

Some nights later, Miss Parson heard the uncertain footsteps of the cook fumbling along her corridor, the slight brushing of her guiding hand, along the wall. When she opened the door, a few moments later, the faint, sour smell of Mrs Rourke's whisky hung about on the air.

In her narrow back bedroom, at the far end of the landing, Mrs Ruby Rourke lay with her coat still on, feet propped up on her pillow, and looked down at her own ankles. A fine pair of legs, for a woman your age, she thought, the finest pair of legs for miles. And her eyes filled with sudden tears of pride, that years of standing beside sinks and ovens had not thickened the muscles or spread the veins. Only her feet were bad now, the bunions sticking out like red noses on their side, under the fine stockings.

A year ago, she had been cooking for thirty-five secretarials in a London hostel, and when they had passed her by on the stairs, going out to dinners and parties with a stream of young men, she had looked at their legs and not had any cause to envy them, had seen over-fleshed knees and thick calves, lack of any shapliness or finesse. And they've other lessons to learn, she had thought, looking at herself in the wardrobe mirror, it takes a woman in her fifties to know how to enjoy herself. *I* wouldn't be in their shoes, wouldn't be eighteen or twenty again, thank you very much.

But in the nights she had woken and heard them clattering up the stairs, laughing inconsiderately, and had not been able to get to sleep again for hours, had been obliged to get up and search about in her wardrobe for a bottle of gin. In the mornings, the skin around her eyes looked puffed and swollen.

When she had been asked to leave the hostel, there had not been another job in London, in the end she had had to travel up here and apply to the Delacourt Guest House.

'Oh, I like old people, I like to see they get nourishing meals,' she had told Mrs Hennessy, crossing her legs to reveal their elegant shape, under the short black skirt. 'I couldn't get along with those young girls, oh, no, couldn't take to their noisy, selfish little ways. It was something like living in a zoo, Mrs Hennessy, and half the food picked and poked at in a *very* dissatisfied way.'

'I daresay they were dieting, Mrs Rourke, that is what young girls all do, nowadays.' Mrs Hennessy was looking at the careful make-up and wondering what age the woman might really be, and if there were not something a little unsuitable about vanity, in an institutional cook.

'I am fifty,' said Mrs Rourke, who was fifty-seven, 'and I am thankful that I have never had to diet, my figure is all that it should be.'

Mrs Hennessy had inclined her head and begun to wonder about the lack of any recent references. But in the end the problem was solved for her, by the absence of any other applicant.

On the last Friday in July the temperature reached 84 degrees and the season for day trippers was at its height.

Sitting in the garden of the Delacourt Guest House, Miss Parson felt restless, felt the summer again passing her by, and was irritated with those around her, by the talk of the Misses Haynes, who were spiritualists, and the snores of old Mr Brotherton. I have no place here, she thought, it is a house for old and dying people and I shall begin to grow like them, the trivialities of everyday life here will assume a greater and greater importance, the times of meals will be all I have to look forward to. And it will be my own fault.

For she had been both startled and aroused by her discovery that Mrs Rourke came home the worse for drink. *She* has some kind of experience and pleasure, Miss Parson thought, some merrymaking and delight in life, she is a woman unafraid of the world, she has the courage of her convictions and laughs in the face of propriety. For the drunkenness of the cook seemed to her entirely romantic, it had no weak or pathetic aspect.

The hard, straight sunlight lay across the Victorian house, and the terrace and garden, it was too hot, now, for any of the residents except Miss Parson herself, and old Mr Brotherton, snoring under a panama hat. From the beaches came the high, sharp cries of children, the sea glittered in ridges for miles out.

I have no courage, I am too concerned about the opinions of others, too afraid of their displeasure. I am anxious to walk down on to the Lower Bay and see the sights, observe the people, anxious to eat cockles and mussels and go along into the Fun Fair, and is that not a very slight, harmless ambition? Yet I have sat here for week after week and only ventured out into the respectable, upper part of the town, only walked the streets and bought from the shops approved of by women like Mrs Hennessy. It is a very poor thing. I do not deserve to have any excitement out of life, any new experiences, I am made of flimsier stuff than a cook!

In her agitation, Miss Parson got up quickly from the striped deckchair and began to walk round and round the garden, rubbing her fingers about in the palms of her hands, wanting to make a decision.

*

On the hot, Saturday evening, Miss Parson ate very little supper, and did not go into the lounge afterwards, to take coffee.

'I have some business in the town – a friend to see,' she said hastily, in reply to the inquisitive expression of Mrs Hennessy, for none of the guests ever went far, in the evenings. But then, she was annoyed with herself, for she paid good money to live here, she was her own mistress, why was it at all necessary to explain her doings in that flustered way?

'On Saturday night, Miss Parson? Oh, are you quite sure that you are wise? The town is so full of rowdy strangers, I am a little concerned as to whether you will be quite safe.'

Miss Parson would have said, and that is why I am all the more eager to go, but little Mrs Pardue, with the pink bald patch showing through her grey hair, said, 'Rowdy people do not come up to *this* end of the town, I am thankful to say,' and in the subsequent murmur of relief and agreement, Miss Parson slipped out.

She felt not merely excited but guilty. The Lower Bay was, in a sense, quite forbidden territory, in the tacit agreement of the residents of the Delacourt, and she could only guess at what they might say of her visit, were they to find out. One or two of them did not entirely like her. 'There is just *something* about Miss Parson,' Miss Phoebe Haynes had said, 'she is not really altogether one of us.'

On leaving Cliff Terrace, Miss Parson made a detour, up to the top of the hill and around the avenue, for someone might be watching her, unseen, from a bedroom window, and then a report would be made at once to the lounge, and to Mrs Hennessy. The ghost of Miss Parson's father warned her, as she altered course and made for the Harbour road, that she was acting a lie. The road dipped and the Guest House was out of sight. And I do not care, Miss Parson said, gripping her pouched black handbag, I have done nothing with my freedom, nothing at all, it is quite time I grasped at my opportunities and enjoyed some small, innocent adventure.

She wore well-fitting leather shoes, and a lightweight coat, in case the evening should turn chilly, for she did not intend to return early to the Delacourt Guest House.

From her back bedroom window, Mrs Rourke saw Miss Parson set out up Cliff Terrace, and then, glancing up again from powdering carefully around her eyes, saw her turn, and go off towards the Lower Bay.

'Well!' she said to her own image in the mirror, and was taken once again by the elegance of her own figure, the shapeliness of leg and ankle. She had always insisted, at every place of employment, upon Saturday as one of her regular nights off, everything happened on a Saturday, you never knew your luck.

For a long time Miss Parson simply walked slowly along the pavements, looking at people's faces. These are the old and the modern young, mingling together, she thought, these are the day trippers, this is life. Middle-aged men in shirts, open over sun-reddened chests, wore pressed-paper hats in imitation of cowboys or undertakers or policemen, and Miss Parson stared into their eyes, anxious to learn the secrets of enjoyment. It was very crowded, very warm in among the booths and cafés, the night air flashed with multi-coloured lights, and along the pier they bobbed, orange and green and red, reflected in the dark sea.

I am very happy, I am watching the world go by, discovering things I never knew, Miss Parson told herself, sitting down on a foreshore bench while she emptied sand out of her shoes, there is nothing to be ashamed of or snobbish about it, that I can see. Loudspeakers sent the metallic beat of popular music out across the street.

Somewhere, far down beyond the green railings and the piled-up deckchairs, the long, pale shelf of sand, the edge of the sea, creaming and stirring a little in the darkness. I would like to walk there, too, thought Miss Parson, it is many years since I have been on a beach at night. Though as children they had spent their holidays at Bexhill, and she had walked the dog Beaver out, after dark, smelling the salt and the green smell of seaweed and imagining her own future, filled with rich, nameless excitements.

A car began to hoot on the roadway, nosing into the back of jaywalkers. Miss Parson got up and went across to the Seagull Milk Bar, to perch uncertainly on a high stool with tubular steel legs and drink a cup of expensive tea. All around her, everyone moved, laughed and chatted across the tables, over plates of waffles and haddock, peas and chips, and every movement reflected brightly in the mirrors above the counter, so that Miss Parson, watching, felt uncertain of which was real and which the image. Under a table, a small child in green bathing trunks dribbled lemonade gently on to its bare legs from the end of a straw.

'There you go, my duck,' a man said, helping her down from the precarious stool, and she noticed the reddish hairs, matted all the way up his arms.

But it was going through the glittering golden archway of the Fun Fair, and standing just a little way inside, which brought home to her where she had come, alone on a Saturday evening, how many unwritten rules of proper conduct she had disobeyed. For a moment, she held her breath and was doubtful, would have gone quickly away, the noise and the clamour of people and machines and lights around her was more than she felt able to take. The smell of the place came out towards her. But then, she went ahead, fumbling in her purse for money, and joined the queue leading to the switchback railway.

On the fourth, reckless plunge over the crest of the metal track and down, down, slicing into the darkness, Miss Parson opened her eyes and saw that the woman next to her was clutching on to her sleeve, eyes huge in her melon-shaped face.

'Oh!' she said, 'Oh!' and the hand gripped tighter, though no sound coming out of the woman's mouth could be heard above the noise, there was only the purse of her lips, purple-looking under the artificial lights. She is laughing, Miss Parson realized suddenly, there is nothing wrong with her whatsoever, she is simply laughing, and she felt friendly, warmed by the careless grasping of the stranger's hand, the gesture of conviviality on the switchback.

As they climbed and plunged again, Miss Parson thought of old Mr Brotherton, and of Mrs Hennessy, stout and managerial in a linen dress, and began to laugh, to feel superior to all of them, as one who has outwitted everyone else in the battle of life, discovered some amazing secret.

Returning to the ground again, she was obliged to lean for some moments against the ticket booth, unable quite to recover her breath. Overhead, the big wheel spun in a flashing circle, as if gathering speed to take off like a top into the sky.

The cockles were hard to eat, she was uncertain which way to prise them out of their hard, little shells, and in her mouth they tasted as they smelled, strong as brine and heavily vinegared. But there was something rich and coarse and satisfying about eating such things, and about queueing up to buy more, to hover in her choice between the brown-pink whiskered shrimps and mussels, rubber-smooth and yet curiously gritty in the mouth.

The foreshore was now more crowded than ever, the voices more raucous, shrieking and cat-calling and squabbling, now and then. Miss Parson got up from her bench when the man next to her began to slip sideways heavily and to snore like old Mr Brotherton, huge hands upturned and loose on his trousers. But, after all, it is only another human being, she told herself, only another aspect of life, and she felt herself expanding and blossoming with new insights and knowledge, open to a stream of experience.

A trickle of juice was left in the paper cone after she had eaten the last mussel, so that, in screwing it up, she strained her coat sleeve. The smell was blotted at once into the cloth, and came up sharply into her nostrils. It would stay there, now, certain proof, in all the months to come, of her evening in the Lower Bay, her new-found courage.

A gang of men and girls came stepping out in a row, arms linked, breasting the whole width of the road, and singing, and for a second Miss Parson was caught up among them, she could see the white teeth and peacock-painted eyes of the girls, smell the men's sweat, and then they parted and went on like the tide, leaving her behind.

In the orange-painted Bingo Booth, open out on to the street, a game finished and, looking up from her unsuccessful card, the cook, Mrs Rourke, saw Miss Avis Parson. Earlier, she had found one or two people to talk to, someone had bought her a drink, but it had come to nothing, the bar had emptied and filled up again and she was left to apply fresh lipstick and do something herself about the empty glass.

'Well, now!' she said, therefore, touching Miss Parson lightly on the arm, for familiar company was suddenly better than none, better than the old routine of trying to strike up a new acquaintance. 'Well, here's a thing!'

Though a thought crossed her mind, to wonder if the old girl might not be a bit unwell, a bit wandering all of a sudden, standing down here and smelling of shell-fish and vinegar on a July Saturday night. She had always had a peculiar fear of madness.

'It has all been a splendid treat, Mrs Rourke, this is a whole new world to me. I have been telling myself for so long, promising myself, you know, that I would be as bold as could be and venture down among the holidaymakers, and now here I am! But I am really just a little bit tired, I do confess to you, my feet are feeling rather swollen.'

It did not surprise her, for nothing was surprising now, when Mrs Rourke, too, took hold of her arm.

'It's the sand,' she said, confidentially, nodding into Miss Parson's face, 'the sand gets into them, plays them up. You can't tell me.'

'Yes? Well then, that is very likely the case and perhaps I have had enough for one day, perhaps I should be getting home . . .'

Miss Parson thought that the cook might be older than she looked, though she admired her care for her own appearance, the brightness of rouge and lipstick and the height of her heels. They were walking uphill now, between the last of the gift shops, and away from the sea, and Miss Parson saw that everyone, here, was arm-in-arm with everyone else, it must be the way of things, the air was close with *bonhomie*.

'My treat, dear,' said Mrs Rourke, making her way firmly between backs and elbows to the lounge bar. 'What's it to be?'

But, sitting at the little, low table and surreptitiously easing a shoe from off one of her feet, Miss Parson felt depressed, thought perhaps it is all a little aimless, all too trivial to count as life, perhaps I have been wrong to come riding on switchbacks and eating strange food and drinking sweet sherry in the Lower Bay.

Mrs Rourke was telling her some story, her eyes protruberant in a flushed face, and Miss Parson thought of the nights when she had found her leaning unsteadily against the Guest House wall, wondered in a moment of panic where it would all end.

Mrs Rourke had forgotten exactly who she was with, was launched, now, into the full tale of her bad treatment at the hands of her previous employers, the London secretarial school.

'Take no nonsense, good cooks are in short supply, my hubbie would have said.' She wiped lipstick carefully off her glass with the corner of a handkerchief. 'He was a chauffeur,' she told the dazed Miss Parson. 'There wasn't anything you could tell Rourke about the tricks of employers.'

'I think I really should like to be getting back now,' said Miss Avis Parson. But when she stood, the lounge tipped and spun round, there was a curious, high-pitched echo inside her head.

In the Delacourt Guest House, Mrs Hennessy switched off the parchment-shaded lamps in the lounge, and closed the top windows, wondering if she had been wise to let Miss Parson have a key.

The whole street seemed to be singing, now, everyone came pouring out on to the pavements as the stalls and cafés began to close, and the smell of beer and human bodies mingled with the faint ozone of the sea.

'Steady she goes,' said Mrs Rourke, stepping off the kerb and on to it again sharply. 'Take it gently.'

'Oh, the nice fresh air, the nice, *nice*, fresh air.'

Can't hold a drink, thought Mrs Rourke with disgust, doesn't know the first thing about it. Aloud she said, 'We're two merry lonely old ladies,' as they came up the Harbour road, leaving the trippers behind them, facing the stairs, 'two lonely old souls.'

There is something wrong, thought Miss Parson, something very wrong indeed, I do not wish to be here, led along the street by a drunken cook, and called an old woman and lonely, there is nothing at all like that about me, and she can know nothing. I would prefer to forget this incident. But, climbing Cliff Terrace, her legs felt weak under her and she was obliged to hold on to Mrs Rourke's arm again for a little support.

'It's a bit of a hole, Miss Parson, a bit of a one-eyed hole. I'm used to a good deal better than this, I deserve it, you know, this is not the sort of carry-on I'm accustomed to.'

I do not trust you, Miss Parson thought, I have learned a very great deal tonight, about the ways of the world, and I do not feel able to trust you, you will not get away with anything with me. But she could not altogether follow what the other woman was saying.

'Come along, old girl.'

But Miss Parson had stopped and bent over to examine her shoes. Behind them, the lights of the Fun Fair were gutted, the whole of the bay was given over once more to the incoming sea.

*

At four, Miss Parson woke in severe abdominal pain, so that, after staggering to the bathroom and back again, she collapsed at the side of her bed and was forced to crawl up, hand-over-hand, and ring the service bell.

Towards morning, the doctor was called, for the pain and sickness had worsened, she became delirious and then semi-conscious.

At breakfast in the dining-room there was an air of alarm and expectancy, questions were asked and speculations aroused, and old Mr Brotherton refused to eat more than a triangle of toast. 'It is the cook,' he muttered, leaning forward and speaking up so that he should be heard quite clearly at all the tables, 'the food is bad, it is not surprising that Miss Parson has been taken ill. Something should be said to the cook, I have said so before, I hope you will all bear me out.'

So that, throughout the next few days, when Miss Parson's condition worsened and, in the end, she was taken to the hospital, the cry grew louder of 'the cook, the cook' as a crowd might mutter, 'Guilty! Guilty! Off with her head!' and Mrs Hennessy, who had discovered the gin and whisky bottles in Mrs Rourke's wardrobe, felt that more than goodwill was now at stake, something public would have to be done.

'It is acute food poisoning,' she told Mrs Rourke, sitting at the desk in her tidy office, 'the doctor is extremely worried, Miss Parson is quite dangerously sick.'

Nor was she pleased when the lies came out so glibly, the long, garbled tale about Miss Parson's eating cockles and mussels and drinking alcohol in the Lower Bay. For surely they *were* lies, she thought, when the cook had been formally dismissed, surely the aloof, prim little Miss Parson would never have been so foolish? Though Mrs Hennessy recalled that there had so often been a strange look on her face, a furtive, secretive expression, and perhaps she had been growing a little senile, perhaps there was a hardening of the arteries and she had begun to act in that way common among the old, as though a new, alien personality had been suddenly assumed.

Well then, it will not do for her to come back *here*, for this is only a Guest House, not a nursing or a geriatric home, I am neither trained nor equipped nor willing to cater for the senile and unreliable, the responsibility would be altogether too great. She thought that there were no relatives of Miss Parson, but somewhere, an old school friend – in Edinburgh? Or perhaps, simply, the doctor could fill out a form and the whole thing be done locally, some suitable home would be quickly found.

In the event, that was not necessary, Miss Avis Parson died in her bed at the General Hospital of a heart attack, following the ravages of food poisoning. The doctor, bringing the news to Mrs Hennessy, warned against any future use of shellfish, cockles or mussels, shrimps or crab, in the cooking at the Delacourt Guest House.

'Old people,' he said, almost apologetically, standing on the doorstep beside his car, 'nothing indigestible, nothing, really, in the seafood line, Mrs Hennessy, take my advice upon it.'

It was only out of respect for the memory of the recently deceased Miss Parson that she did not speak of her own, long-existing ban on all crustacea from the menus of the Delacourt.

On the train, Mrs Rourke lifted her coat up on to the rack, tidied up her face in the tiny, rectangular mirror and then walked along to the buffet car for a drink. She had found, only the day after her dismissal from the Guest House, an appointment as cook to a boys' approved school in rural Norfolk. They had not asked for an interview or anything more than verbal references simply because they were, they said, desperate, they would take her on a month's probation.

Like one of the bloody inmates, Mrs Rourke thought bitterly, imagining the remoteness of the countryside, the absence of any Gaiety and Life, like a bloody prisoner myself. But then she rebuked herself, for she did not like to swear, it was a sign of weakness, a loosening of her grip. Instead, she looked down into her glass for a moment, and then drank, quickly, to the memory of the seaside, and of Miss Avis Parson.

Somerville

Even the sight of the envelope terrified him. For he did not receive letters now – only a few household bills and their receipts, a random circular. This was what he had planned, that he should retire here and nobody should disturb him, that he should be forgotten. There would be no letters. The envelope terrified him.

So that, for comfort, he went to his desk and found that other letter and sat with it on the terrace in the early morning sun, weighing it in his hand, and he despaired again.

He had no need to read it, knowing the words by heart, but he read it and the shape of the letters upon the page helped him, the familiarity of the emotions they aroused. The sun was already hot upon his face, though it was not yet ten o'clock. These days, it was always hot.

'Somerville', it began, the twenty-seven-year-old letter, 'Somerville', as though they had reverted to the formality of first acquaintance, as though this were no time for the frivolity of Christian names. 'Somerville', and he looked up, and into the sun, remembering how it had been, how he had sat at his desk in Whitehall and seen his own name upon the scuffed page and already known, for over two months, that Barton was dead. 'Somerville' . . . The sight of the envelope had terrified him. Beyond the tall windows St James's Park, and a steel-blue sky, the January sun glinting on the lake and the stiff backs of ducks, down between bare trees. 'Somerville' . . .

Now, he took the letter out of the envelope again and unfolded it, and still it seemed that nothing so appalling could ever come to him again, that he would never be so troubled by the sight of handwriting upon a sheet of paper.

Somerville,

I can't write much now. I can't think. My fingers are almost gone – I mean, frozen. They swell up and stiffen. Though holding a mug is the worst – hot tea – they warm up and you can't stand it, the skin cracks open. You don't care about anything here, except the bloody cold, and keeping yourself moving, on your feet, keeping on. I think about you when I can. Sorry.

Listen, yesterday we dug Lewis Higton out. I mean dead, he was frozen, he'd gone in up to the chest and you don't last long in this, if you go down – ten, fifteen minutes? I don't know. I suppose he fell. You can't notice anything in this, you can't think of anything except yourself. We went back for him. But we dug him out and he was dead. I thought you'd want to know. Though there are enough of us dead aren't there, for Christ's sake, how many of us are left? You're left, I suppose. I don't know. We don't get news.

I can't write, not much, I can't hold the pen, but I can tell you, I know what hell is and it isn't hot, it's cold, it's this frozen, bloody country. You want to lie down and just go off, you know, just give up. They won't let you. But maybe he did that, Lewis Higton. Maybe. I don't know. I don't know how long we'll be either, they don't tell us anything. We'll be no use when we get there. They say it's pretty bad, there isn't any food. But you can't tell, you don't care, not about anything except yourself, keeping yourself going. Yesterday one of the prisoners went mad with a can-opener and they shot him. Dunkerly shot him. He had strange eyes, walnut-coloured eyes. I can't get him out of my head. Dunkerly shot him and I remember him, I dream about him, the colour of his eyes. It's bloody silly things like that you remember. I've changed, you wouldn't know me, you won't ever know me, not after this.

I can't write, my fingers are hopeless, I can't move the others, the ones on the left hand, can't feel them at all. Only

thought you'd care to know about Higton. He played the piano,
didn't he? The one in your rooms. Bloody silly things like that
go through your head. Higton playing your piano. We
shouldn't have dug him out, should we, we should have left
him there, just left him.

    Jesus, this cold, Jesus.

After that, Somerville had wanted nothing to do with letters. He
did not want this letter, today.

    Shortly after coming here, six years ago, he had realized that
he could no longer remember what Barton looked like. There
had once been a photograph, a single snapshot, of the three of
them, Barton and himself and Lewis Higton who died in the
snow, they had stood together awkwardly, in tennis flannels and
with white pullovers tied about their necks, racquets dangling
from long arms, and all of their faces looked oddly similar, bony
and eager, and blurred, the hair of all their heads appeared thick
and pale. But the picture never served to remind him of anything.
Barton had not looked like that, and in the end the photograph
had been lost or burned or thrown away, and now he could not
remember. There had only been the letter, coming to him like a
ghost, weeks after Barton's death.

    On his own sixtieth birthday, when he was already retired and
settled here, the shock of imagining Barton, alive and of the same
age, Barton, at the mercy of stiffening joints and weakening eyes
and greying hair, had been very great. Though later he had been
comforted, knowing that, after all, it was not true, that Barton
was dead and therefore could not change, was now as he had
always been. Only that the image of him was faded and dispersed
as the flesh itself, now, within Somerville's mind. And every so
often, he took out and reread the letter.

    'Somerville' . . .

    All his life, he had planned to live here. He had seen it first on
the day he was taken to meet his great-uncle, the famous general,

they had driven past the tall gates in his father's car and he had looked through them and up the long drive between the beech trees, to the rose-brick house. The car was an early de Dion, slow upon the hills, he had hated it from the beginning, sitting in the front upon his mother's lap, and feeling as though they were on the back of some monster. But that day, climbing up slope after wooded slope of the Chilterns, into the sun, he had been soothed, began to come to terms a little with the terrible car and with the driver, his father, as he might, after many hours of cautious watching and stroking, with some wild animal. And then he had seen the gates and, through their black patterns, the drive, and the garden and terrace and rose-coloured brick, the glint of the lake and the magic shape of the chimneys. Moving very slowly past in the car had been better than walking, for there had been enough time, but none in which the sight of the place could become over-familiar, they had not gone up too close.

Though perhaps he realized none of it, until he was grown up, perhaps imagination supplied this and that detail. Certainly, he remembered nothing else about that day, nothing about the visit to the famous general. Only the fact that his father had been, for once, good-tempered, and then the slowly moving picture of the house, glimpsed through gates at the end of a drive.

Years later, he and Barton had come walking here, day after day through the whole of one summer, searching. But when the house was at last found, he would come no nearer than the gates, not wanting the place to deliver up, before he was ready to take them, any of its secrets. He had returned to Oxford, and later to London, to his mathematics, a spare, rational, ascetic man, a believer in the symmetry and clarity of life, obsessed by the beauty of the knowledge that the world contained five regular solids, no more and no less, a romantic.

So that when he was almost sixty, and he read that the house was for sale, he was unsurprised, he bought it and relinquished his public posts, the advisory positions in Whitehall, his fellowship at the university, his membership of committees. He was untroubled, too, by the fact that the house had come to him rather earlier than he might normally have expected to retire, looking upon these extra years as a gift, the margin of incalculable bounty for which one allowed, in a calculable world.

He negotiated the entire purchase through an agent and from a distance, in order that the day after his official retirement should be the first upon which he walked any further than the tall gates, walked up to and into the rose-brick house, from the long drive. He thought, I have everything that I shall ever want, for the rest of my life. Though, in his breast-pocket, there was the letter from Barton, which he knew by heart.

I have everything.

From that day he wished to receive no more letters. Few came.

Early that evening, he walked down the slope behind the house, to the lake. It had been made out of a gravel pit, more than a hundred years ago, long after the building of the house – to be filled with fish, for the entertainment of week-end sportsmen. Now, whatever fish might be there, he left alone. It was a small lake, entirely surrounded by a grassy path, and then by the beeches. In winter, through the pale trunks, the house could be seen, and in the opposite direction, a mile away, the village. But now, the leaves were dense green, layer upon layer. The water of the lake was completely still. Down here, the heat gathered, kept in by the trees, so that by the end of the day the air above the surface of the water shimmered, playing tricks with the light.

Somerville sat down and at once felt the letter again, stiff and flat inside his pocket. He had not opened it, he was still terrified by the sight of the envelope.

He thought, no, nothing more can happen, it can be nothing, nothing at all, no one shall come.

If he half-closed his eyelids, the lake seemed to expand and thin out, far away, he could see no end to it, which was what he would have liked, for there to have been some mystery on the other side.

The sun slipped down further, so that the water flamed.

He remembered, as he persistently remembered, the story, in Beowulf, of the burial of Scyld Scefing.

At Oxford, it had been Barton who made him read, he had come to his rooms sometimes, when Somerville was out, and left a book upon the desk, with a marker, on which would be a page, or a chapter reference, and what the book contained was always a surprise. At first, he had begun to read reluctantly, dutifully, for at that time he cared only for the preciseness of figures, not for the formlessness of words, spread about the page. But later, he always read on, caught by this or that image, amazed by what Barton was showing him, needing to discover the end of a story, the secret of a character. He read on, too, because he could never bear to leave anything incomplete, could not set down even a very bad novel, once begun, because the recollection of the loose end would have continued to irritate him. But Barton never gave him very bad novels.

After a time, he had understood that the form of words was as precise and complete as the form of numbers, and then he had become adventurous, begun to look in the windows of bookshops, try this and that for himself, and Barton had smiled and shaken his head, gently triumphant.

From the beginning, Beowulf had obsessed him, and for the rest of his life the image returned again and again, without warning, to his mind, of Scyld Scefing, the dead Danish king, laid in the ring-prowed ship among his own treasure, the riches of a lifetime, and sent off to some unknown destination across the water.

> Then high above his head they placed
> a golden banner and let the waves bear him
> bequeathed him to the sea.

Now, the thought of burning, or of earth burial, repelled him. It was this, the ship across water, which had meaning. And he had been stirred by the thought of honour. 'A golden banner,' he had said occasionally, to Barton, as his name in mathematics became celebrated, his opinion sought after. 'A golden banner, be good enough to remember that, that will be the way to go!' Barton had smiled and shaken his head, not an envious man.

These days, Somerville found his mind filling suddenly with the image as he was doing some job, making coffee in the early morning, pruning forsythia, watching for the hedgehog, and he would be momentarily troubled, as he realized what it was that he was seeing, in his mind's eye, the burial ship moving slowly across water, the golden banner.

He thought, I have everything, I am altogether alone, there are no letters, no one calls, I have everything, and perhaps I will not be able to bear it, such an absence of anxiety and striving, perhaps this will make me mad.

But he was not truly alarmed.

The lake had darkened again, blood-red in the centre. He eased his legs, began to think of the walk back up the slope, of lighting the lamps and cooking the mackerel for supper, of the hedgehog's coming.

It was then that he heard the footsteps behind him in the grass. As he did so, he remembered, again, the unopened letter.

She had been to this house before, perhaps half a dozen times in all his six years, but never this way, only up the drive, to leave the box of groceries at his side door. Generally it was her father who came, a little, bossy man in an old green van. Or her brother. Occasionally, Somerville had caught sight of her in the shop, when he took his order, or else from a distance, walking down the street, or out along the Hadly road, towards the bus-stop. They were people with whom he had nothing in common, nothing to do, dull people whom he wished well and did not understand. He knew the name of the girl, Martha, and he had seen, some weeks before, that she was pregnant. He thought nothing of it, was uninterested. He was alone here, he had the house, everything he wanted. Nobody came.

She said, 'This is where they catch fish.'

Somerville got awkwardly to his feet, a little stiff and damp from the grass, and terrified of her, bewildered as to why she might have come. He could think of nothing to say.

The sun had gone altogether now, there was simply the declining evening, still warm, smelling of leaves.

'Do you?'

'I?'

'Catch the fish. Is that what you do here, all the time?'

'No.' He hesitated. 'No.'

She laughed. 'You're about the only one that doesn't, then, aren't you?'

'No one comes here, there is no one to catch the fish.'

Her face shone with a rather benign amusement. Somerville felt uncomfortable, at a loss.

'That's all you know, then!'

He lifted his hands up and down inside the pockets of his jacket, wanting her to go away, unwilling to talk.

'You'd be surprised who comes up here. They *all* come. Fancy you not knowing!'

'Who comes?'

'Oh, people, this one and that one. Boys from down the village.'

'To fish?'

'Why not?'

He said, 'No,' and shook his head, 'I see no one.'

'Well, you don't suppose they come dancing about your lawn, do you, they don't make a great deal of noise. It's like a game, sort of, like poaching. Except they all think you know, really. Everybody thinks that.'

'I know nothing of any of it.'

'Oh, I suppose you'll go and stop them now, then.' Her mouth was sulky. 'You'll get a dog.'

'I dislike dogs.'

'Well, something. Come down and send them off, spoil it for them.'

He looked out across the lake, thinking. Then, after a moment, he said, 'I do not care. I do not care who catches the fish, I am not interested in fish. It is not the fish that matter.'

'Look, they wouldn't touch anything else, don't you start thinking that, they're not out to burgle you, are they? They're not like that, it's only catching fish, they're not going to come thieving.'

'*Who* are they?' He turned and looked at her closely for a moment.

'People. I told you. Lads from the village. Dave, sometimes. Well, not so much now, he's got older, he's got other things to do. He used to.'

'Your brother came here?'

'Yes.'

'Do you come?'

'I'm not bothered about fishing, am I? Not that they are, really – well, not about the fish. That's not what they come for. It's like a game, I told you, creeping up through the trees and sitting here, knocking off some of your stuff from the lake. They sling them all back, generally. They come up at night. It's nothing. It's a lark, that's all.'

'No.'

'I shouldn't have bloody said anything. You'll come down and put up wire, you'll stop them, now, I know.'

'No.'

There was silence. He felt her staring at him, examining his hair and face and clothes, the way he stood, the shape and size of his feet. He would not have it, would not be looked at.

He said desperately, 'I have no interest in them, I do not care what they do. So long as I do not have to meet them. So long as nobody comes near to me.' For he was suddenly panic-stricken, imagining hordes of strangers trampling up through the woods, shouting and calling, setting up rods and lines and green umbrellas, eating picnics and then overflowing up the slope towards the house, into the house, invading him, his silence, passing the word round, importing friends. About the fish he cared nothing. He looked at the girl, Martha. She grinned. 'They won't bother *you*. It's not you they're interested in, is it? You just said. You never saw them up till now, never heard them. Besides, it's only once in a way. They won't bother you.'

When he had first come here, he had seen her playing about in the yard at the side of the shop, or walking to school, and she had been a child, then, with thick, short hair cut level to her chin and straight, heavy limbs. It did not seem to him long now, not more than months, though it was six years. But she was very young now, the flesh of her face was soft, still disguising the bone structure, though there was something new in her expression, a knowingness, and her eyes were narrower, tired at the corners. The child she was carrying seemed not to be part of her, it was simply a swelling, a weight carried as a bag might be carried, and behind it, she was herself, her bones and flesh were the same, unaffected, and when the child was gone, she would look as she had always looked. He supposed she might be seventeen.

She came forward abruptly and stood, hands in the pockets of her yellow dress, looking down at the water. She said, 'I couldn't stick it.' Somerville did not answer, he was thinking again of the house, and the lighted lamps, wanting his supper. It was time to put out milk for the hedgehog, to sit and wait on the terrace. The best time of the day.

'They don't stop, you know, that's what made me come out tonight. They can't seem to give it a rest. Round and round and round, as if we haven't had it all before, all said, right from the start. I don't know what they'll do after, when I've had it, there'll be nothing for them to talk about, will there, not for any of them?' She glanced up quickly. 'Only you.'

'Me?'

'Oh, they talk about *you*. You're like the weather, always good for a chat, you are.'

He was astonished, and angry, too, for he had not thought himself of any interest. He was entirely separate, he did not want to exist in the minds and mouths of any of these people, it was as though a part of himself had been broken away and scattered about like crumbs to the birds, he felt diminished.

'Well, it's only natural, isn't it? You're different, you're not like anyone else round here. They can't make you out, they're always wanting to know what you're up to. I suppose I do, as well. I want to know.'

She stirred her toe about in the grass. A slight breeze moved towards them, over the surface of the lake, Somerville felt it and was made anxious.

'Only just for the moment, it's me, and that's a lot more interesting, they've got me down there, haven't they, all the time, they see me every day, so it reminds them, and off they go again. It's all right for you. They hardly ever see you.'

'No.'

'I'll be glad when it's over and everything's back to normal, I will.'

He was amazed by her, he thought, I know nothing. And then, I do not want to know.

'I was thinking about you today,' she said, 'I've thought about you a lot just lately. Funny that. I never did before, not much.'

'You know nothing about me.' He spoke stiffly, for that was what mattered, nobody should know.

'I wished I was you though, all the same. Up here all by yourself, doing what you like. Nobody says, don't do that, who was it, what are you going to do now, what did I always tell you, what do you think everybody's going to say? You don't have that, not any of it. I thought, that's what I'd like, to be up there all by myself, just like him. I wouldn't give tuppence for any of them then. That'd be all right.'

Somerville smiled. 'Yes.'

'Only I couldn't. It's not the same for me.'

He shook his head, for he did not know, and he felt battered, now, by her flow of talk, the questions and comments and desires, it was years since he had spoken for so long with another person.

'Don't you go mad, though? Don't you get lonely?'

But she scarcely paused for answer. 'I would. That's why I'd never do anything like it, not really. I did wonder, I did think I might go off somewhere, on my own. I can't stand being with them. Only I'd go potty. If I were *you*, I'd go potty, up in that great house with nobody to talk to, nothing to do.'

'Oh, there is everything to do!'

'What?' Her face was sharp as a monkey's. 'What is there to do?'

Somerville moved a hand vaguely, not replying, trying to think of what he did. He thought, nothing, I do almost nothing. I read a little, things I have read before, I do the garden, walk about, I spend hour after hour trying to make the acquaintance of a hedgehog, I cook and clean and wash and dress and sleep and sit in the sun. Everything. Nothing.

'They all think you live in a pigsty. Up here. You don't even have anybody from the village to do for you. They think you must live in a right old muck-heap.'

He was angry. 'I am extremely fastidious. I am clean and tidy and neat, I care a great deal about those things.'

'Oh yes. I can see that. Just by looking at you I can see it. It wasn't what *I* ever thought.'

It was almost dark, the sky above the copse was only a little paler than the water of the lake. Moths had come out.

Somerville said, 'You had better go home.'

'I'm all right.'

'No. You should not do this, walking about on your own in the woods at night, you should go home. Think – think of what might happen to you. You should not be here.' For though his ideas were vague, about the behaviour of young girls, the dangers of this countryside, yet he remembered things, said years ago by his mother and his sister.

She laughed, and then she spoke again, the tone of her voice was changed, there was the hard edge of adult experience and irony, making him again uncomfortable.

'There's nothing much else can happen to me, is there? Not just for the moment.' And she laughed again, so that the sound of it echoed around the circle formed by lake and trees and sky. Somerville turned and walked abruptly away. And then stopped, for should he not do something, see her back on to the road, take her home, make some gesture towards her welfare? She was a child, he felt somehow responsible.

When he looked back again, she had gone. Her dress and face and limbs had been pale, and now there were only the dark spaces between the beech trees, he could scarcely make out the place where she had been standing, across the grass.

He began to walk back to the house. But the pleasure was gone, he cared nothing for the thought of sitting on the warm terrace waiting for the hedgehog, for cooking the mackerel, smelling its rich smell, he felt dissatisfied, sour.

'They talk about you.'

All the same, he lit the lamps and took out the fish and made the bread and milk in the blue saucer. But then he was restless, so that he sat outside for only fifteen or twenty minutes, and for the first time in weeks, the hedgehog did not come. Though perhaps it came later, something came, for in the morning the bread and milk were gone.

It was on waking, a little before seven, that he remembered again the unopened letter.

The sun was already hot. He went down into the kitchen and filled the kettle and made his coffee, and later, went to spray the greenfly from the roses.

That day, the postman did not come up the drive, there were no letters.

For two nights, the hedgehog stayed away. Somerville sat on the terrace in despair. Something had changed, a pattern was broken, with the arrival of the terrible letter. He had hidden it now, at the very back of a drawer in his desk. Unopened.

The days were still hot, all of that summer had been hot, he began to imagine how it would be in the world beyond this house, people talking on and on about the weather, the sun, the sun, you felt a new person, didn't you, when the sun shone, felt you could cope with anything really, so long as it didn't get too hot, because we had everything, didn't we in this country, provided you got your weather with it, everything.

He opened all the windows of the house and ate and read and sat and slept outside on the terrace, his shirt unbuttoned. In the early mornings, the air smelled of the Loire valley. But he was anxious. The hedgehog had been coming every night since the middle of April, and now it did not come.

In the end, he went down to the bottom of the garden, to the tree with the hollow. There was a lump, covered with bits of twig and leaf, which might have been the hedgehog, sleeping, but he dared not disturb it, for fear of frightening it permanently away. Once, he had seen it in full daylight, down in the grass by the old shed, basking on its belly in the sun. He changed the food in the blue saucer, cooked strong-smelling fish. He was fascinated by what the animal would and would not eat, by the way it snuffled across the terrace, towards the saucer with its moist pink snout.

Still it did not come. For comfort, he read the Japanese poetry book.

> In my boat that goes
> Over many salt ways
> Towards the open sea
> Faintly I hear
> the cry of the first wild goose.

At midday, the temperature went up to eighty, cracks opened in the lawn. He spent hours watering the rose Albertine, flowering like pink snow over the south wall.

*

The next time she came, he was sitting on the terrace, limbs loose in the chair, doing nothing at all, thinking nothing. He heard no footsteps. The lawn and the beech trees and the sky faded into one another like the blotted edges of a watercolour, green-blue. Then, the girl's pale shape at the top of the path.

Ever since Barton's death, he had been troubled by dreams of ghosts, rising out of mist and water and softly piled snow. Whenever he walked to the lake he expected to see something, the arm that held the Sword Excalibur. He was haunted by these few images, they had become part of him, like the burial ship of Scyld Scefing. Terrifying. He needed Barton to mock him.

Now, he stood up, knocking over the flimsy deckchair as he did so, furious, wanting to lift up a newspaper and flap the girl away, like some insect, to shout at her. He began to sweat, feeling himself spied out and known.

I have finished with your world, I have come here, chosen this place, I would be entirely forgotten.

'It's cooler up here, anyway.'

Somerville bent and retrieved the deckchair, struggled to replace the awkward struts and they defied him, going over backwards so that the canvas billowed out.

'I like your garden.'

He tipped the chair, dropped it down flat, began again.

'I like those flowers. What are they? Those blue ones?'

'Larkspur.'

'I like those.'

A willow warbler started singing from the blackthorn, at the bottom of the lawn.

'It's all of a piece, this garden, you know? There's hundreds of different things, plants and bushes and that, and they all look just anyhow, but really they're not, are they, not when you look? It wasn't like this before you came. You should have seen it in the old days.'

He was still standing, hovering, as a man in a room waiting for a woman, who has just entered, to sit down. Except that he wanted her to go away.

'We used to come up here, after school, a whole lot of us did. It was empty for quite a bit, wasn't it? Well, all of one summer, anyway. It was up to your middle, then, in grass and stuff. That's years ago, though.'

'No. Six years.'

'Well . . . !'

He looked at her. When she was born, I was a middle-aged man, Barton was long dead. The best things were already over.

'I like it up here.'

Somerville sat down heavily. She reminded him of the child who had belonged to his London neighbours. Their garden had adjoined him, part of the fencing was down, and the child, a girl, would come through, walk up to the tall, uncurtained windows of Somerville's study and stare in. If he went and sat in the garden, she came to stand a few yards away from his chair, saying nothing, asking no questions, only staring, until he felt that he could neither move nor breathe, he had stayed indoors and bought a blind and rammed it down hard in the child's face, loathing it. He realized, one day, how he loathed it, and was overcome with disgust at himself, and with guilt, too, for the child did not trouble him, it made no noise, touched nothing. Only came up to his window and stared, still-faced.

In the end, he had sold the house.

'My Gran's on the way out.'

'Your . . . ?'

'Gran – *you* know her, you've seen her, in the shop. Everybody knows her.'

'She lives with us. Well, she did. They've had to take her now, though, into the hospital at Cittingham. We couldn't stand it.'

She sat down on the terrace, her long thin legs sprawling out from under the yellow dress.

'I didn't think it'd bother me, not at all. Well – she's old, everybody dies when they're old, don't they? Everybody has to. Only when you go and see her you feel awful. When they ring the bell for the end of visiting, she starts pushing back the covers, you know, trying to get out of bed. "Where's me clothes, where's me clothes," she says. They had to hold her down, the time I went. That makes you feel awful, you coming out of there and just carrying on, everything carrying on and her staying in the hospital to die. Especially in this weather. It makes it seem worse, somehow, everything seems as though it's more living, doesn't it, in the sun?'

Somerville thought, do not tell me this, it has nothing to do with me, I want to hear nothing of your grandmother. I have thought of all that, gone through all those questions and solved them, years ago, the problems of living and dying. It is sealed and packed away, that knowledge. I will not listen to you. It is nothing to me.

Yesterday we dug Lewis Higton out. I mean dead. He was frozen stiff, he'd gone in up to the chest . . . We went back for him. But we dug him out and he was dead . . . We shouldn't have dug him out, should we, we should have left him there, just left him.

'It's funny about my Gran. I mean, she's old, she's gone seventy, and she's a bit funny, you know, about some things.

You've to be careful what you say to Gran. But she was the only one of them who didn't go on and on at me about this.'

This.

'She just gave me a look, you know. One look. You'd have thought she'd be worse than anyone, wouldn't you? I did. Really shocked, that's what I thought she'd be. Well it's that generation, isn't it? It's what you'd expect. But it wasn't her at all, it was them, they were the ones. My God! *She* went to bed for the whole day, she had hysterics, you'd have thought it was her that'd caught again. And my brother, he was the same. And that's a laugh, as well, if you knew what he was like himself in that direction. You can't tell me. No, it was only Gran that didn't bother. I went to see her yesterday. She looks all shrunk up, and she kept calling me Cissy, as well – that's my Aunt Cissy, the one that died. She thought I was her daughter, only young again. Her mind's gone all confused. That really upset me.'

Somerville began to hear her voice as though from far away, it went on and he heard it and yet did not hear it, he ceased to listen. It was almost dark. The drawing-room lamps threw long fingers of light on to the terrace.

'It started in her womb, they said, so far as they could tell anyway. I suppose it'll just creep all over her.'

He thought, she is not here. I can close my eyes and ears and then she does not exist in this world. Everything is the same. *She is not here.*

'It's a terrible thing, I think, cancer, it's like a sort of hand, isn't it, spreading out inside you. That's what it's like.

'The crab,' he said distantly. 'Cancer the crab.'

She turned her head and he closed his eyes again at once, not wanting to be seen by her, not wanting his secrets known. *She is not here.*

'I tell you what else, as well. I found out something from my Gran, today. I found out that it happened to them.'

Her voice was thick with satisfaction.

'They had to get married because of our Dave. It happened to them! You'd have thought I was the first and last, you'd have thought they never knew anyone so bad, the way they went on at me. Only I know all about it now, don't I? My Gran told me. She thought I was my Aunt Cissy, she started talking all about it, telling me, I couldn't believe it, not at first. Well, you can't be sure of everything she says now, I told you, not with the injections they give her. Only in the end I did believe it. And do you know what I did? I went home and I went in that kitchen and I just asked them, I just said it, out loud, I said, it happened to you, didn't it, only you never told me you had our Dave like that, just the same, everything the same, and the only difference is you got wed and I'm not, that's all. I stood there and said it. They were having sardine salad for tea, all sitting there. My hands were shaking, you know, all trembling. I didn't care though, not about any of them.'

Somerville half-opened his eyes. She was smiling, looking away across the garden.

She said, 'That did for them.'

He began to think about it, the scene in the kitchen at the back of the grocer's shop, sardine salad on white plates, the face of the girl, and then was horrified at finding himself interested at all in what she said. He wanted to wave his arms at her again, to shout, why do you come here, why do you talk to me, *why*? For she spoke as though she had always been his familiar, as if they inhabited the same world.

'It upset me, seeing my Gran in the hospital. I didn't expect it to. Not so much as that.'

He thought in panic, she will come here again and again, there will be nothing I can do, she will come and bring the child and the child will know me, she will come here. I shall have to move away.

'I can't talk about it to them. I can't say anything about any of it.'

Then high above his head they placed
a golden banner and let the waves bear him
bequeathed him to the sea.

But now he had a terrible image of the old woman in a hospital bed, struggling to get up, pushing back the blankets, struggling against such a commonplace, public death. 'Where's me clothes? Where's me clothes?'

'They've had to put her in a room by herself now. She was with all the others, you know, in the general ward, but they've put her on her own now, because of the smell. That was why they couldn't stand it at home. That's the worst of it, isn't it, the way it smells?'

We shouldn't have dug him out, should we, we should have left him there, just left him . . .

Then he remembered, he saw Barton, exactly as he was. Not Barton the ghost, Barton of the photograph. Barton. The colour of his eyes and hair, the precise mould of flesh over bone. Barton, hands in pockets, shaking his head.

'Look at that!'

A yard away, the hedgehog was drinking from the blue saucer.

He would say, quite firmly, you must not come here, I do not wish to see you, I do not wish to have any visitors. For he began to imagine how it would be, summer merging into autumn and winter, and then she would bring the child up here, crying and crawling, and it would be too cold for the terrace by then, he would have gone inside the house, and she would come there to find him. He wondered how many of the others already knew that she had been up here, to whom she had talked about him, about the way he lived.

He felt helpless. He realized that he himself had spoken almost nothing, half a dozen disconnected sentences, in his anxiety to be rid of her. She had talked.

You must not come here. I have always been alone. I will be alone now. You have nothing to do with me.

He walked up and down the garden in the early morning, rehearsing phrases. I bought this house, gave up my public life . . . I do not wish to see you, to see anyone.

The rose Sanders White had climbed and spread up and along the whole of the west wall, and now it was tumbling over the other side. When he came here, it had been nothing, a few thin, stray branches. In the autumn, he would have to cut it hard back. Or perhaps not. Perhaps leave it, let it riot as it chose. He was certain, from time to time, that he should do this, should simply leave the garden, apart from the ugliest of the weeds and the cutting of the grass. For perhaps to be a gardener was not an honourable thing, perhaps he ought not to impose his own private, artificial order, upon the land.

He walked about for a long time, soothed by the familiar argument, for he knew down which path this and that and that extension of it led, knew the various conclusions. He turned his back upon Sanders White and looked ahead, into the dark green, watery light, between the beech trees.

But it was not true that no one at all had ever been here. His sister had been.

Even now, even four years afterwards, he remembered the feeling he had had, on waking, the knowledge that someone else had slept under his roof, that his sister was breathing up the air in a room two floors below, the sudden panic. He had run out of the house and down the path to the lake, pushing his arms out in wide circles through the air, trying to get away. There had been a buzzing noise within his head, a confusion, he had felt, for the only time since coming here, that he did not have any hold upon himself, that he was spread about, his skin could not contain him. His sister had come, someone was here who shared his blood and knew about his past, someone who spoke of rights and duties, awakening in him the old, childish feeling of threat and dread.

He shook his head. The garden was empty, the leaves rustling about against one another, inside the beech copse.

Once, he had said to Barton, 'I hate my sister.' It was the first year they had met, the first time they had gone abroad on holiday.

'I hate my sister!'

They had been standing in the pink- and lemon-coloured early morning, on a hill above Assisi. Barton's face, as he turned slowly and looked up at him, had been smooth and pale with a kind of horror at the words, his skin seemed to be pulled more tightly across the bones. Below them, the beautiful roof-tops of the town, rose- and sand- and slate-sea-coloured in the southern sun.

'I hate my sister!'

'You can't say that!' Barton had stood up. 'You *cannot* say that!' But he spoke more quietly than ever, so that Somerville had not recognized anger, had laughed.

'Oh, I can! I know her, I've spent a good deal of my life with her. I can say it. "I hate my sister!" '

Then, Barton had simply walked away from him, on and on down the hill, not pausing or looking back, had vanished into the town. Later, towards the evening, Somerville had found him, sitting on the steps of a church. They did not yet have any place to stay. Nothing had been said about the morning, nothing. He had not understood, Barton continued to bewilder and at times to frighten him. His own sister had not been mentioned again.

Afterwards, he knew Barton, knew everything about him, afterwards, they grew older. He learned that Barton never spoke grandiosely, as the others did, about humanity, about the general good, about society, but that he cared for those people he knew, and above all, cared about family, the ties of blood, for the closeness of mother and sister, cousin and grandfather and aunt, in a way Somerville could not begin to understand. Somerville, who hated the claustrophobic feeling of shared blood and bone, hated to look in his mirror and see 'the family nose'. He said, I am alone, I am alone, my skin is a bag containing everything of me, and outside there is nothing, no one who has anything to do with me.

As a small child, he had gone about saying that he had not been born, as others were. One moment, there had been a world without him, the next, he had simply been altogether there. In adult life, he recognized the depth of his longing for this to be true. He felt pried upon, and lessened, remembering that he shared a relationship of flesh with others.

'I hate my sister!'

Barton, he had jealously thought, Barton and his sister were too close, they wrote letters and sent one another cards, each sought out small, ridiculous trophies and tokens for the other, they shared jokes and spoke a private language, thought one another's thoughts. So that, over the years, he had wondered which of them he hated most, his own, or Barton's, sister.

Except that Barton knew and laughed and shook his head, mocking him. And he was a little reassured, seeing that in any case Barton was the same with all the others, with the most distant members of that enormous family.

'I hate my sister!'

But his sister had come. She had not written him any letter, knowing, perhaps, if she knew anything of him at all, that he would find time to make some excuse, to go away, that he might even fail to open the envelope at all. She had not written, therefore. He had not seen her for almost eleven years. She had come, driven up to the house one afternoon in September, by taxi from Cittingham station. She had arrived.

Because she had grown much fatter, not thinner, with age, she no longer looked very much like him. Except for the nose, 'the family nose'.

'And *haven't* you looked after yourself? *Haven't* you made yourself comfortable?'

He had forgotten it and now remembered, the way she talked, he heard her voice sounding down his childhood. She went about the house, his house, in and out of rooms, stroking the furniture, lifting this and that, the expert eye valuing.

'Oh yes, it is only what I would have expected of you, it is entirely typical. *Haven't* you got just what you wanted!'

She had turned suddenly to face him, standing by the drawing-room windows, so that the incoming light flattened her features even more, gave her a bland, characterless look, he could attribute no past to her, no experience. Though he could imagine her in the shop, driving a bargain over an occasional table, talking very fast and assuredly about silver, selling a bad steel engraving to a fool.

Once, he had been there, had gone right up to the window of her shop, peered in, at lustre-ware jugs on oak dressers, at corner cabinets full of air-twist stems, at screens and stools and beaded cushions. Even standing outside, he had been able to smell the smell of the shop, and to imagine his sister within it, moving her hands about as she talked, catching sight of herself in a cheval mirror, of 'the family nose', and looking away, for she was a woman embarrassed by herself. She wore clothes which did not suit her, roughly textured tweeds or busy patterns on dark silk, with small feathered or fruited hats. He had been passing through the town on his way to some conference and remembered that she lived there, had driven about looking for the shop. But after having seen it, he had gone away at once, not liking this place, not wanting to meet her.

'You had better come and take what is yours away,' she had said that day. 'It is all there, everything is left. You had better come down for a day.'

Somerville stared.

'There are only the two of us, we see nothing of one another. Well then, you had better get it over with, come and take away what is yours, of the family property.'

Outside, the beech leaves were drifting up the lawn in the wind, piling softly against the rose-red brick of the house.

'*The family property.*'

He had wanted to kill her, to make her disappear, this thick flat-faced woman in his house, his room. His sister.

He said, 'I want none of it, you must do as you think best, it is your own affair. I have everything here, there is nothing at all I would possibly want.'

'The house is sold. I took it upon myself to do that.'

He shrugged.

'You had better have what is yours by right, I wish to do what is correct. There are only the two of us. You should come down and choose.'

'No.'

There were things he remembered suddenly, from the house in Kent, things he had touched and stared at and known daily, through his childhood, the patterns upon carpets, the knobs on particular chairs, things he did not wish to see again.

'I have everything I want here.'

She began to look about her again, the keeper of the antique shop, so that Somerville wanted to hide things, to shut the doors of cupboards and mask over the glass, to close the lids of his own eyes.

'Well, I am not surprised by you, whatever others may think. You behave strangely as you have always behaved strangely. Nothing you did has ever startled *me*.'

He had tried to say that he did not care, that he wanted her to feel nothing towards him at all, to put him out of her mind, but he could only make half-remarks, only repeat, 'I have everything. There is nothing I would have.'

She had stayed for another day, and he had scarcely been able to bear it, to bear the smell of her about the house, to hear the movement of silk stocking against silk stocking on her thighs as she walked.

She had said, 'You should knock down that wall, make this drawing-room longer.'

'You should pave that side lawn, neaten things off, save yourself trouble.'

'You should have these things properly insured.'

'You have done well for yourself. But then, you have had no responsibilities, no family cares.' Though her own husband had died, before the war, before they had been married a year, had left no children, no trace of himself upon her.

She said, 'Do you remember that man you once knew? That man Barton?'

When she left, he had gone up to her bedroom and found hairs on the dressing table, pale beige hairs, dry and curling at the corners like dead things. His hands had been trembling.

Every day for weeks afterwards, he had woken and heard the wind, the leaves rattling down, and been lifted up by his sense of new freedom, and the emptiness of the house, by the sight of his books on the shelves and of Barton's charcoal drawings framed in rows upon the walls, by the long tunnel of cool air down between the beech trees leading to the lake. He had thought, I am here, I am myself, I have everything. Nobody shall come.

That is what he would say then, to the girl, what he would tell her.

'You must not come here again. No one shall come.'

She said, 'What happened to the hedgehog, then?'

She was wearing the same yellow dress, puffed out over her stomach, the same expression of face, pert and world-weary.

Somerville straightened his back slowly, sucked a rose-thorn out of his thumb, said you are not to come here, I will not speak to you, you are to go away, summoning up words inside himself, staying silent.

'There was one I saw on the road the other day, all squashed up where a car had hit it. They're not very bright are they, hedgehogs?'

His head thundered, in his anxiety, he felt violently protective towards the hedgehog, desperate to make her understand everything about them, to know what he knew. He began to speak anxiously. 'It is a defence, they curl up – it's their spines – they sense danger and roll up at once . . . it is to protect themselves, it is . . .' He lifted a hand hopelessly, imagining the small body burst open, the stumpy, inquisitive nose, upon the gravel road. 'How can you expect them to know of cars and lorries, of the speed and power of the engine? How should they know that?'

She had settled herself on the terrace, legs like those of a wooden doll, stuck out straight in front of her.

'Oh, no. They're little vermin though, aren't they? I mean, they're very nice, pretty and that, I like them. But they're vermin, all the same.'

'*No!*'

'They suck the milk from cows in the fields at night. Did you know that?'

He had reached her and now was pacing up and down the terrace. He wondered how he would be now, trying to address some meeting, to give a public lecture, for he could not make the words jell together and come clearly out of his mouth, could not use them in a neat, clear line to express his thoughts. He saw them marshalled like rows of soldiers, but the soldiers were felled by cannon, there was a confusion, blood and mess and smoke, a tremendous noise. He breathed in deeply, held the breath. He said, 'The hedgehog is the most maligned, the most misunderstood animal . . . it . . . listen . . . the *lies* told about . . .'

'Well, what about the fruit then? They like fruit, hedgehogs do, they eat that. People might be right about the fruit.'

'No. They only eat fruit when they are obliged to, when there is nothing else at all. Hedgehogs are flesh eaters, hunting animals, destroyers of insects and snails and garden pests. Even of snakes. Did you know that the hedgehog is almost entirely resistant to the poison of a snake? Did you know that?'

She drummed her heels impatiently upon the terrace, like a child. 'What about the *fruit*, why couldn't they carry it that way, if they wanted it? I don't see why they mightn't.'

He took up a piece of stone and began furiously to make marks upon the terrace. 'These are the spines, stiff, all down the back, all over the skin . . . but when the hedgehog rolls over, *if* it does, then the back muscles relax, and the spines just go loose, they fold over like . . . No, no, can't you see? It would be impossible, no matter what the fruit. A man would have to hold the animal and press an apple down on to one of the spines from above, he . . . No, it is simply another lie, a lie everyone tells. It could not be *done* in that way.'

Somerville heard the echo of his own voice, almost hysterical.

'It could not be *done*!'

'Not even if they wanted the fruit.'

'No.'

'And they don't?'

'No.'

The willow warbler started up, and a thrush from the bushes. Somerville looked down at his own hands, at the faint, tobacco-coloured freckles between his thin fingers, at the marks made with his bit of stone upon the paving.

'You know a lot, I must say. About hedgehogs. You do know an awful lot.'

He wondered whether she were laughing at him.

'I suppose that's what it's like though, living up here, in this place, all on your own, you get interested in funny things like that, you get carried away, don't you?'

He stood up awkwardly. 'Yes.' He thought, I should not have begun to speak to her, I do not wish her to come here. Except that he had felt it important, he had spent so long, watching the hedgehog, it distressed him beyond bearing to hear the old, repeated lies.

'You ought to write a book about it, then. Be something for you to do, wouldn't it? Take your mind off things.'

Things . . .

He said, 'I am very happy . . . I am . . . I have everything here.'

'Still . . .'

She leaned back against the wall, closing her eyes, Somerville watched and the anxiety began to rise in him again, seeing the patch of yellow dress against the rose-red brick. When she arrived, he had been about to go down to the lake, he wanted to smell the close, sweet soil-smell, down between the beeches, to see the water.

'It's a pull now, coming up that hill. I really noticed it tonight. It's a pull on my back.'

He stood, uncertain, silent.

'It's lovely and warm against this wall. Lovely. Only I really did notice it, walking up. It's like having something in a sack tied round you, that's what it's like. Like being a cow.'

The thrush had moved nearer, to the roof of the garden shed.

'It's about time it was over and done with, that's what. I'm about ready for that, I can tell you. And that's another thing, we've had all *that* again tonight, as if I'm not sick of it – that's another reason I had to get out of the house. You wouldn't think I'd already told them, would you, over and over. They've got no respect for me, no respect for my mind, have they, they think they can just argue and order me about and I'll change it to suit them, do just what they want.'

Her eyes were still closed, she talked on and on, as easily as a child, relaxed against the wall.

'"*We'll* look after it, *we'll* have it here, keep it, the both of you," that's how they go on. "You ought to let things like this stay in the family, it's got nothing to do with strangers, you listen to what we say, we know, we're older than you, we know what's best. We'll have the baby and you, you'll live here, just the same. That's what you *ought* to do, what's right and anything else in your head is wicked, it's unnatural." '

She opened her eyes. 'There was Mrs Mason's girl, you know her – Mrs Mason up at the bungalow? Well, her daughter had a little girl, that Sally, and she wasn't married, and she brought it home you see, lived with her mother and father, they all lived together. Until she upped and married someone else in the finish and they've gone elsewhere now. It was all one big happy family though, till then. Catch me!'

She glanced down at the puffed-out yellow dress. 'It'll be over and done with and gone. There's plenty of people waiting for babies, aren't there, I know all about it, plenty of people like that and welcome, in this world.'

Somerville felt dazed, standing in the evening sunlight, felt lightheaded. He thought, I know nothing, understand nothing – and looked at the girl in amazement and dread.

His head was full of pictures, columns of numbers and snatches from half-remembered tunes, full of the sound of dead voices, full of images – nothing. He felt that he might blow suddenly away, like one of the brown curls of beech leaf on the terrace in October, leaving no trace.

She said, 'I've got it all worked out.'

He would say, I do not wish to see you again, or talk to you, I do not wish you to visit me.

But a fortnight went by and the girl did not come again. Somerville cut the blooms of pink and red and orange roses and crammed them into bowls and vases in all the rooms of the house, the air was heavy with the smell of roses, and in the copse the leaves of the beech trees yellowed in the heat.

A picture came into his mind, and stayed with him through those hot days of July, of his mother, who had been ill with this or that indefinable complaint, for most of the summers of his childhood. He saw her, from the window-bench on which he was sitting, half-propped upon fat pillows and turning her head restlessly against them, in the bed. Beyond this window there had been a garden, with too much rockery and flat lawn and privet hedge, and a cedar tree standing squat in the middle of its own black shadows.

'How *boring* the summer is!' his mother said, 'and this heat, glaring on and on. How I hate the summer!'

He had stared at her and been amazed, and when he had looked back across the garden, it was to see everything differently, he tried on his mother's eyes as though they were spectacles, he thought her thoughts. 'How *boring* the summer is!' But the summer became his favourite time, then, for it had taken him only a short while to perceive the truth about his own mother, and then he could not bear to stay with her, could not bear the languid, dissatisfied voice, though he was obliged to bear it, for she demanded his company.

Now, he thought, I have no need to remember that, I am an ageing man, I am able to do what I choose, in my own house, my own garden. I have everything. He began to get up even earlier in the mornings, while a thin mist still clung on the air between the trees, and sat on the terrace reading – Beowulf and Skelton and the political novels of Trollope, the grey-bound book of Japanese poetry, he thought that he would read everything Barton had ever given to him.

The hedgehog, too, was often about at this time, trailing sleepily away over the lawn, or snuffling in the mulch underneath the roses for a snail.

But it was an evening, when he came back up the path from the lake and remembered the lemon-yellow dress. He stopped dead, looking up towards the house. He thought, the child is born and the grandmother is dead and I am here, I am as I choose to be, I have everything. I am a wicked man.

The following day he walked down the hill to the village.

'Oh, they talk about *you*, don't they? You're like the weather, you are, always good for a chat.'

So that now, he felt them staring at him, he walked along the dull main street and the windows of the houses were like eyes.

'It's all I can do just to keep going, I can tell you that, it's about all I can do, I've wondered if I ever would manage it, these past few weeks. Leave her, the doctor says, don't fuss her, just leave her be, don't take any notice. How am I supposed to do that? It upsets me, it really does, watching her. She does everything for it, feeds it, bathes it and it might be a lump of putty, the way she looks, Mrs Haswell, it might just be a lump of putty. It's not natural that, is it? I can't make her out and there's something wrong, whatever he says. And then that hospital, night after night, and you wonder when *that'll* end, and half the time she doesn't even know us, you see, when we go, doesn't even know who we are. I'm just about up to here, what with that and the way she is, over that baby. It's about all I can do, just to carry on. It is.'

In the end, Somerville came out of the shop without speaking at all, he left his grocery list on the counter and pushed his way out into the hard sunlight of the street, trying to get his breath, wishing that he had not heard the voice of the girl's mother, had not discovered about the old woman, still dying in hospital, and about the girl who fed and bathed her child and looked at it as though it were a lump of putty. They were both silent as he went so abruptly out, the girl's mother staring at him, fat and hostile in a blue nylon overall, the customer contemptuous, bored, he felt tainted by their staring and their voices, by the mess of other people's lives.

The heat shimmered just above the roadway, as he walked back up the hill.

Then, he went inside the house and was restless as he had never been here before, going from room to room and hearing the silence, fiddling with the roses in their bowls. He thought, I should write a book, about the hedgehog, do what she told me, I would answer all their questions, make some use of my own knowledge, of those months of observation. I should justify my life.

'Give you something to do, wouldn't it, take your mind off things . . .'

Things.

He went to his desk. He would sort out all the notes he had made, on scraps of paper and in diaries, he would begin.

At the back of the desk, he found again the unopened letter. He thought, the child is born and is not wanted, the old woman is dying. He read, 'September 2. Hedgehog ate milky custard from saucer (sweet). Fish later. V. cold morning and evening. Hibernation?'

I can't write, not much, I can't hold the pen . . . only thought you'd care to know about Higton. He played the piano, didn't he? The one in your rooms . . . We shouldn't have dug him out, should we, we should have left him there, just left him . . .

Somerville walked out of the house on to the terrace, and the heat came up from the flagstones like the blast of an oven, full in his face. The shadows were hard and black-edged. Nothing moved.

He thought, I have everything here, no one shall come. I have everything. I am a wicked man.

It was years since he had ridden in a bus. He had forgotten how the seats smelled, made hot by the sun through glass, and the rough white tickets that came whirring out of the machine. He had forgotten how close the other people were, and how much they stared. He was like a man newly released from years of imprisonment. When he got off the bus, in the main street of Cittingham, he had no idea in which direction to go, the rush of the cars confused him. Only Woolworths looked the same, the lettering of the sign, gold on red, as it had always been. He stood for some time, in the doorway of Woolworths, feeling safe.

Having made his decision, early that morning, he had thought little about it. It was simply clear to him that he had a duty to come to this place, to see what he ought to see. If he did not, his life would sour like the roots of a plant, left for too long in an old pot. He was guilty of too much happiness.

He had known what kind of building the hospital would be, the shape of each block, like so many cut-off squares of cake, set down at angles to one another, had known about the buff colour of the outside paint and the green of the inside corridors. He knew how it would smell and the sounds he would hear, of metal against enamel and the shriek of wheelchair rubbers upon polished floors.

Walking up the driveway of this building, his bowels turned in a moment of fear, he thought of the beds hidden claustrophobically behind screens, and the massed petals of hothouse flowers. But he had not thought of anything else, beyond these softly swinging doors, did not know what he was to say.

'Her name is Mrs . . . ?'

Oh, God. He tried to picture the letters of the name, written above the village shop.

T-R-

T-A . . .

T-R-A-B . . .

'Trabe.'

'Mrs Trabe? And you are?'

He stared.

'Your *name*?'

Somerville leaned his hands on the edge of the desk, pushed his face forward, he said desperately, 'My name is Somerville, I am . . . I am her brother. The brother of Mrs Trabe . . . she has cancer . . . she is in a room alone . . . I am . . .'

The wasp began to vibrate on the glass.

'You are Mrs Trabe's *brother*? You have come some distance? But why did you not tell me that to begin with?'

Because I am afraid, he would have said, because I am a liar, for I do not know why I have come here . . .

'This way . . .'

'Mrs Trabe? Wake up, dearie, come along, let's have you sitting up just a little bit, make you nice and comfy. Let's wipe your mouth. Mrs Trabe?'

The room smelled hot and septic.

'Here's your brother, Mrs Trabe.' She bent down very close to the old woman's ear. '*Your brother*. Here's your brother come to see you.'

There were bones and skin and glistening eyes. No flesh.

'Not too long, now, I can't give you too long, not in the morning, however far you've come. *It's your brother, dear.* Don't expect too much, Mr Somerville. Don't expect too much.'

The eyes opened, very dark and glassy, like marbles under water, set in the sockets of the face. Somerville stood back, hands locked inside his pockets, smelled the suppurating smell. Then the neck poked forward, the skin unfolding like a tortoise. She said, 'It's our John,' and then laughed, or coughed, terrifying him.

'I told them, didn't I?' The eyes slid away and then back again to his face. 'I told them. I said, he'll come, you wait, I know him. He'll come. I told them. It was her, she was the one, trying to make out you were dead. She's never liked us, not really. But I told them . . .'

Somerville ran.

'We do what we can, Mr Somerville. You do see how it is? We do what we can.'

She had caught up with him, at the glass door of the entrance hall, blocked his way out.

'It can't be long. I'm sorry to have to tell you that.'

Tell me nothing, he thought. Do not speak to me.

'I'm glad she's seen you. It's always best, isn't it, always nice, when everyone can get to see them, all the relatives. I am glad. She recognized you, didn't she? Knew you straight away. She's not always done that, you know, not just lately. I'm sorry to have to tell you that.'

She walked with him out of the glass doors, ushered him to the top of the drive, spoke to him of the weather and of how they did their best for his sister, so that it seemed that he had, after all, mysteriously kept the rules and won the game, had found favour.

The air in the streets was thick with the fumes of traffic, so that the difference between this world and his own seemed to be entirely one of good and evil smells, good and evil noises.

In the bus his hand shook violently, he spilled the fare money in between the dusty treads of the floor.

He had told a lie and gained access to the room of a dying old woman who was not known to him, he had cheated and won, and she had taken him for her dead brother.

He began to weep, the other passengers stared at him and a fat woman moved from his side, to a seat further up the vehicle in the opposite aisle.

Walking up the drive towards the rose-red house, it seemed to him that there was, after all, no answer, and he was bewildered, for he had made the terrible journey because he expected to find one, to have the problem solved. Barton would have known what to do, would have sat quietly in the sun and shaken his head, Barton would have told him the answer. So he relied, then, upon a man who had been twenty-five years dead?

The flowerbed beneath the drawing-room windows blazed with mesembryanthemums, flat and bright as medallions in the mid-day sun.

But I am here, I have this, I have everything, Somerville

thought. Nothing is changed. No one shall come to trouble me.

Inside the front door, on the mat, lay a second letter.

Just after dawn, he woke from the last of the nightmares and got up, he could no longer bear the pictures that lay in wait behind his closed eyelids.

Out on the lawn, the early sun glinted silver as a razor between the grass-blades. The air smelled damp.

Gradually he felt calmer, his hand no longer shook, holding the mug of coffee. He thought of the lake.

When he emerged from the green tunnel of beeches, he saw that the grass around the margin of the water beside the path had already been disturbed, the footprints lay dark as bloodstains in the dew. He stood, listening, looking out across the water. Down here, it was still quite cold.

After a time, he began to walk slowly around the edge of the lake.

He found the body of the baby in a hollow at the base of one of the trees. She had scarcely bothered to conceal it, only cursorily covered the face with handfuls of leaves and grass. The torn ends were still wet and green with the sap.

Somerville found that he was neither surprised nor appalled, only certain, at once, that he must do something, and of what it should be. There were no marks upon the child, only the flesh was faintly blue-white, about the face and throat, the eyelids a little swollen.

She would have known that before long he would come down here, that he was the most likely person to discover it. He felt curiously proud, that she had trusted him. He wondered how distressed she was, where she was, now.

On the far side of the lake there was the wooden shed, though he had scarcely been into it since coming here, he had no idea in what condition the rowing boat was by now, whether it had rotted altogether from seeping damp and disuse.

For a moment, he stood, looking down at the body under its scattering of leaves. It occurred to him that someone else might come here, the boys she had told him about, who poached his fish from the lake. He carried the baby over to the shed. It felt limp and strangely heavy and when the back of his hand brushed against its face, the flesh was cold to his touch. He wondered what she had done.

After that, he went back up to the house, and he felt nervous, and excited, too, wanting to do anything in order to make a pattern, he was following a chart, laid out in his head.

Behind the plant pots in the toolshed, he found the largest of the wooden trugs, and sawed the handle carefully off at each end. The wooden slats seemed plaited tightly enough, overlapping from end to end, he thought that it would do. In the linen cupboard of the house, he found a freshly laundered cotton pillowcase.

The sun was much higher, and the mesembryanthemums had already unfolded. When he reached the lake again, the dew was dry, and the water gleamed like brass at the rim.

Lifting the child up and wrapping it, laying it in the wooden trug, he felt his heart begin to race, for fear anyone should come before he were finished. But it was not out of any sense of guilt.

Once, there had been a gravel slope running down from the shed to the edge of the water, but now it was thickly overgrown, so that he could scarcely drag the boat through the grass and weeds and protruding tree roots. The oars lay in the bottom, tangled with dust and the old webs of spiders, woven to and fro. At the edge, he stepped inside and moved his feet about, walked from end to end, tested the wooden seat. It was a small lake, he thought that the boat would take him to the centre of it and back again, and if it did not, the water was still, he could swim.

He set the basket, into which the baby's body exactly fitted, in the bottom of the boat.

For a moment, he thought he had forgotten how to row, he

could not remember which way to fit his hands round the oars. They had spent long afternoons of each summer on the river. But then, Barton had always rowed.

Barton.

Now, there were other people, the girl mattered to him, and the old woman in the hospital bed and the dead child. He thought, I am doing what I can.

In the centre of the lake, he let the oars rest. The water went still. All around him, the beech trees, lime-yellow where the sun shone through them, and dark at the heart, and between them he could see the rose-red house. Nothing moved.

From his breast-pocket, Somerville took the two unopened letters, and laid them in the trug, at the side of the baby in the white pillowcase. When he lowered it over the side, it touched the water without a splash, hovered for a second, and then began to glide almost imperceptibly away from him.

At once, he began to turn the rowing boat around.

When he had almost reached the edge again, he looked back. The trug was almost out of sight, sinking lower and lower in the water, and still moving away. He waited until it had completely disappeared.

In the house behind the village shop, the girl moved quietly about her room, emptying drawers and wardrobes, filling a suitcase. It was a little after six o'clock. She worked methodically, her thoughts vague. She had planned everything, long before.

Somerville made a fresh pot of coffee and took it out on to the terrace. He began to read. But in a little while, he saw that the hedgehog had come over the lawn, towards the blue saucer, so that he laid down his book carefully and began to watch it.

Nothing troubled him.